THE LEGEND of the NINE-TAILED FOX

Also by Katrina Kwan

The Last Dragon of the East

Romance

Knives, Seasoning, and a Dash of Love

THE LEGEND of the NINE-TAILED FOX

KATRINA KWAN

LONDON NEW YORK TORONTO
AMSTERDAM/ANTWERP NEW DELHI SYDNEY/MELBOURNE

1230 AVENUE OF THE AMERICAS, NEW YORK, NEW YORK 10020

This book is a work of fiction. Any references to historical events, real people, or real places are used fictitiously. Other names, characters, places, and events are products of the author's imagination, and any resemblance to actual events or places or persons, living or dead, is entirely coincidental.

First Saga Press trade paperback edition February 2026

SAGA PRESS and colophon are registered trademarks of Simon & Schuster, LLC

Manufactured in the United States of America

1 3 5 7 9 10 8 6 4 2

Library of Congress Cataloging-in-Publication Data is available.

ISBN 978-1-6680-5132-0
ISBN 978-1-6680-5134-4 (ebook)

For the little girl I once was who found escape in worlds of fiction,
may the stories you write offer others the same refuge.

Three hundred li farther east is Qing Qiu Mountain, where much jade can be found on its south slope and green cinnabar on its north. There is a beast here whose form resembles a fox with nine tails. It makes a sound like a baby and is a man-eater.

—Excerpt from the *Shan Hai Jing*
(*The Classic of Mountains and Seas*)

1

Yue

Hunting Log #142:

They bleed black. They have no soul.

I like watching them. Humans. It's a cheeky little pastime of mine.

Most stand alone, individualistic. Selfish. But I've seen what they can do—what great feats they can achieve together—if they feel so inclined. They remind me of ants, though I mean that as neither slight nor compliment. Merely an observation.

I've watched them build taller than any mountain, how they nourish the land to nourish themselves in turn. Music, poetry, art . . . I've seen them accomplish a great many things. It's such a shame they're always so busy fighting among themselves. They could have achieved godliness ten times over in the years I've been observing them. But they won't have my pity.

There's no sense in feeling sorry for my food.

I slink through the narrow streets, mindful of the intricate network of canals that section the city into neat square blocks. Longhao, they call it. The capital city of the Southern Kingdom of Jian.

A mouthful, if you ask me.

I round the corner, alert. The balance between predator and prey can shift in an instant. I may be the one on the prowl, but there's nothing more fatalistic than believing yourself untouchable. It's one of the many reasons why I work under the cover of night. There's no better way to sneak up on my next meal.

The moon sits low and heavy amidst a bed of stars, its silver glow reflecting off the water's surface in a silky shimmer. Paper lanterns hang over the walkway barricades, floating like lightning bugs over the sleepless city. Even at this late hour, the water markets buzz with activity. Vendors sit upon gently rocking longboats, their hulls half full of all manner of spices and vegetables and imported trinkets, haggling wildly to earn themselves an extra bronze piece before the day's end.

There's an art to it, I've noticed. Too aggressive, and the customer walks away. Too accommodating, and you're taken for a fool. What a fun little game.

The sour smell of decay lingers in the thick, humid air; the sound of seabirds screeching not too far off from their precariously balanced nests wedged into every available nook and cranny. I don't understand how the humans put up with the lack of elbow room. I'd sooner suffocate in this dark, watery pit they call home.

At the center of it all—a palace made entirely of jade.

Tall pillars carved of deep green stone, white veins swirling through like clouds. Even the tiles upon its roof are made of the precious mineral, the sharp points of the gable and hip structure accented in gold. Where I have only ever known the shelter of the underbrush, those within have their pick of whichever pavilion they so choose. It's a bit much, if you ask me, but there's no denying its magnificence. Especially when surrounded by the sprawling city of smaller wood buildings, all looking upon their jade neighbor with a mixture of jealousy and awe.

Upon the water, a group of young maidens blow kisses at a

night watchman as they float by on their canopied boat, giggling sweetly when the man's face turns a sheepish pink. He could be a tasty treat, I think, but one glance at the sharp dao tied to his hip gives me pause. I don't mind a good fight—but only if I know I'll win—and he looks much too strong for my liking. To make matters more complicated, he's not alone, walking alongside two of his compatriots who appear just as heavily armed.

I move on, allowing my eyes to wander. Not all are ripe for the picking. The haggard old man begging near the moon bridge looks easy enough, but I find that men past fifty leave a strange aftertaste. Stale, more often than not. He has little meat on his bones to begin with, and I'd prefer something with more sustenance. Nobody stops to help when a quick-handed thief steals his small cup of tarnished coins and makes off into the night.

There's a group of young boys playing near the water, seated on the stone edge of the canal, sending paper boats coated in wax sailing down the murky current. It would be a simple enough task to lure one of those tasty rabbits away, but I don't harm children as a rule. Not because I have a bleeding heart, but because it isn't worth the trouble. Humans lose their minds when a child goes missing, battening down their doors and hatches. I'd much rather not make future hunts more difficult.

Smarter to let them grow into larger meals, besides.

What I need is someone who won't be missed, with enough meat on their bones to satisfy my belly, and whom I can easily overpower in a pinch.

"Quit yer naggin', bitch!" a man slurs.

My sensitive nose can parse him from here, reeking of alcohol and the acidic trace of vomit. Picking up my pace, I sneak around the corner and find myself in a narrow alleyway, the path cutting through the block on a diagonal. He stands at the end, swaying foolishly from side to side as he takes another hefty swig of his rice wine. With thin, greasy hair, pock scars marring his cheeks, and yellow, rotten teeth, it would be fair to say that he possesses a face even his mother couldn't love.

Soft orange light spills from a nearby doorway. His shanty home. It seems his family lives in relative squalor, judging by the filth and detritus piled on their stoop. Even the den I've made up for myself in the neighboring jungle boasts more space than this hovel carved of rotten wood.

A woman clings to the frame, a wailing babe at her breast. The lamb's cheeks are covered in red patches, terrible boils, and bumps covering his skin. Its breaths come labored. I can smell the sickness creeping through its veins. I turn my attention to the woman next. Even in the inky dark, I can see it, my sight sharper than most. Her bruised eye is fresh, a violent red that will only darken in the coming hours. Bruises mark her throat, too. One does not require an impressive intellect to imagine how she came to sustain them.

"You can't keep doing this," she hisses, tears streaking her puffy cheeks. Snot drips from her swollen nose. Not exactly appetizing.

The drunkard pulls his hand back and the woman flinches. "Piss off. I'll spend my evening however I damn please."

"Always drinking our money away. I'd be better off without you, you worthless pig!"

He scoffs. It's a wet, ugly sound from deep down in his throat. At his hip dangles a leather purse pregnant with coin, bronze pieces jingling with his clumsy steps. "Leave me alone, woman."

"If you leave, you'd better not come back."

"Fine!"

My ears perk up. I'm nothing if not an opportunist.

I give him the courtesy of a head start before shadowing his trek through the narrow alleys. I have no qualms about his intoxicated state. In fact, I prefer my meals marinated. It makes the meat more tender.

The man roams aimlessly, muttering obscenities under his breath about his "*hag of a wife*." I don't make my move. Not yet. There are too many witnesses around, and I prefer to eat in privacy.

So I stalk my prey until he's well and truly lost, turned around in a neighborhood that's fast asleep. The moisture in the air clings to my skin, but I don't mind the heat so much as I do the smell it brings. Hunting in the city has its benefits: plenty to eat, and plenty of places to hide my work. It's unfortunate that it smells of rot and sweat. Unnatural and restricting. I miss the days when I could smell the earth readily beneath my feet.

There was a time when this peninsula remained untouched by human hands, covered in a thriving jungle where my sisters and I would nap beneath warm sunspots filtering through the heavy green canopy. Now the humans have carved the land to their will, built a city upon the waters flooding in from the seaside all in a matter of decades.

When the man tilts his head all the way back to drain his bottle of wine, that's when I decide to end this boring, one-sided game of cat and mouse. I can't ignore my growling stomach any longer. It's been almost two moons since I last ate, and my mouth is watering with anticipation. I've gone much longer before—nearly four moons, to be precise—but those were desperate times. I see no reason to continue my hunger with a buffet so readily available. I smack my lips together to keep saliva from dripping off my front teeth.

Quick and painless should do the trick. I may not pity them, but I draw the line at playing with my meals. I find no pleasure in prolonging their suffering.

I bring a hand up to my face and readjust my mask, making sure to keep the hood of my cloak pulled low over my head. The mask is made of polished porcelain, as smooth and perfect as a doll. Every painstaking detail of her face has been painted by hand.

Like a fisherman's lure, it's a tool at my disposal. From the mask's perfectly straight black brows, the soft rouge upon her carved lips, and the light blush that stains her cheeks, she's the most tempting of lures indeed. I feel the magic within the mask rooting in place, seamlessly blending her features over my own as a second skin. No prey can ever hope to escape me now that I've been made beautiful.

With the illusion cast and steady, I step forward.

"Excuse me?" I call out, lifting my voice so that my words rival the saccharine notes of a bamboo flute. I pull off my hood slowly. My long black hair pools over my shoulders like calligraphy over the finest parchment. "Excuse me, sir, it seems that I've lost my way."

The drunkard turns, lips curled into a sneer. I can tell he's about to curse me out when he suddenly freezes, his eyes locked upon my visage with an almost haunted reverie. I'm the most exquisite face his miserable eyes have ever looked upon. He almost looks heartbroken by my beauty, his eyes glassing over with tears of awe.

If only he knew the horrors concealed just beneath the surface.

He starts toward me, entranced, mouth hanging open to add to his general air of stupidity. "Where are you going, my lady? I can show you the way."

I bat my lashes, a delicate hand over my chest. Gone are my claws, replaced with dainty human fingers. All the easier to pluck his eyes out with. "I hope it isn't too much trouble. I would hate to be a bother."

"No trouble at all!" The man offers his hand out to me, suddenly a gracious gentleman. I pretend not to notice his bloody knuckles, remaining perfectly still. The goal isn't to go to him, but for him to come to me.

"These streets are so terribly confusing," I continue. I slowly reach for him, my movements graceful and enticing. "Won't you come a bit closer? I fear I'll trip on these uneven stones."

He stutters pathetically. "Y-yes, I'd be happy to—"

The moment he's within range, I pounce.

My daggerlike nails pierce through the flesh of his wrist, slicing through tendons and grating against bone. I yank him toward me, already unhinging my jaw to tear at the side of his throat. He doesn't get a chance to scream as we fall to the ground. There's no fight in him now that the wine on his tongue has dulled his senses.

The metallic twist of blood coats the inside of my mouth, smears across my lips, drips down my pointed chin. It's not just the taste I enjoy but the energy that comes from a mere bite. For all life, from the smallest insect to the mighty dragons far out east, is made up of qi. It flows through every breathing creature and gives balance to the world. It's the invisible force that turns flowers toward the sun, which helps our bodies heal from sickness . . .

And it's something a demon like me doesn't have.

Perhaps that is why I crave it so. It's only natural to seek what we lack—and this man is full-to-bursting with qi to share. The wine in his system lends its intoxicating effects, and before long, my head is spinning with inebriated bliss. Where most might find it vile, blood to me tastes better than a hearty beef stew. It quenches a thirst so deep I can feel the relief and satisfaction in my marrow.

I release his neck with a gasp, so engrossed in my feast am I that my lungs burn from lack of air. I can't help but hum as I swipe a finger over the corner of my mouth. My sisters used to tease me for being a messy eater. Now that I have him in my clutches, I can tell this isn't the man I'm looking for—why is that cursed Maskmaker so damn hard to find?—but he'll make a scrumptious meal all the same. The drunken man beneath me sputters and twitches, his little eyes staring up at me in pure horror. He uselessly clasps his hand over the gaping hole I've left in the column of his throat. Red pours freely. I must have chewed through his artery. He won't last long.

I take off my mask and set it down beside me, not wanting it to stain. It is one of a kind, irreplaceable. The magic pulls away like the thick strands of honey between two broken combs, and what once looked like skin returns to its rigid porcelain form.

I catch my reflection in a growing pool of blood beneath his quivering mass. I try not to look, but it's no use. Now that the illusion has fallen away, I can make out the curve of my severely hunched back, the shape of my dirty claws, and the pointed, hairy ears sitting atop my head. My nine tails sweep out behind me, stretching out like a hand-painted fan, my fur bushy and a dirtied white. I now stand above the drunkard, my bones creaking as I grow to almost triple his height—a behemoth by comparison—as tall as the shanty homes that surround us.

But what I hate most isn't my jittery figure or my knobby joints. A fox stares back at me. The right side of my face is horribly burned, the skin pulled back so tight that it exposes my fangs to the cold evening air. My six eyes are slits of dull obsidian and stark gray irises, no soul of my own to shine through. I look like a dead thing. Roadkill. A beast that should remain banished to the shadows.

I look away to eat. I'm not here to lament my hideous features.

First to go are his ears and nose and both his eyes, all wonderfully chewy. Every bit of bone and every crunchy piece of cartilage. Organs, skin, teeth, and hair. I peel away his layers until I get to the main course: the heart. For within the heart resides the soul, and that is where the true feast lies. Richer than a persimmon, juicier than a peach. I don't bother chewing, relishing the way his heart slides down my throat and settles in the pit of my belly. Hot like bone broth and thrice as nurturing.

I'm about to leave when I remember the appalling state my appearance is in. I reach for my mask, pressing it to my face to allow the magic to melt into my skin. I look back at the pool of blood, as a human might with a mirror for a little reassurance, and find a beautiful woman with long raven hair, rosebud lips, and bright, sparkling eyes. The face of an innocent. Someone who definitely didn't just devour a man.

There isn't a scrap of my meal left behind—only, perhaps, an errant knuckle bone and a single molar. No one will ever be the wiser. The evening is young, and humans are far more entertaining to watch under the cover of night. There's plenty of time left to indulge in my favorite pastime.

But first, I snatch up the man's coin purse.

I retrace my steps, following the scent of squalor. When I find the little hole of a home I'd arrived at earlier, I see that the door is shut tight and the lights within are out, though I can still hear the infant's soft sobbing. Easy targets, the both of them, but I think they've dealt with more than their fair share of bad luck tonight.

Maybe I do pity my food. Just a little. In the same way one might feel sorry for a wounded rabbit squealing helplessly in a snare.

Coin purse in hand, I hop up onto the stoop and tie its strings to the door handle. I have no use for money. Whatever I want, I steal. Most are too slow to realize what I've pocketed, and those that aren't can't keep up with me should it come down to a chase.

With two swift kicks at the bottom of the wooden door, I bolt around the corner and duck out of sight. I watch from the shadows as the woman nervously opens the door a crack, peering out for someone she never finds. She notices the coin purse almost immediately, taking it with a sharp gasp. A quick look left, then right, suspicion etched into her cry-swollen face. I smell relief, a sweet note lingering beneath the surrounding decay, but it's mostly masked by the bitter tinge of her distrust. I don't leave until the woman returns safely inside.

I've had my fill this night. There's no need to feast on lambs when there are wolves to satisfy my belly.

2

Sonam

Hunting Log #151:
They will consume until nothing remains.

T***he reports these last six*** moons are troubling. People have been going missing at an alarming rate. Men, women, and children—regardless of wealth, age, or creed. The count is pushing into the low hundreds; though for all I know, it may well be higher. The one thing I *am* certain of is that this work has all the markings of a demon: not a hair left behind, yet the unmistakable twinge of blood in the air.

"Remember to stay close," I instruct Wen and Sooah as we arm ourselves for the night ahead. "Don't give it an opportunity to pick us off one by one."

We've gathered in the storehouse, though the building's unimpressive size and molding exterior would suggest that it's been all but abandoned. It was one of the only places I could secure upon my return. Our cache of weapons was too valuable to leave unattended. And since I was not welcomed by a host at one of the pavilions due to the dishonor of my rank, this was the best I could manage. So long as the creaky roof over our heads keeps out the rain, and therefore the threat of rust, I can find no complaint.

Laid out upon the wooden table before us is a wide selection of weapons. Sharpened axes, steel-tipped spears, double-edged swords, arrows with fletching of sleek dove feathers. I have to choose wisely. To be over-encumbered is a disadvantage, so it's better to only take what we need. No matter the weapon—they will all kill demons just the same.

"You reckon we'll be done by dinner?" Wen asks. He inspects the sharpened tips of his arrows before sliding them into the bamboo-carved quiver at his hip. "Ling's making dumpling soup tonight."

I suppress a chuckle. There are few things Wen enjoys more than talking about his wife. Give him a long enough stretch of silence and I'd wager my every coin he will find a way to mention her. "I'm offended you haven't extended an invitation," I say dryly.

Wen snorts as he rubs his wrist. The tremor in his hand is slight, but I notice these things. Their well-being is my responsibility. I pray for all of our sakes that this is the last hunt we will endure.

"You can join my table any time you want, Cap'n. You know right well my kids prefer you over me."

"Of course they do. I bring them sweets, and it's your job to scold them."

Focus, Sooah signs with her hands. Her movements are somehow both fluid with practice, yet stiff with urgency. *The sun is setting soon.*

She's right. In all my years of hunting, I've observed that demons are most active after nightfall. It makes sense, given their opportunistic nature. When better to strike than while we're asleep in our beds, unaware and defenseless? If we don't hurry, we may face another string of disappearances before the sun rises once more.

I run through my usual checks. Daggers, sharpened. Dao, at my hip. Rope dart wrapped tightly around my waist. Just as a fisherman never leaves shore without his line, I have the tools of my trade at the ready.

"Move out," I order. "Before it strikes again."

If they leave no bodies, there may be witnesses. If there are no witnesses, there might still be tracks. And if there are no tracks, there's always the faintest chill in the air—a gut instinct that tells me something vile has walked the path before me.

A woman sits on the stoop of her shop, the local seamstress, biting her nails down to the beds. Her face is pale, her eyes red and puffy from crying. She stands the moment she sees us, apprehension furrowing her thin brows.

"Have you come back to mock me?" she asks, her voice rough and cracking.

I set my jaw. "Why would we mock you, madam?"

Her bottom lip trembles. "The officers tell me I've gone mad, but I swear I speak the truth. Something snatched up my daughter. A *demon*."

I take a deep breath and will my heart to remain calm. Sightings in the city are rare these days, no doubt in part because of my team's efforts. Demons tend to target smaller, more isolated villages where humans make easy pickings. The fact that one has made Longhao its territory bodes ill. The authorities here aren't equipped to combat such a danger, which was why I returned home in such a hurry at His Majesty's behest.

It had been years since he'd sent me a letter. I contemplated—only for a moment—ignoring his summons, though I decided it was unbecoming of a man my age to throw a tantrum. Besides, whether the king wishes to acknowledge it or not, I may be the only one equipped to handle situations such as these.

"Did you lay eyes on it?" I ask the seamstress. "This demon."

"No," she replies. "I mean, just a hand. That is all."

"A hand?" Wen mumbles.

"It shot out from around the corner," the woman explains. "My daughter was playing by an alley near the water markets. I looked away for but a moment, and when I looked up, I saw someone beckoning to her. I tried to call her back, but before I could, they grabbed my girl and dragged her away." The woman shakes her head, fighting back tears. "I gave chase, but by the time I made it to the alley, they were already gone. *Vanished*. All that was left was—"

She breaks into a sob as she pulls something wrapped in silk from the pocket of her dress. She hands it to me with trembling hands. Wen and Sooah both give me questioning glances as I unwrap the package.

Inside, two severed fingers belonging to a child.

A chill courses through me.

"Allow me but a moment," I say as gently as I'm able. Reaching toward one of the pouches attached to my belt, I retrieve one of the talismans I remembered to pack. Pressing the edge of the paper to the cold fingers, I frown in dismay when the slip immediately ignites, burning a foreboding black.

Sooah shakes her head slowly. Wen sucks in a sharp breath.

"W-what does it mean?" the woman asks, trembling.

"Tell us what it looked like," Wen says. "Was it a claw? Did it have fur? Feathers? Scales?"

The seamstress shook her head. "It was just a hand. Human. A woman's, I think."

Sooah frowns at this, signing quickly. *A skin-wearer?*

I grit my teeth and pray it isn't so. The last time I had the misfortune of encountering a skin-wearer was three years ago near the northern territories. By the time we arrived to banish the cursed beast, it had decimated the local population, peeling humans like little more than ripe fruit.

"Did its flesh appear rotten?" I ask her. "Deformed. Miscolored in any way?"

The woman, understandably, appears disgusted. "No. She had beautiful skin, like porcelain."

Good. Not a skin-wearer, then, but that only raises more questions. I might have dismissed this case as an unfortunate kidnapping-turned-murder, yet the talismans never lie. They may appear like nothing more than strips of parchment, but the spells written upon their surface have proven effective wards for centuries. It only burns black in the presence of a demon's aura. But a demon who looks human, capable of hiding in plain sight?

I want to say it's impossible, but to deny the possibility will only hinder my efforts. I must be pragmatic in this—no matter how terrified I may be.

Carefully, I wrap up the remains of her daughter and return them to the seamstress. "We shall handle things from here," I say firmly.

"Please find her, sir. *Please*, save my daughter."

It's far too late for that. Her child now rests in the belly of a monster, one incapable of satiation.

"We'll do everything we can," I lie fluidly. There's no sense in upsetting her further. Better to offer her hope—as false as it may be—and try to stop this beast from making a meal of yet another poor soul.

We head for the water market, which bustles with late-night activity. Maybe we'll find more clues near the alley where the girl went missing. My hands grow clammy at the sight of so many people still out at this late hour. They don't understand the danger they're in, blissfully unaware that they're offering themselves up for dinner. I want to warn them, to tell them to return to their homes and lock their doors tight, but I would much rather avoid inciting panic.

"How much are you willing to wager it's the same demon eating all the rest?" Wen asks, and rather crassly at that.

Sooah huffs. *I don't know what's worse. One rabid beast, or an entire horde.*

"What do you think, Cap'n?"

Admittedly, I'd only been half listening, too engrossed in the notes of my hunting log. It was open to the entry pertaining to the skin-wearer we encountered all those years ago. "It takes three to five days for skin to rot," I say. "Even if it were a fresh kill, there'd still be identifiable discoloration. What if the demon we're after has found a way to prolong their disguise? Or maybe it's the result of some other strange magic."

An illusion, Sooah suggests. *Or perhaps hypnosis?*

"Possibly," I murmur, flipping the page. "Or maybe it's—"

"You there!" calls a woman's sweet voice.

My attention is drawn to a canopied longboat lazily drifting down the canal. Beneath the shade sits a gaggle of young women, dressed in fine silks with bejeweled adornments shining in their hair. They titter to one another behind hand-painted fans, batting their long lashes at me with obvious interest.

"Can I help you?" I ask bluntly. There's no time to spare for pleasantries. Not with a man-eating monster on the loose.

"Will you come join us for tea?" one of the women asks unabashedly. I wonder if they're drunk. "My sister here thinks you're *very* handsome."

I clear my throat, hot under the collar. I don't much care for their attempted advances. There are far more pressing matters I must attend to. Even if I do find their smiles pleasant, duty comes above and before all.

"Not interested," I answer. Best not leave room for argument.

As the ladies let out jeers of disappointment, Wen nudges me in the arm with the tip of his elbow. "Let them down easy, Cap'n. You're hurting *my* feelings."

"I'll buy you flowers later," I offer dryly.

He doesn't deserve them, Sooah protests with a roll of her eyes.

"Course I deserve them. In fact, I should get a medal for dealing with your nagging ass day in and day out."

Sooah gestures rudely, her imaginative string of signs translating to something along the lines of, *Go fuck a hungry tiger*.

While the two of them bicker back and forth, I notice something curious out of the corner of my eye. Across the water on the other side of the canal, I spot a figure skulking in the shadows. They wear a heavy wool cloak, its hood drawn low over their heads to obstruct their face from view. Strange, given that we're in the middle of the summer months. They must be sweating buckets in that thing. Unless . . .

Unless they don't know this isn't how humans act in the muggy heat.

The figure turns their head, as if something in the distance has caught their attention. They pivot with hawkish precision, disappearing like a specter into the night. The fine hairs on the back of my neck stand on end, my heart racing. I don't need a talisman to confirm my suspicions—I just know. It's in their gait, in their posture. Eager, yet careful; a predator stalking prey.

Whatever is prowling the streets of my home, I have every intention of running my sword through its heart.

"Sooah, Wen," I call. "Come with me."

3

Before him, a wasteland. The parched ground cracked and crumbled beneath his arduous steps. There were no trees in sight, no flowers in bloom. Even the weeds, normally steadfast and conniving, had shriveled up and forsaken the land.

"Houyi, my husband, please wait!"

He turned to find his darling wife clinging to the shadows of their abode, though she dared not venture out into the sunlight. The rays were far too harsh for her ivory complexion to withstand a moment's exposure. He himself was covered from head to toe in white linens to protect his flesh from charring, and even still, he could feel himself beginning to burn.

He placed a hand on her round belly. They were expecting their child any day now, though with the world outside on the cusp of disintegration, it was difficult to enjoy their impending gift. "Chang'e, my love, you need not fret. I shan't falter in my mission."

"At least take this along with you," she said as she produced a dried calabash. It was full and heavy, liquid sloshing within. These days, fresh water was worth more than gold. She likely spent weeks collecting what little could be drawn from the underground stream beneath the mountain—a feat in and of itself.

"Please take caution, my lord. You must promise your safe return."

Houyi pressed his lips to her cheek, relishing the momentary coolness of her skin. "For you, my lady, I will move Heaven and Earth."

With that, he adjusted his grip on his bamboo bow and quiver before setting out to do what many had deemed impossible—to kill the very stars above.

The heat was unbearable, the air horrendously dry. He could hardly draw breath without the back of his throat cracking and his lungs burning up from within.

Ten star gods hung low in the sky, all of them as brilliant as they were blinding. They laughed at his efforts to climb to the tallest peak of the tallest mountain, and laughed harder still when Houyi readied his bow, nocked his arrow, and aimed toward the sky.

"Begone!" he shouted toward the stars. "Lest I pierce you each through the heart."

"Do you mean to amuse us, little archer?" the first star replied mockingly. "Your hubris shall be your undoing."

"I shall only warn you once!" Houyi declared, steadying his breath as he prepared to loose his arrow.

The ten stars only burned brighter in response, setting the land ablaze and evaporating the remaining rivers. So hot was the air around Houyi that his sweat dried the moment it formed upon his brow. Crops shriveled and turned to dust. Critters burrowed deeper into the ground in search of relief. His warning unheeded, Houyi fired his bow—

And pierced the first star in the heart.

Startled by the archer's impossible aim, the star god stumbled from his place in the sky and plummeted beyond the horizon with an earsplitting scream. Before the rest of the stars had a chance to react, Houyi let loose another arrow, and then another—and then another. One by one, the stars fell from their seats in Heaven until only one remained.

"Still thy bow, Lord Archer," the final star pleaded. "A grave mistake it would be to kill me as you have done my brothers."

"Tell me why I should spare you after the torture you have wrought."

"You cannot survive in total darkness, mortal. Spare me, and I will ensure your forests will flourish and your bountiful harvests will bloom. Without my aid, all will freeze and die."

As angry as he was, Houyi knew the star spoke the truth. Life and light went hand in hand, as did Death and darkness.

"How do I know you will not retaliate?" Houyi asked. "I let you live, and you use the rest of your magic to burn me when my back is turned."

"Then this, too, I shall promise," the star god replied. "I will bestow upon you and your line my godly blessing. Seal my magic within your souls to protect you through all endeavors, and in turn, you will be the protectors of mankind forevermore."

Houyi could not be sure if this was a ploy. The gods, after all, were a crafty sort. With this offer, Houyi's wife and child—and the rest of the world, for that matter—would finally be unburdened.

"Very well," he said. "Let it be so."

Slowly, he lowered his weapon and shrugged off the overbearing weight of his linens. Houyi was pleasantly surprised when his skin did not immediately burn and blister.

He welcomed the delightful warmth of the singular star, where it would remain for the rest of time—known solely as the Sun.

4

Yue

Hunting Log #159:
Trust your instincts. Not all is as it appears.

I ***find my way back to*** the main street, pulling the hood of my cloak up and over my head. The merchants of the water market are packing up for the night, while the local teahouses grow rowdier as the evening drags on, the orange light spilling out through the latticed windows to paint the cold ground outside. I've never been inside one, for I'm sure the beauty of my mask would bring ill-wanted attention, though a part of me likes to dream. What do sweet bean buns taste like? What gossip might I overhear?

I wander, as I do so many nights, nothing more than a leaf drifting upon the current of people. I'm drawn less so to the crowds than to areas of noise, where folks gather merrily beneath the flickering golden glow of paper lanterns. It's a special sort of thrill to walk among their kind undetected. Sometimes, I can pretend I'm one of them. Especially now that my stomach is full.

I peer into homes through cracks in their windows, spoiled with the sight of families enjoying their nightly meals. A few blocks away, I spy a mother tucking her children into their beds by candlelight, lovingly combing her fingers through their hair as she wishes them sweet dreams. The home after that, I peek in to find an elderly couple, their bodies frail and little, curled up together beneath a shared blanket. Their faces are peaceful in sleep, the gentle rise and fall of their chests in time with one another.

I don't stop until I accidentally find myself in what the humans call the Pleasure District, pulled in by the scent of floral perfumes and the melodious songs of painted women. A column of large buildings stands on either side of the single street, their walls painted red with heavy golden accents. It's so bright and ostentatious that it hurts my eyes. Ladies stand by ground-floor windows in sheer dresses, making flirtatious eyes to the men and women browsing as they would in the markets. It never occurred to me that pleasure could be a commodity—both bought and sold like any other good.

Settling into the mouth of a narrow alley, I take a seat behind a stack of abandoned crates, soaking up the movements and sounds and colors. Across the way, I spot a young couple stumbling out the front doors of a pleasure house. The buck looks drunk, likely on both wine and kisses, the doe on his arm giggling sweetly against his ear.

"Promise you'll come again tomorrow?" she asks him.

He whispers something. Although my hearing is better than most, I can't make out what he says at this distance. It's a secret, just for her. One that causes her cheeks to flush pink and her eyes to widen in delighted surprise. Did he promise to whisk her away? Or did he murmur something scandalous in nature?

The man takes her hand, carefully threading his fingers between hers, all the while holding her gaze with a tenderness that makes my chest feel . . . strangely tight.

Curious, I hold my own hands up before me and thread my fingers together. They are soft and warm, but it's hardly as magical an experience as the couple makes it seem. I laugh bitterly under my breath. How pathetic am I, yearning to have my hand held like a child?

"Are you lost, madam?" a deep voice reaches my ear.

I nearly jump out of my skin, turning so quickly I almost lose my balance. I look up to find a night watchman.

From what little I understand about human aging, I estimate him to be in his early to mid thirties, though his steep frown makes him appear a decade older. He's dressed in armor—a leather chest piece pulled over mulberry red robes—with his dao at his hip and black leather gauntlets pulled up to below his elbows. Strong and regal and much too serious, his features teetering just on the other side of unfriendly. His hair is cropped short at the sides, where the length on top is pulled back into a neat bun in typical Southern Kingdom fashion. I note his thick brows, square jaw, thin lips, and rough stubble. Some might call him a rugged brute.

But his dark axinite eyes and impressive stature aren't what beguile me so . . .

It's his *smell.*

Crushed cinnamon, star anise, and sweet dried mango. An assaulting combination of sweet and earthy. I wonder if he's been spending time with the spice traders near the markets. My mouth waters. My stomach growls with a painful ferocity. I fight the urge to unhinge my jaw and swallow him whole, my baser animal instincts rising to the surface of my skin.

I damn near lash out to bite him when he suddenly says, "It's a little late to be wandering the streets alone, madam. Do you require an escort home?"

My hands tremble and my nostrils flare. I've never come across a human who smelled more delicious. His scent blanks my mind and leaves my body numb. I could finish him off in seven bites, I think. First his throat to silence his scream, then his head, both arms, his legs, and then torso. A meal like him would keep me satisfied for two whole moons.

My sudden lack of control horrifies me. I'm trapped within myself, so consumed by this desperate hunger that it reduces me to the beast I truly am. What if I lose myself and go on a rampage? I'd feast on every soul I could find until hunters are called to find me.

The watchman observes me with obvious curiosity. I recognize him now. He was the one I spotted on the other side of the canal earlier this evening, fending off the attentions of the young ladies in their boat. Has he been following me? Does he know what I've done? My eyes flicker down to his weapon now.

Sharp. Dangerous.

"What is your name?" he asks.

I bite my tongue. He tries to offer his hand, but I flinch away like I've been burned. I don't know what's come over me. I need to escape, to get as far away from here as possible.

And yet I can't move. My war-drum heart hammers against the ladder of my ribs, the rush of blood past my ears putting a terrible pressure behind my eyes. If I don't eat this watchman, I feel like I might die.

Even worse than that—I think he knows. He *knows*. It's in the tension of his shoulders, his stance, prepared and alert and ready to fight if need be. This man may look the part of a night watchman, but I know for a fact that their patrols don't take them out this far. In fact, I've seen the local proprietors pay good money for the privilege of a wide berth. Either this man has been newly hired and is not yet in someone's pocket, or he isn't a watchman at all.

I've remained silent for far too long. His hand falls to the hilt of his dao—

I lunge at him, my jaw unhinging as the last remnants of my sanity wash away. He throws an arm up and my teeth sink into the leather of his gauntlet, barely scraping skin. I see him reach for his sword, but I knock it away with a well-placed kick, using the momentum to throw myself under and then over his arm serving as a pivot point—all while my teeth sink in further. I throw him off-balance, dragging him down. The hard *thud* of his body against the stones rattles my skull. If he tries to move, all it will take is one hard yank to separate arm from socket.

Unlike the drunkard, however, I smell no panic. No fear. Surprise, perhaps, but the watchman is quick to counter, moving with an almost practiced ease. He gathers dirt in his free hand and throws it into my eyes. Such a nasty trick. His arm falls from my mouth as I hiss and reel back, blinking away the debris stinging my vision.

"Wen! Sooah! Do it now!"

His gaze flicks up to something behind me. I realize my mistake—I've let my guard down. I don't even have a chance to turn before someone throws a weighted net over my head. There are two other watchmen, closing in to pin my arms and legs down with their pointy knees. No matter how much I thrash and scream, they show no remorse as they press yellow strips of parchment to my wrists and ankles—binding talismans—to magically immobilize my limbs.

"We have the animal secured, sir," one of them announces, his words thick with a distinguishable countryside accent. "What should we do now, Cap'n Sonam?"

Sonam. So that's the name of this monster. An uncommon one around these parts. I've only ever heard it once before, though now is hardly the time to reminisce.

Onlookers begin to gather, horrified to see three grown men forcibly restraining a helpless woman. I lean into their alarm, crying and wailing and pleading in the hopes of manipulating their sympathy. My performance is convincing, but their disgust with the watchmen quickly dissolves into curious shock as Captain

Sonam steps forward, crouches down before me, and reaches beneath the net to pull off my mask—and the magic along with it.

I transform against my will. Now they see me for what I am: a revolting beast. I can't stand to have them look.

"Give it back!" I gnash my teeth, swallowing my burning shame.

"I've only ever caught a nine-tailed fox once before," he says thoughtfully. The captain inspects my mask with great interest. "But it never had something like this. Where did you find this piece of cursed magic?"

My voice is a growl from the very back of my throat. "Give it back right now, or I'll eat your heart whole!"

He doesn't seem remotely threatened. Or even alarmed, for that matter, to lay eyes upon my hulking, demonic form. Instead, he calmly turns to one of his friends. "Secure its binds and bring it to the Jade Palace. I need to present it to the king. It'll be safer there for the shamans to banish it away from prying eyes."

"Banish me?" I snap. "Banish me where?"

"To Hell."

5

Yue

Hunting Log #164:
They often resemble animals, which helps them hide in plain sight.
A list (non-exhaustive): hawks, tigers, hounds, boars . . . foxes.

T***hey force me into a*** barbed muzzle, the suffocating leather straps twisting around and over my head like thorny vines. The dull metal isn't strong enough to cut my flesh, but it's uncomfortable nonetheless, biting into me like vicious horseflies in the summertime heat.

I'm crammed into a cage so small that I can't stand, nor properly sit; crouched over painfully as I awkwardly balance myself on my paws. Every corner is sealed with talismans designed to trap me as the guards pull me forward on a rickety wooden cart. No matter how hard I fight against the bars, rocking myself from side to side, the magic refuses to relent. As we draw closer to the main gates, an ugly chill shreds its way down my spine.

I've never been this close to the Jade Palace before. There's never been any need. Too many guards, too many constricting walls. A death trap more than a hunting ground. It can only be described as a city built within a city—built within another city.

Its massive courtyards and palaces nest on top of each other, the walls of each section circling around the next. The king's abode is located directly in the center, the main pavilion overshadowing every other building in its vicinity. Everything from the pathways to the guard towers to the moon bridges arching over man-made streams is carved of polished jade, but I'm the furthest from impressed. A pretty shell does nothing for the rot within, and I can smell its repugnance all around me.

Something isn't right about this place.

We come to a stop in the middle of a wide, open courtyard. Armed guards are everywhere, their swords drawn and ready to swing. Royal archers surround us atop the inner city's walls, at the ready with their bows nocked and arrow tips aimed in my direction. One wrong move and they'll slice me to bits and riddle those same bits with holes. I despise the way they look at me—as if I am equal parts freak and nightmarish horror. If only Captain Sonam hadn't taken my mask, I'd be able to hide from their judgment.

One of the captain's men pokes and prods at me through the bars with his scabbard, laughing in cruel delight whenever he manages to pull a growl from my throat.

And they call *me* an animal.

"Leave it alone, Wen," Captain Sonam snaps.

Wen doesn't heed his warning. Instead, he reaches through the bars and strokes one of my tails. I lash out against the cage, but I'm unable to reach him. He'll be the first I devour when I get out of here.

"But look at this fur. I could wash it! Make one of its tails into a pretty scarf for my wife. Ain't like it don't have any to spare."

He's the youngest of the group, his immaturity accentuated by his boisterous nature. He stands at least half a head taller than his captain, but his shoulders are narrow and his limbs lanky. His armor doesn't fit well, hanging off of his frame like garments left out to dry on a clothesline. Hand-me-downs, if I had to venture a guess. I pity him his wonky nose and gapped teeth, but I pity the woman who agreed to marry him all the more.

The other guard under the captain's command has yet to utter a word. A woman, not a man as I first believed, though her masculine appearance certainly lends itself to the assumption. She stands tall and dutiful, wearing just as severe a frown as her leader. This is not a lady of refinement, but one of battle, the deep scars of angry red upon her cheeks and across the bridge of her nose a written history of all the violence she's seen. It isn't until she motions to Wen with her hands, stringing together a sequence of signals as she produces shapes with her mouth, that I realize she's missing her tongue.

Did she lose it in a fight, I wonder, or was it punishment for some unknown crime?

Whatever the guard says, it causes Wen to roll his eyes. "It ain't gonna bite me," he replies arrogantly. "Would you quit being such a worrywart?"

Sonam stands firm, arms folded over his broad chest. "Sooah is right. Leave the demon be. The king will be here soon."

Mildly disgruntled, Wen bows his head. "As you wish."

My heart skips a beat. The king is coming? Why in the nine suns would the King of Jian deign to see someone like me?

At the sound of a palace eunuch's boisterous call, Captain Sonam bows steeply, hinging at the hips toward a figure I can't yet see. Wen and Sooah also bow, though they drop to their knees into a full kowtow, foreheads smacking against the jade stones—an indication of their unworthy station. What I wouldn't give to tell them to do it over and over again until they shatter their own skulls.

"You've done well, Demon Hunter of Jian."

I strain my neck to see who the voice belongs to. Standing at the bottom of a jade staircase is a man practically swimming in the finest silks in all the land. He contrasts sharply against our all-green surroundings, his white robes accented with embroidered designs of delicate golden thread, appearing almost like a cloud at sunset. He is nearly double the captain's age, his long beard streaked with white and his mianguan expertly placed to conceal his receding hairline. Thick rings of jade decorate each of his fingers. There's a heavy sink to his jowls, and the crow's-feet at the corners of his eyes become more pronounced as he smiles with approval.

Behind the king stands a group of young men, all dressed nearly as lavishly as he. There are seven of these peacocks—all brothers, judging by the same shape of their lips and width of their eyes. Qualities, I notice, that Captain Sonam seems to share. But that's where the similarities stop. Where they stand with lax, haughty airs, Sonam is rigid and tempered. A collection of fine silk against the edge of sharpened steel. I don't miss the way he clenches his filthy, calloused palms and hides them from view behind his back.

"Our people are all the safer thanks to your efforts," the king says.

"Thank you, Father," Sonam replies. Stiff. Almost rehearsed. "This demon has plagued our city for far too long. My only regret is that I failed to catch it sooner."

My ears prick up. *Father?* How very interesting. While I'm curious to understand Sonam's lack of a princely title, I'm more concerned with finding a way to escape. I have no interest in human affairs, least of all the affairs of my captor.

"What's done is done," the king says as he approaches my cage, inspecting me from head to tails with wide-eyed fascination. "You're certain it's the last one in the city?" he asks Sonam.

"Yes, it is. I've been careful to kill or banish all the rest."

My stomach twists. This can't be. Of all human flaws, I've always despised their ability to lie above all else. There's no way a single, mortal, weak little human could have achieved such a feat.

But what if he speaks the truth?

It's not that I care for the well-being of other demons. They are hardly my concern, nor, I'm sure, am I one of theirs. We are mountains, built of the same cold earth, but we stand alone to brave the world all on our own. I look after myself. Though I'll confess to feeling a strange numbness at knowing I'm the last one to walk the mortal plane. *Special* isn't quite the right word I'm looking for, but I can think of no other way to describe it. I outlasted them all—until today, it would seem.

"Very well. I expect nothing less from a son of my court."

The princes whisper among themselves, clearly unimpressed or disbelieving. In the same way Sonam looks down on me, they do the same to their brother. Sonam may stand tall and proud like the rest, but he also stands apart. His clothes are utilitarian, no excess fabric or hefty pieces of jewelry to show off his wealth. The weapons strapped to his belt are not simply for show. There are signs of wear and tear on the worn hilt of his sword, as well as the grooved leather loops of his belt. My curiosity burns. If he is a son of the king, surely his station can afford him the life of a prince—so why does he look a mere foot soldier?

Even his title as a captain makes little sense. A man of his birth should have a whole army at his command, not two measly guards. And surely he should be able to afford finer armor. Where is his chest plate carved of gold, and his heavy helmet complete with ridiculously long head feathers to flaunt his importance? Humans love to boast—so why not this one?

Sonam's expression brightens a touch, hopeful. "Does this mean that I'm welcome back?" He sounds so much like a boy at this moment. Too eager, too transparent.

The king pats his son on the shoulder. "We shall discuss things further once we have dealt with this beast."

Reminded of my plight, I struggle within the confines of my cage, my hackles rising. The self-righteousness in their tone infuriates me. I'm nothing but an object to them, something to discard if they so choose. And they will. Even with the muzzle pulled tight over my face, I scream and growl with every ounce of fury burning in my chest. The more I lash out, the more the talismans sear my flesh. The heat is excruciating. Hotter, even, than the fire that maimed me all those years ago.

With a quick wave of his hand, the king summons the palace shamans.

They emerge from the shade of a nearby building, apparently awaiting their cue. They smell unnatural, so sickeningly bitter it makes me gag. Humans have no magic of their own, but they've learned to harness it for themselves through potions and incantations and the manipulation of qi; teachings passed down through the generations from a time when the gods still walked the earth.

"Wait," Captain Sonam interrupts. "I wish to speak to it."

"Speak to it?" one of the princes scoffs. "Whatever for?"

"Hurry up and get rid of the thing. It smells horrible," grumbles another, pinching his nose with a sneer.

Curse him.

Despite the captain's protestations, the shamans approach the cage, wearing their necklaces of bird skulls and dried herbs, their irises a milky white. Their bodies may be of the mortal realm, but I can tell by their distant gazes that their minds are worlds away. They chant in unison, a spell recited in a dead tongue, their low murmurs equal parts haunting and threatening. There's static in the air, a rising charge causes my muscles to tighten and clench. An invisible force chokes me, scorching the air in my lungs and boiling my blood.

The sky darkens, a sudden storm manifesting overhead. It brings with it a wind strong enough to whip the entire palace aside. Dark clouds swirl as the jade beneath my cage begins to warp. I'm sinking, the ground beneath my feet transforming into quicksand. This is what they meant by banishing me to Hell. They've opened a gateway, and now they intend to throw me down and the key along with it.

Darkness engulfs me, claiming my body as I'm dragged beneath ground. It would be easy to give up, to let these monsters do what they want. But I haven't survived all these years by literally tucking my tails between my legs.

I force an arm through the bars. The talismans' magic is so intense it feels as though it singes through my fur, my flesh, my muscles, and all the way down to the bone, but I fight. I fight with every ounce of my being, and with one last desperate swipe, I dig my claws into the captain's shoulder. It all happens so quickly that the king and Sonam's mob of brothers can only blink as I drag him down.

The ground swallows us up, the banishment now complete.

At least I can die knowing I brought this insufferable human with me.

6

Yue

Hunting Log #370:
There is little known about nine-tailed fox demons, as encounters with the beasts are rare . . .

No doubt because they consume any witnesses before records can be made.

I think about death often, as morbid as that may be. The permanence of it.

Unlike humans who have souls ready for reincarnation, a demon cannot boast such luck. The first gods of creation did not craft us with souls in mind. Whether this was their intent or due to forgetfulness, I cannot say. What I do know is that if I die, my very existence will be wiped from the land, no soul of my own to rejoin the circle of death and rebirth. We're removed from karmic justice, destined to *cease*. The onus of remembering my family lies solely on my shoulders, but it troubles me to know that there will be no one to remember me. It will be as if I never lived at all.

And that's why, when I see the ground coming up to meet me, I scream bloody murder.

Landing isn't so bad.

It's everything that comes afterward.

It's a uniquely chilling experience to listen to every single bone in my body break, the crushing of a bundle of twigs underfoot. Black stars speckle my vision, threatening to fill the entire canvas of my view. I spit out a mixture of blood and shattered teeth. I'm certain that both of my knees are hinged in the wrong direction, but I'm in so much shock that I cannot feel anything. The smallest of blessings, that.

I'm dying. Afraid and alone. My heart twists knowing no one will mourn me.

And then I catch a whiff of something sweet. Crushed cinnamon, star anise, mangoes.

I know this scent. I *hate* this scent.

Captain Sonam has landed not five arms away, his eyes fluttering as he struggles to wake. The fall should have killed him, but I can hear his wretched, wet breathing. Barely holding on, but most definitely alive.

Good. I want the pleasure of killing him myself.

I'm unable to move, however. The cage has broken open as a result of the fall, but its bars have warped themselves around my limbs and rib cage, rendering me immobile beneath its punishing grip. Pulling against my restraints is useless. My fox form is simply too big to escape this confinement.

If only I were a little smaller. Human-sized.

Out of the corner of my eye, I spot my mask. The captain must have dropped it. It's mercifully fallen to my side and appears to be intact, no doubt thanks to the magic within. If I put it on, my body will remain broken, but at least I'll be able to wriggle free from this cage.

I reach for it, flexing with a claw and clipping the mask with a nail. It nearly rolls away, dragged down by the slope we've landed on. My broken bones scream with the effort, but I refuse to relent. No one's going to help me, so I need to help myself.

My sisters were the last who tried, and look how well that ended.

When I finally manage to tip the mask toward me, I snatch it up. Pressing it to my face, my beastly form shrinks in an instant, the spell transforming me into a young woman, a tragic beauty since my body is but a mangled heap.

Now that the bars of the cage no longer have a hold on me, I drag myself over to inspect Sonam. I must look horrifying, my sweat-soaked hair over my face, awkwardly using my forearms and elbows to shift me forward on my belly like a beetle whose hind-legs were plucked off. I grit my teeth and fight through the pain.

The captain's survival is nothing short of a miracle, though I might argue it a curse. He's in far better condition than I am, just the one arm dislocated and twisted beneath him. Deep cuts mar his face, dark purple bruises around his eyes, his jaw, his nose. I can hear his strained heart thumping, his pulse irregular and weak. I hope he's bleeding inside. I hope it *hurts*. Killing him may actually be a mercy.

I sink my fingers into the captain's injured shoulder, determined to tear him open. Sonam cries out, eyes flying open, his face crumpling as he tries to shove me away. Now is as good a time as any to exact my revenge. The easiest meals come when they're injured and alone, and the captain happens to be both.

The only problem is this meal knows how to fight.

Where I targeted his weakness, Sonam does the same. He kicks at my ruined knees, sweeping an arm to grip my side and squeeze my sore ribs. I fall back, gasping for air. He is on top of me, pinning my back to the ground as I scratch and hiss, the wild animal that I am.

I hit him, he hits me back—an explosive conversation with our fists.

It's not that he's strong enough to overpower me, but that our injuries have rendered us both equally weak. There's a monstrous anger in his eyes, fiery and vicious. Burning with righteous hate. It's nothing new. Mankind has looked upon me with disdain for so long that it would be shocking to see anything but.

He has the upper hand like this, but not for long. I drive my thigh up and kick him in the groin, watching with exhausted satisfaction when Sonam crumples, giving me a chance to push him away. I struggle to prop myself up on to my elbows. He does the same, his lip curled up in a bloodied sneer. He's a vicious thing—even more vicious than I.

I've never been more terrified.

This man is going to be the death of me. All the more reason to finish him first.

But I don't get the chance. Just as I gather the strength to pounce, Sonam pulls himself to his feet and scrambles away into the bleary dark.

"You bastard!" I scream, crawling after him. "Come back here and fight me, you coward!"

My voice breaks, shoulder-wracking sobs shoving their way out through my throat. Iron-hot tears race down my cheeks, and my heart twists violently in my chest. I don't know what's worse—to be left alone in the dark to die, or the fact that I wasn't worth a killing blow.

Forcing air into my lungs, I will my nerves to steady. This is no time to cry. If the human wants to run, then let him. I will simply do what I do best. I push past the pain and drag myself forward on my stomach, my feet leaving bloody, dragging marks along the ground. They could very well be the only evidence I leave behind to prove my existence here.

Once more, I set forth to stalk my prey.

7

Sonam

Hunting Log #373:
From what little I have managed to parse,
nine-tailed foxes are known seductresses.
They use their beauty to lure victims into their waiting jaws.

T***he beast called me a coward,*** but I know better than to react. Any hunter worth his salt knows it is always better to retreat and regroup. Once I manage to catch my breath, I'll eagerly return to kill it. Survival and strategy go hand in hand.

It's closing in, maybe two li behind. I don't dare stop to look and see. It's in far worse shape than I am, the terrible scraping shuffle of its broken legs against the cold ground filling my ears like a taunt. A nightmare incarnate. The fall should have killed us both, yet it follows, ever hungry.

In truth, I haven't the faintest idea where I'm going. There is only a sea of shadows swirling around me in a cold, dense fog. So dark are my surroundings that, when I hold out my hand, it disappears into the gloom.

Before me stands an endless abyss. Behind me crawls my demise.

I stumble over uneven ground, falling forward with no time to catch myself. I land on my dislocated shoulder, shards of glass scraping their way up my nerve endings. I try not to cry out, but a pained grunt squeezes through my clenched teeth.

The fox cackles. It's an unnerving, manic laugh—high-pitched, like a child's. "Come out, come out, wherever you are," it sings, the tune echoing into the measureless expanse.

My body screams in protest as I force myself to rise, every fiber of my being begging me to stop, to rest. Running is futile, but what other choice do I have?

Reaching out aimlessly, my fingers jam up against a rough, solid surface, scraping the skin off the back of my knuckles. I wince, ignoring the sting in favor of feeling around. It's part of a crumbling stone wall. Squinting, I notice what look to be the ruins of an old building, worn away to its foundation. How odd. It never occurred to me that anyone would make a home of Hell, though they've clearly left long ago.

My knees buckle, exhaustion and panic whiting my mind. By some miracle, I'm able to prop myself up against the wall, struggling to stay awake. I need to escape this place, but I don't know how. The palace shamans understand the magic required to cast demons away, but I've always understood it to be a one-way door. Even if I possessed magic and knew the spell to open a gate, I have doubts it would even let me pass through.

It's okay to be scared, little brother, Jun once told me. *I'm sure even the Legendary Archer feared the wrath of the stars.*

How did he do it, then? I remembered asking, still small enough to sit across his lap. My eldest brother had come home injured from a hunt, and because he did not cry, I felt compelled to cry for him.

Jun had simply laughed as he pinched my cheek. *How does anyone do anything? Afraid but willing.*

I silently repeat the mantra to myself until my heart finally begins to steady. Sweat drips from my brow and down my neck, soaking into my clothes. I can't hear the fox anymore. Hopefully it's died somewhere, but I know better than to leave my fate to luck.

What I need to do is reset my shoulder. I will want full use of both my hands if it comes down to another fight. Taking a deep breath in through my mouth, I thread my fingers together to form a loop with my arms. I prop my leg up and through, hitching my wrists over my knee. I thrust my leg forward while pulling my torso back, swallowing my agony as the joint snaps into its socket.

I make no sound. No scream, no groan, not even a whimper. I must endure in silence or else risk giving up my position. It takes a moment for the horrendous dizziness to fade. Even when it does, the terrible churn of my stomach threatens to make me lose my lunch. I think of Wen and Sooah, of how we were making dinner plans only hours ago. I'm thankful, at the very least, that the demon didn't drag them into Hell with me. I wouldn't wish this fate on my worst enemy any more than them.

Although my arm throbs, I can move more easily now. I draw my dao, the sharpened edge of the blade singing against the scabbard's throat. My brothers all have their own, most of them gifts from Father, but they are decorative and wholly useless: worn at the hip the same way the court ladies flout their jewelry and custom-painted fans.

My blade boasts no name or glittering accents, only triumphant kills. This nine-tailed fox may be the fiercest, vilest, and most grotesque monster I have ever faced, but I am the Demon Hunter of Jian and there has never been a beast I could not vanquish.

Reaching for my belt, I produce one of my throwing needles, mindful of the poison-coated tip. I may be afraid, but I am willing. If I cannot banish the fox, I will outrun it. If I cannot outrun the fox, I will fight it. And if I cannot fight the fox, I will simply have to outsmart it.

I untie my scabbard and grip the end tight, throwing it a few feet ahead of me. It lands with a dull *thud*, but in this silent void it may as well be an ear-bursting clamor. I'm rewarded with a snarl from somewhere to my left. The fox, still disguised as a human woman, must have been lying in wait. She picks up my scabbard and screams—a high, bloodcurdling howl—when it realizes it's fallen for my gambit. It turns in search, but it's too late. I lunge, throwing my arm around its throat to trap it in a headlock.

I squeeze and squeeze and *squeeze*.

"Get off!" she rasps. "Filthy human—*get off*!"

"This is for all those innocent souls you feasted on," I hiss against her ear. "For that little girl you snapped up."

"What"—she croaks—"girl?"

"The seamstress's daughter."

"I've never—I don't eat children!"

There's no reason to hesitate. To believe its desperate lies. I've killed countless demons without a second thought. I could easily snap her neck—a quick and harsh pull separating head from shoulders—yet this feels different somehow. It's . . . jarring. *Wrong*. Especially when her eyes roll back and she attempts to suck despairing gulps of air. I've never killed a demon who looked and felt this human before. Even the skin-wearers were easier to dispatch, for they lacked the life and warmth of the people they impersonated.

This feels too real, too much like murder.

"Please," the fox demon whimpers, her cheeks wet with tears. "Please—*I don't want to die*."

8

Yue

Hunting Log #374:
Risk comes with reward.

This is it, I think. The human is going to kill me.

His hold loosens from around my throat.

With my remaining strength, I throw my elbows back and push him away. He falls to the side with a wet cough, blood spilling from his lips.

And we just . . . lie there.

Our minds are exhausted and our bodies destroyed. Black creeps from the edges of my vision, my eyelids are too heavy to keep open. It would be so easy to give in. To let myself rest until there's nothing at all.

"If you didn't eat that little girl, who did?" he asks me gruffly.

It takes me forever to catch my breath. "I do not know, but it wasn't me."

"And I'm supposed to believe your word?"

"Believe whatever you wish. I'm telling the truth."

I feel a dull stab of pain against my forearm. Little more than a pinprick. Given all of my other wounds, I could have imagined it.

"Make a deal with me, demon." The captain's words come hoarse, barely above a whisper.

Whatever snappy remark I have wilts on the tip of my tongue as a sudden scourge of dizziness grips my mind. I lift a hand and press it to the back of my head. My fingers come away black and sticky. A head wound, severe at that. It must have happened when I fell. Running on pure adrenaline has seen me this far, but now my injuries are finally taking their toll. I'm sluggish, every thought and movement laced in confusion.

"What?" I croak.

"A deal. With me. Demons make deals, do they not?"

It's a little-known truth that, when asked a direct question, demons cannot lie. For what reason, I haven't the faintest clue. It's written into our beings, a trade-off of sorts for our strengths. Perhaps the gods looked upon my kind eons ago and feared the twisted lies we'd whisper in their ears, and so condemned us to speak the truth when questioned as one of our only shining qualities.

"Yes, we make deals," I answer tightly.

He speaks between labored breaths. "Spare my life and help me escape this place."

I want to laugh, but the sound comes out as a squeak. I think one of my lungs is punctured. "Why"—I wheeze—"would I ever agree to that?"

"Would you prefer to die?"

"No, but this is nothing," I murmur. "I'll heal. It will take time, but it's going to take more than a fall to do me in."

"I'm not talking about the fall."

I strain my neck to glare at him. "What are you on about?"

Even through swollen eyes, the captain glances down at my forearm. I follow his line of sight, startled to find my fair skin has begun to fester. That pinprick . . . it wasn't a figment of my imagination after all. A black ooze spreads beneath the surface of my arm, tendrils of ink reaching and squirming like a squid marooned on land. The ghastly sight brings with it a burning sensation. Liquid fire spreads through my veins, searing everything in its path.

"What have you *done*?" I seethe.

"Poison," he replies, almost smug. "Derived from the feathers of a Zhenniao bird. I always"—he coughs—"keep a needle or two on hand."

All I can do is glare, my heart hammering. I'd seen a handful of those pretty birds before, back when my sisters and I still called the jungle our home. They might be extinct now. I haven't seen one in ages. It wouldn't be a surprise if the humans had hunted them to death, or perhaps they did the smart thing and left the jungle for safer skies.

I remember its body was small, as were its wings, but its tail feathers were so long that they spilled out from over their nests and almost touched the jungle floor. I easily recall the brilliant violet of their plumage. Lighter near its head, with an impressive crimson beak and a gorgeous, green-tipped tail. I almost made the mistake of eating one as a pup, but my sisters saved me from a most horrific fate, for their feathers are so poisonous they could kill even a dragon stone-dead. Even the gods are said to fear them, from the tales I've heard—one of the only things in existence strong enough to kill them.

And now I have a pin's dose filtering through my bloodstream.

"I have . . . an antidote," Sonam says around another breath. "Spare my life and see me from this place. Agree, and I'll give the antidote to you."

"You conniving little—" I speak around burning lungs. The poison is taking effect. I'll be dead in a few minutes. Maybe sooner, given the state I'm in.

The reality of my situation finally settles. I've been thrown into the pits of Hell with the very man who banished me here. I don't know if there's a way out, and we may well end up killing each other first, even if there is. Striking a deal with this heathen is the last thing I want to do, but I'm desperate enough to do it. The fact that Sonam didn't hesitate to bring his sword down upon my neck gives me pause, however. He spared me, that much is true, but to willingly work with this human could be my death sentence. He tried to hurt me once; who's to say he won't try again the moment he's free to—I will not risk my neck on a human's fickle whim.

My body seizes, every muscle suddenly pulling tight. I try to scream, but the sound is choked out of me. I can't see clearly, can't even hear the sound of my own thoughts. My arm has turned completely black, the poison spreading up and over my shoulder toward my neck and chest. If it reaches my heart, I'm done for.

Death sours the air around us. We're both running out of time.

Curse it all.

"Fine," I finally answer. "We have a deal, but give me the antidote first." He eyes me warily, prompting me to say, "You can't get what you want if I bloody well die first."

"How do I know you won't run off? We'll do it at the same time."

A growl rumbles in my throat. What a loathsome little ant. At first opportunity, I will crush him beneath my heel. "So be it."

Gritting his teeth, Sonam reaches for something tucked into one of the loops of his belt. A needle of some sort. He plucks it between his fingers. As he does so, I snatch his dagger, only for Sonam to grab my wrist.

"What are you playing at?" he snaps.

"Spare me your whingeing," I snarl. "I require an offering."

"What—"

I take his hand roughly and drag the blade across his palm before doing the same to mine. While his blood flows red, mine comes in a startling onyx. I grab his hand and press his wound firmly to my own, allowing our blood to mix. Where humans have no magic of their own, and the gods are an infinite well, demons can boast only a handful of spells—blood oaths being a particular specialty.

"*Gods above and devils below, witness us our accord. A cure for escape, escape for a cure, command our bodies be restored.*"

The moment I've finished my incantation, he jams the antidote into my thigh. Relief comes in the form of a wave. It swells, crests, and then crashes into me. I can finally breathe again, the firestorm raging within now quenched by the overwhelming flood that follows. I'll admit I was worried he wouldn't follow through on his promise.

Healing is a violent storm. My bones crack back into place like lightning. Every inch of my skin burns as if pelted by ice shards. Sonam writhes in similar agony, though I only hear him cry out once when the shattered bones of his ribs crunch into position. His cheeks are flushed, and his brow is slick with sweat, but at least he's alive.

"You look horrendous," I grumble once I've managed a breath.

"You're one to talk," he replies pointedly, struggling to sit up.

"Are you feeling better?"

"Yes, I—"

"Good."

I clench my fist and punch him square in the face. I never said anything about keeping my hands off of him. So long as I keep him breathing, I'm not in violation of my contract.

He groans loudly, pinching his bloodied nose. "What in the nine suns was that for, Fox?"

"This is all your fault! None of this would have happened if it hadn't been for you. If you wanted to go to Hell so badly, you could have just asked me to kill you."

We're back at each other's throats. He reaches for his dagger; I kick it away. I bring down my hand to strike; he throws his weight at me and tackles me to the ground. We spend a good few minutes like this, a give and take with no clear victor, until we're both thoroughly exhausted once more. I have never felt a more destructive loathing. I don't even hate the Maskmaker at this moment as much as I do this pitiful human stain.

We sit apart, fuming. Sonam rolls his head from side to side, stretching his neck. "Pulling me through the gates with you was wholly unnecessary."

"I thought I was going to die!"

"Am I supposed to feel sorry? Monsters like you—"

"Stop calling me that."

"Why? It's what you are."

"Don't test me, human."

"What's the worst you can do?" Sonam snaps.

"I'm going to rip your damn heart out."

"I would love to see you try, Fox."

I think about it. I truly, genuinely think about it. I can beat him black and blue all I want, but if there's ever a moment where his heart stops, I will suffer the punishment. The blood magic that binds me to him will obliterate me in the blink of an eye. I've seen it happen. I know the consequences—not that I'm keen to tell Sonam any of that. He might try to lord it over my head somehow.

"You're insufferable," I mutter.

"Whine all you want, but your stubbornness is going to see us both killed."

"I don't trust you."

"Nor I, you." Sonam takes a deep, slow breath before exhaling sharply. "We're not going to make it far if we don't work together. We need a . . . truce." The last word sounds like he's fighting back a gag.

"Your enthusiasm strikes great confidence," I say, eyeing him up and down suspiciously.

"The sooner we work together, the sooner we can leave." The captain's face is impassable, as hard as the carved jade of his family home. There's a heavy tension in the air, our eyes locked onto one another—two vipers ready to strike.

I lean in as close as I dare. "You may have your truce," I whisper, "but the moment we get out of here and our deal is done, I'll kill you."

"Likewise, Fox."

"Yue."

He frowns. "What?"

"My name," I tell him as I stand. "It's Yue, since you never bothered to ask."

"*Moon*?" he translates. "That's far too delicate a name for a demon—"

I kick him in the chest. Not hard enough to break what's just been repaired, but with enough strength to get the message across. He lands on his back with an unceremonious grunt, glaring daggers up at me. I ignore him and turn away.

I'm stronger than him. Faster, too. The only reason he managed to capture me in the first place was because he had help. But he's all alone down here, not an ally in sight. He'd be foolish to forget that.

I take in my first few glimpses of my surroundings through renewed eyes. Tales about the Ten Courts of Hell are common among the human folk. It was hard not to overhear stories whenever I'd come to the city to hunt. They'd pray to their gods, pray for their souls, fearing the oceans of devils and storms of liquid fire. Where suffering is a universal language, agony a common song.

How wrong they were.

It first appears that we've arrived back at the capital city of

Longhao. Except it isn't quite. It's empty, abandoned of all life and drained of color. The air is still and quiet. There are no songbirds to fill the silence, no idle chatter by the water markets, not even a whispering breeze. My breaths come too loudly. I'm afraid that if I speak, I may shatter my own eardrums.

There's little to no light here. The sky above is pitch-black. No stars, no clouds, no moon, no sun. It's as though someone's taken a thick blanket and sewn it in place. There is, however, a faint green light emanating from somewhere in the city, casting an almost sickly glow against the surrounding buildings. I crane my head back to get a better look, feeling the segments of my spine pop one by one.

It's the Jade Palace. A version of it, at least. It shines as a lighthouse on rocky shores, but I know not whether to run from it or be drawn to it. This place isn't right. It's strange and dark and cold. It smells rotten, putrid. The same horrible scent I detected back on the surface. The Jade Palace above, the one on the mortal plane, must have been built directly above this hellish abomination. As above, so below.

"How do we get out of here, then?" Sonam asks.

"How should I know?"

"Don't play games with me. All demons come from Hell."

"You're wrong."

"What do you mean?"

"I was born on the surface."

He shoots me an incredulous look. "How is that possible? I thought—"

I snort, hands on my hips. "You humans and your twisted tales. Demons are not born in Hell. We are born from human suffering. Be it rage, sorrow, pain, or lust—we come to be by your pathetic hands."

The captain frowns deeply. "I don't believe you."

"If you're not going to listen to me, don't bother asking stupid questions."

Sonam sets his jaw, too proud to speak his mind. I, however, am not above prodding. "What?" I ask. "Go on. Say it."

"I look forward to killing you," he replies bitterly.

"The feeling is mutual."

We both eye Hell's Jade Palace in the distance. It's as good a starting point as any. Surely its jarring green glow must be some measure of its significance.

"Let's head over there," I say.

He takes the lead without discussion, his long strides making it difficult to keep pace. Something tells me that our reluctant alliance will test every ounce of my limited patience.

"Don't fall behind, Fox," Sonam calls over his shoulder. "Don't expect me to carry you."

I bite my tongue and swallow my growing anger.

Oh, I cannot wait to eat him.

9

Yue

Hunting Log #375:
If what it says about being born of human suffering is true,
this could explain the increased demon sightings after every flood,
famine, and battle. I'll have to corroborate my findings
with the palace historians upon my return.
A troubling thought, this. Could it be that my work
may never truly be done?

T***he captain and I have*** been wandering for hours, venturing through the narrow streets of this empty city in bitter silence. Even in the gloomy green glow of the Jade Palace, I can see that every building, canal, and bridge stands as they do above. The path forward lies unobstructed, our destination clear. It's almost identical to the one on the mortal plane.

Almost.

No matter how many turns we take and roads we follow, we always seem to find ourselves back where we started. Something strange is going on. What, precisely, I cannot say.

Sonam reaches for something in one of the pouches attached to his belt. Is he trying for a weapon? One of those blasted needles coated in poison? I'd rather not deal with one of those again.

To my surprise, he pulls out a thick notebook bound between two pressed covers of bamboo, its spine tied precisely with twine. He flips open to one of the pages, his brows furrowing as he studies its contents before shutting it once more.

"What is that?" I ask.

"None of your business, Fox."

His tone is the cold, sharp edge of broken glass. Striking me across my face would be more polite. Prying information out of him is going to be like pulling teeth. I suppose I should be content with his standoffishness. I'm going to kill him sooner or later, so getting to know him serves no purpose.

I want to make a mess of him. Will I be satisfied tearing him limb from limb? Maybe I should make him scream first. What pleasure can I find clawing pathetic cries from his lungs and scraping tears from his eyes? I'll make him regret everything—every injury, every nasty word.

Turning toward the rickety wooden hut to my left, I tilt my head back to inspect the roof tiles. They look sturdy enough. The question is if I have the strength remaining to pull myself up. Even when I jump, I'm two heads too short of grabbing the ledge.

"What do you think you're doing?" the captain asks gruffly.

"Dancing—what does it look like?" I reply dryly. "I need a better look, so give me a lift."

"No."

I take a deep breath and swallow my simmering fury. Is this what insanity feels like? "Heaven forbid you should break a nail." When the captain once again meets me with silence, I roll my eyes. "I'm not going to run off, if that's what you're worried about. You've trapped me in a blood oath, remember?"

The muscles in his jaw tick, but he makes no move to help me. I turn away with a huff and try again, this time giving myself a running start. It's no small accomplishment when I clamber onto the roof of the building, my new vantage point offering a much better sense of the labyrinthine layout of the city.

That's when I notice something most curious.

The walls move of their own volition like a nest of gray snakes, or perhaps a knot of ashen worms, slithering and shifting as one giant creature. The roof tiles *click-click-clack* as they rearrange themselves, terra-cotta vertebrae snapping back into alignment. No wonder we haven't been making any progress. There's magic here. Magic that's actively conspiring against us, keeping us trapped in an endless loop. It would have driven me to madness, had I not discovered the truth.

"What do you see?" Sonam shouts up at me.

I glower at him. What I wouldn't give to run off on my own. Dragging a human everywhere is only going to slow me down. It's such a shame that blood oaths are unbreakable. There is no loophole, no clever wording to sway things to my favor. This magic is absolute and binding. The one I have with the Maskmaker has yet to release its hold, in fact.

"Some sort of enchantment," I tell the captain. "Seems our path changes as we make our way through. The only way forward is over."

I carefully lean over the edge of the roof and offer him my hand. The moment he reaches for me, I pull back.

"What are you doing?" he snaps. "Help me."

I cackle bitterly. It's a fox's laugh, chilling and raspy. Even the magic of my mask isn't enough to disguise the sound. *"No,"* I taunt.

I take great pleasure in watching the man climb up after me. Sonam uses the ledge of the window as a step before hauling himself onto the shanty roof, his breath labored and his face sweaty. I pay no mind to his hate-filled glare and start toward the palace without him.

The soft green glow grows more intense the closer I get. I'm mindful of the gap between buildings, jumping from one roof to the next with ease. From this height, I'm better able to see the snaking walls slither and slide. I see an upcoming wave, the shifting tiles almost . . . angry at my newfound tactic. I jump to the next rooftop, only for it to slide out from under me. I hit my ribs on the edge as I fall. As if sensing my sudden loss of footing, the building shoves its way back like a horse attempting to buck its rider. It's then that I realize this is no enchantment.

The city itself is *alive*, a sentient being.

I watch, slack-jawed, as the city grows into an amorphous mass of loose stones, bamboo planks, and metal pipes. The world shakes with enough force to knock me off of my feet. The canal drips from loose gaps like blood through pores. Two broken moon doors sit unevenly to form gaping eyes, a broken fence of splintered wood arranging itself into rows of teeth. The trembling mess expands and contracts as though breathing, smothering me in the stench of sewage and foul water. I lose sight of the Jade Palace as the beast swallows it whole, its eerie green glow pulsing like a heartbeat from within.

Sonam stands behind me, his hand hovering just above the hilt of his sword. Like it'll do us any good. Neither we nor the writhing titan makes a move. The moment we lift a finger, we will face decimation. It's almost befitting, I think. I've survived being burned and hunted, but what better way to die than to be eaten like all my victims before me?

Some might call it justice.

I say it's just my luck.

My ears detect movement before my eyes do, the faintest creak of the city's rolling body inching forward at a snail's pace. It continues to grow, bigger and bigger until it towers over us, a tidal wave ready to crest. A mountain ready to crush us underfoot.

It's time to run.

The city surges forward in an avalanche of debris, pelting us in loose rubble. Shards of glass rain down on our heads, iron nails embedding into our skin. The hulking mass gives chase, its imposing shadow darkening the path forward. We can't outpace it. The captain is falling behind. Where once I would have relished the thought of seeing his comeuppance, I'm now bound to him. If he dies, so do I.

An idea sparks in my mind, piggybacking off an old memory I thought long since forgotten. I recall a time when I was playing too close to the sharp slope of a mountain face with my sisters. One of the rocks must have given way as a result of our rambunctiousness. The resulting slide nearly saw us buried, but instead of letting the stones chase us, we split off to the sides like a branching river.

"This way!" I scream at him, snatching up his hand.

He resists at first, disgust seared into the lines of his face. There's probably nothing more repugnant to a demon hunter than a demon's touch. For what it's worth, I can't stand it, either. Humans are too soft, awfully squishy. But I can't run and explain myself at the same time. Better to yank him along than to be crushed to death—that, and pray he isn't thick enough to start yelling at me for it.

I leap to the side and pull Sonam with me. It's the furthest thing from a graceful landing. I stumble and roll, scraping my knees and landing on my belly, breathing in plumes of dust. The grotesque creature, top-heavy and lopsided, spills out in a raucous crash, stones and splinters left in its wake.

I dare to look over my shoulder and breathe a sigh of relief. We would have been done for, but now is hardly the time to rest. The magic here in Hell is unpredictable. For now, it seems the city has simply gone back to building itself up piece by piece as if nothing happened. We've landed on the outskirts of the city's perimeter, the little progress we managed to make now dashed.

"Are you still in one piece?" I ask Sonam.

He lies beside me, gritting his teeth. The quick rise and fall of his chest betrays his usual stony composure. "Regrettably." He shakes his head in dismay. "What was that thing? I've never seen anything like it."

Sonam sits up in a daze. He fumbles around for something. That same small notebook and a bit of thin charcoal. He cracks the book open and brings the black stick to the paper's surface to draw, so engrossed in his work that I'm convinced he's forgotten all about me.

I keep my distance—because I frankly wouldn't put it past him to turn this into some sort of trap—and peer over his shoulder.

To my genuine surprise, he's drawn a quick sketch. An impressive one, at that, replicating the horror we just encountered with precise detail. In the corner, he's scribbled down an estimated weight and height, along with a few notes written along the edges. Sonam has neat writing, elegant script one would expect from someone with access to capable tutors.

It's a hunting log, I realize with a shiver. In the event that he should come back later and finish the job, or perhaps share what he's learned of Hell with his compatriots once we find a way back to the mortal coil. Whatever fascination I had for his artistic prowess quickly drains away.

"Get up," I snap, nudging his thigh with the tip of my foot. "Now's hardly the time for pretty pictures."

With a deft hand, Sonam grabs me by the ankle and squeezes hard. "Touch me again and you will regret it."

"You think I would willingly sully my hands?"

"Demon filth."

"Human scum."

I drag my leg away from him and stomp off a few paces. I

should have known escaping Hell couldn't have been that easy. "Now what are we supposed to do?" I grumble.

"You're so loud. You're giving me a headache."

I spin around and snarl at him. "What did you just say?"

Sonam blinks at me in confusion. "I said nothing, Fox."

Something behind us cackles, concealed by the seemingly endless expanse of shadow. I can hear skittering feet. Ghostly whispers. I even feel the faintest brush of something cold against my cheek. Sonam and I are being watched, but by what exactly? I hold perfectly still, caught between fight and flight, when I lock onto a pair of empty black eyes staring at us from the darkness.

"Who's there?" I yell. "Come out where I can see you, coward."

"Who're you calling a coward?"

A figure steps out into the dim green glow of the Jade Palace. A little girl, her skin so pale it appears translucent. She has abnormally sharp teeth sticking out from beneath her bottom lip like tusks. Her wild brown hair is matted on one side and windswept on the other, nothing but a thin gray sack draped over her body like a shirt. She's barefoot, her soles and toenails stained black. It's her stench that overwhelms me. Like sweat, manure, earth, and something distinctly not human.

Most notable of all, however, is the mask she wears. A mask just like mine, only it's half broken and sits on one side of her face, a fraction of its illusionary magic at work.

My heart skips a beat.

I take a single step toward her, alarmed. "Where did you get that?" I ask. There's a slim chance she might have found it on her own, though I'm not sure how that's possible. Last I knew, the Maskmaker was hiding somewhere on the mortal plane. How did one of his masks end up down here?

If she can lead me to the Maskmaker . . .

"Do you know the man who gave—"

"You made the Sleeping City angry," she says, ignoring me.

"Sleeping City?" I echo. "Is that what that . . . *thing* is called?"

"Mm-hmm." The girl picks at her overgrown fingernails. They're long and curling, yellowed with time and improper care. "No one's allowed to leave. Not without their permission."

"Who?" Sonam asks.

"The star gods, the star gods," the little girl chants. "Everyone knows. Death made them the key."

Her nonsensical rambling makes my head spin. There's a good chance that she's lost her mind, trapped down here in Hell for gods know how long, but a tiny voice in the back of my head wonders if there's an inkling of truth in her babbling. After all, we can't *lie*.

"You mean to say that there's a way out?" I ask.

"Oh, yes. Everyone knows," she repeats. "But I'm not telling you any more, human. You smell as bad as the ones we caught today."

"There are other humans here?" Sonam asks.

The child crosses her arms and snorts at him. She sounds like a boar. "Filthy, stinky humans. We're going to eat them soon. We just need to find the right spices."

"'We'?" I press on. "Who's—"

"Not telling, not telling!" she says, turning to run away.

I'm quick to crouch down and pull off my mask. Not entirely, just lifting a corner to expose my true face. "You can trust me," I say hastily.

She gasps softly. "The Maskmaker gave you one, too?"

I hold my breath. She *knows* of him, which means that bastard must be somewhere down here in Hell. No wonder I was having such a hard time tracking him down.

"That's right," I say, swallowing the swell of triumph in my chest. This is the first major lead I've had in ages. "We're the same, you and me. What's your name, little one?"

"Lin." She glances nervously at Sonam behind me, who looms like a sentry. I can sense her mistrust, and I don't blame her. The captain is a miserable sack to look at. "The ones we caught," she says. "They look just like him. One with an ugly face and the other without her tongue."

Sonam looks furious. So much so I fear he will strike me down here and now. "You dragged my guards down with you?"

I sneer back. "I did no such thing."

Lin chews on her disgusting nails. "Can we eat this mean one?"

I almost laugh. I'm starting to like this one. Unfortunately, it's out of the question. "This one's mine, I'm afraid."

"But there's so little for the rest of us." She pouts her lips. "Live humans never come this way."

"He's . . . special. I need to keep him around."

"Like a pet?"

I do laugh now, an ugly little sound from the back of my nose. "Yes, exactly. He's my pet."

"Mind your words, Fox," Sonam grumbles. I ignore him, taking great pleasure in his irritation. "Bring me to these other humans, girl. It's important."

Lin sticks out her tongue, causing Sonam to frown deeply. It's a privilege to see the captain cut down to size by someone who barely comes up to his hip.

I personally don't care what happens to the captain's guards. I'm more than happy to leave them behind to rot. Sonam is the only one I'm bound to see out of Hell. Bringing another pair of humans along isn't a part of the deal. I barely trust Sonam not to kill me when my back is turned, and I certainly don't trust his lackeys.

Looking behind us, I see that the city has reassembled itself stone by stone, no trace of that monster anywhere. The palace looks like a glowing green heart in the middle of the rib cage of city sprawl, ready and waiting to tempt its next victim forward.

Perhaps rescuing the guards could prove useful. There's might in numbers and all that. Who knows how long it will take us to leave this forsaken place, or how many other nasty creatures lie in wait. I do stand a better chance of seeing our deal to completion with a few helping hands. They'll protect their captain at the very least, and in doing so, unknowingly protect me. It may be worth the risk.

I turn to Lin. "Will you help us? We're terribly lost, and we don't want to anger the guardian again."

"Very well," she says, offering me her hand. "Just make sure your pet doesn't wander off."

"Don't worry. He's not going anywhere."

Sonam sneers. "I hate you."

"Oh, how I weep, " I reply dryly.

10

The stars screamed their way down to Hell and awoke together engulfed in complete darkness.

This couldn't be. They were gods, after all. Destined for the Kingdom of Heaven. To be felled by a mere mortal was insulting enough, but to be banished to Hell despite their divinity was a slight of unforgivable proportion.

They confronted Death together, seething with self-righteous fury.

"Remedy this at once," one of the brothers demanded.

"An outrage, an outrage!" cried another.

"We deserve better than to wallow in all this filth!" wailed a third.

The lord of the underworld merely looked upon the star gods one by one, seeing neither higher power nor lowly life-form. In the eyes of Death, all were equal—and the star gods were no exception.

"It is not I who keeps thee trapped here," he explained, "but the heavy weight of sins bearing down on thy souls. Redeem thyselves in servitude and earn thy place once again among the Heavens."

With a sweep of his hand, Death trapped them within the shifting structure of his palace, separating the nine brothers to nine different courts, standing in the way of the Gates of Hell at the very center to make ten full circles. They were sentenced to serve out the next millennia among those whom their cruelty once touched in life.

That was, until one day, when the youngest star god made his daring escape. He quietly slipped through the gate between worlds, vowing to one day return to free his dear brothers.

11

Yue

Hunting Log #376:
I know not the consequences of breaking a blood oath, but the fox appears bound to its word.

W***here once I thought Hell*** was empty, I quickly learn that it is teeming with life.

Or perhaps, more accurately, the antithesis of it.

They're everywhere—ghosts—thousands of lifeless black eyes blinking at us through the gloom. Nearly liquid and formless, they shift and flow like the ocean tide over sand, ebbing away when we draw too near, shaped by nothing more than shadow. I wonder how long they've been trapped down here, forgotten in the dark.

I stay close to Sonam. Not because I care, but because there's no telling what would-be demon may try to snatch up his soul. It's mine to devour, mine to stake claim. If what Lin said is true, they might have sunk their teeth into the captain's compatriots already.

I am curious to know how she came to exist down here. I wasn't lying to Sonam when I spoke of being born from human suffering. But there are no humans down here. Not whole ones, at least. I suppose that if a soul's suffering were significant enough to follow them to the afterlife, it might explain Lin's existence. How else am I to explain vengeful ghosts and poltergeists? Some souls are simply too stubborn to let go, even in death. The pain they carry runs so deep that it may well follow them into the next life, all the while creating monsters in its wake.

Lin takes us away from the city, venturing out into the abyss that seems to stretch for miles like an endless sea caught in eternal night. I never thought that such a stark nothingness could be so overwhelming. It isn't difficult to imagine losing one's mind in this expanse, forced to wander forever without any hint of where you're going, or any sign from where you'd once come. I'd honestly prefer being eaten by the Sleeping City.

"This is a trap, Fox." Sonam's voice grumbles from somewhere behind me. "I can feel it."

For once, I don't argue. I feel it, too. And as much as I hate the thought of Sonam being right, I care for my self-preservation more. Lin skips on ahead, muttering under her breath, talking nonsense. She could have been weaving tales before. Yet her description of Sonam's guards, Wen and Sooah, was too accurate to pass off as a coincidence.

"Are you listening to me, Fox?"

"What did you say, Lunch?"

"I said—"

"A *jest*, human. It was a jest."

"Are you incapable of taking anything seriously?"

"I can, but what a joyous occasion it would be to see that vein in your neck burst." I run my tongue over my teeth and grin. I'm delighted when his nostrils flare in annoyance.

"This way!" Lin exclaims, pointing a finger at something in the distance. A faint light. Barely perceptible if not for my above-average sight. "Our camp is over there."

The little hairs on my arms stand on end. "Our?"

Less than a li away stands a small cluster of soft orange orbs. Lanterns, somehow floating in the air of their own accord, arranged in a wide circle around the perimeter of their so-called "camp." A simple spell, easily cast. There are bedrolls of dried straw, but no tents. I suppose there's little need for it, given the fact that there's no discernible trace of weather here in Hell. There isn't much of anything, now that I think about it, apart from the Jade Palace and the monstrous city who guards it.

I notice two things at once. A group of roughly ten other demons, the largest congregation of my kind I've seen in a very long time; and the two humans they have bound and gagged at the center of camp, both tied to a thick wooden post.

Wen and Sooah are a dichotomy. While Wen struggles against his bound wrists and screams over the filthy cloth unceremoniously stuffed into his mouth, Sooah sits there calmly, albeit begrudgingly, observing with keen eyes and steady focus.

I have no memory of dragging them down with me. Could it be that they fell in?

A part of me is curious to know how these two buffoons wound up in Sonam's service. Then again, I don't much care. The only thing I want to know is the whereabouts of the Maskmaker. Lin is the closest to a clue I've managed to find in nearly three decades, and I'm not about to let this lead pass me by.

The little girl rushes forward, giggling as she skips toward a boar demon. I've never seen one this close before. He's huge and rotund, his horns overgrown and curling, tusks sticking out of his mouth in ugly yellow spikes. His wild green eyes are red rimmed and caked in a crusty mud, both sitting askew within deep sockets. He stands on his hind legs like a human, hooves digging into the earth while he grips a lofty spear with pudgy human-like hands.

He's a sickly old thing, but still strong and vivacious enough to become a problem should things take an aggressive turn. They all are, now that I've had a chance to look at them.

The captain was right. This is definitely a trap.

Yet another reason for me to hate him.

We haven't even exchanged words with the demons yet and I'm already running through the possible scenarios. Everyone is an enemy until proven otherwise, and even then, I'm not foolish enough to give them the benefit of the doubt. If things go sideways, where will I run? How will I manage to drag Sonam with me? The other humans are of little consequence, but they may prove a beneficial distraction if it comes to it.

"I made a new friend," Lin says to the hulking boar demon.

"I told you no wander off," he replies, voice so deep and rumbling that I swear I can feel the ground shake beneath my feet.

"They tried going to the Jade Palace. I watched the whole thing. I was hoping they would get crushed, but they didn't."

I chew on my tongue. She doesn't have to sound so disappointed about it.

The boar demon regards me tensely. I don't miss the way he sniffs the air. Distrust abounds.

Dealing with demons is entirely different than dealing with humans. We are a scheming sort. Dangerous by nature. There's always something to gain, always a delicate balance to strike. I could be honest and tell him the truth, that we're seeking a way out of this place. But what I'm more curious to know is why this horde of demons looks so much like a small army. I suppose even the worst of us seek out company rather than wander alone.

The boar demon and his goons don't respond. Instead, they brandish their weapons and take a step closer. The muscles in my neck tense when Sonam slowly places his hand upon the hilt of his sword. Humans—stupidly reactionary. He needs to calm down. Any sudden movement may see to our quick and painful demise.

"Lower your weapons," I say to the boar demon. "It hardly encourages friendly conversation."

The boar demon snorts, nostrils flaring wide. "Conversation?" he says stupidly. I don't think he has enough wits about him to understand more than three syllables at a time.

"I want to *talk*," I clarify, speaking slowly so my words stand a chance of getting through his thick skull.

The boar, who is very obviously the leader of this strange demonic pack, shifts his gaze toward Sonam. "Human." He grunts. "We kill."

I wave a hand dismissively instead. "He's harmless. Just a boy playing soldier."

"Fox," Sonam mutters tightly. I think I've offended him.

"He'll behave." I turn and fix him with a hard glare. "I just have a few questions, and then we'll be on our way."

Despite his ego, the captain gets my message. He relaxes his hand, though his posture remains bamboo-straight, his eyes flitting back and forth between the demons now closing in and his two trusted guards.

The boar stares at me for a beat or two, but eventually gestures for the rest of the horde to stand down. Satisfied, for now. "Lin say you anger guardian?"

"More like we stumbled into it."

He snorts, his snout wet and dripping. "Bao think you stupid to face it," he says. "It kill Bao's friends every time we try get past."

My ears perk up. "'Every time'? How many times, exactly?"

"Ten," Bao answers without resistance. "We give up now. Make camp here. Eat human souls we can find."

He takes a step forward, looking like he might attack, but I quickly catch him with another question. "Has anyone ever made it out before?"

"Bao can't say. Never seen happen. The way through too hard, but Bao think it maybe."

"How do you mean?"

"See Jade Palace? Look at ring walls. Each one a Court of Hell. Only souls good and brave can make it through. The Gates of Hell are in middle, like an egg yolk and you get through the shells. The Maskmaker say he only want smart ones. Only smart ones get through."

I allow Bao's words to sink in, goosebumps spreading up the back of my neck. So the Maskmaker really *is* here, hiding somewhere within the city. But what could he possibly want with demons? What awful plan is he stitching together?

And, most importantly, how am I supposed to get to him without being crushed to death first?

"The stars," I mumble. "Lin mentioned the stars being the key. Do you know what she meant by—"

Wen screams something unintelligible around his gag, drawing everyone's attention in his direction. I'd almost forgotten the fool was there. With my question interrupted, Bao appears to regain his composure.

"Enough!" he snaps. "Bao head hurt! We eat now!"

The demons close in on us. For the first time, Sonam gives me an almost pleading look. He's been nothing but cold and distant, downright standoffish since our unfortunate encounter. It's the weakest I've ever seen him. The most vulnerable.

"Help them," Sonam whispers.

I'm used to listening to humans beg. Mostly for their own lives, though, never for the well-being of others.

"You've already made one deal with me," I whisper back. "You cannot strike another."

His jaw tenses, the muscles in his face twitching. *"Please,"* he says, so soft and quiet even my exceptional hearing almost misses the word.

I don't understand the slight tightness in my chest. I feel strangely . . . sympathetic. Like I'm seeing someone pluck the wings off a bird while its family watches on. He reeks of desperation.

A part of me wonders if this is an unforeseen side effect of our blood oath. The longer Sonam holds my gaze, the more my resolve crumbles. I try to justify it. Many hands make quick work, as the old saying goes. Wen may be a bumbling idiot, and Sooah has yet to prove her worth, but if I don't do something to save them, the captain might do something stupid—like attacking ten demons head-on.

In the end, I suppose this could serve me well.

"I wouldn't eat them, if I were you," I say smoothly to Bao. "They're utterly foul."

The boar demon's nostrils flare. "Foul?"

"Terrible," I clarify. "Disgusting. That one there? A demon turned her tongue into a stew. One bite, and they were sick for weeks. Isn't that right?"

The captain bristles but ends up nodding quickly. "It—she speaks the truth."

"You lie," Bao replies, though the hesitation in his tone bodes well for us.

"You're welcome to check her mouth," I say casually. He's right. I *am* lying. But since he did not ask me a direct question, I'm free to spin my web. So long as he doesn't realize the context of my mistruths, I can say whatever I well please. It comes down to a matter of skill, twisting words and their meaning to my advantage. "Humans these days leave a terrible aftertaste. I think it's something in the water they drink. They pollute everything they touch."

The boar demon nods toward another among his group—a river spirit, judging by the silvery scales he has instead of flesh or fur—who grasps Sooah sharply by the chin and forces her mouth open for all to see. There's a murmur of agreement, perhaps even intrigue. The guard doesn't shy away from the attention, puffing out her chest instead of shrinking away. Her lack of tongue is nothing to be ashamed of. To her, it's a badge she wears with pride.

Unfortunately, my carefully chosen lies aren't enough.

"Meat is meat," the boar says with a huff. "Someone start fire and—"

"Absolutely not," Sonam snaps, drawing his sword. Impulsive as ever.

"What are you doing?" I hiss. "Let me handle this."

"Use your head. They never had any intention of letting us go."

I look around at all the sharpened blades and axes the boar's little troupe wields, grips knuckle-white and muscles ready to swing. They're practically vibrating out of their skin looking for a fight. Hunger—true hunger—is easily spotted. It's in the smacking of lips and erratic breathing. It's in the way they can't stop looking at the three humans in the center of their camp.

I run my tongue over the front of my teeth. What a pain. Sparing Sonam a fleeting glance, I shift my weight and bend my knees, allowing my sharp nails to grow. He nods in understanding.

Together, we strike.

Sonam runs toward the center of the camp, and with a quick swipe of his blade sets his friends loose. They're quick on the uptake, snatching up the weapons the demons confiscated and threw into a pile a few paces away. Our odds are better now that it's four against ten, but I can't afford to be complacent.

Wen picks up a discarded bow and a quiver of arrows, swiftly running to the opposite side of the encampment to offer himself a better vantage point. I'd all but written him off as nothing more than a loudmouthed fool, but he's quick on his feet. A slippery little thing. He curses when his first few arrows miss. With a quick shake of his hand, he readjusts his grip to try again. He picks demons off one at a time, each of his arrows finding their mark, though the fool doesn't hit anything vital.

Sooah, I notice next, prefers to fight with a pair of twin daggers. It's no wonder she's covered in all those scars. She's practically a one-woman army, given her sheer size and impressive strength. She uses her mass to her advantage, charging demons at full speed. There's nothing to do but pray when her unstoppable force comes barreling toward you.

And then there's Sonam. That awful, curt, genuine eyesore and unwanted blot on my life.

He's . . . mesmerizing.

In a violent sort of way.

Coated in blood, teeth bared like an animal, his blade screaming as it slices through flesh and bone and air. His movements are fluid, chaining together in an onslaught of well-placed cuts and stabs. Well-practiced, but not rigid with formality. He fights like it's a dance, every step as effortless as the flow of a stream. It hurts my eyes to look at him, so bright and brilliant that I may as well be staring directly at the sun. The Demon Hunter of Jian. I suddenly understand why he holds such a title. He kills my kind with impunity. No hesitation, no remorse. He is uncatchable smoke, a specter with a pulse, slitting throats and skewering hearts as though it were a race against Death.

He moves in to strike a three-eyed tiger demon, but his enemy is quick, ducking out of the way before the captain has a chance to sever. With a powerful swipe of its claw, the demon sends his dao flying out of hand; it lands out of reach with a cold, hard clatter. The captain stumbles back, falling out of the way as the demon attacks again.

My heart leaps into my throat. I refuse to die because of this bastard's overconfidence. I rip and tear and maul my way to get to him. Just as the tiger opens its jaws—

Something whips out, lashing the demon directly in the eye. A weighted dagger tied securely to the end of a long, thin rope. The captain is already back on his feet, handling the rope dart with startling control. It is a viper at his command, snapping out and around with the faintest guide of his hand. The pointed tip of the dagger screams with fury as it slices through the air, the sharp crack of the rope as he releases and pulls back as formidable as lightning.

He deliberately snakes the rope around his legs, his arms, even his neck to create constant momentum, flagellating anyone who attempts to draw near. Sonam stands in a maelstrom of his own making. With one final swing, he sends the dagger flying out. It embeds itself into the tiger's skull, killing the demon in an instant.

I don't know whether to be impressed or afraid.

"Eat them!" the boar demon bellows as he charges toward me.

My sisters always used to tell me that the best defense is not fighting at all, but I'm without choice. I shake my head free of distraction and get ready, ripping off my mask to reveal my true, hideous self.

I leap. Aim for the throat. The boar demon's thick neck is too hard to bite through. There's nothing exemplary about demon flesh. It's tougher, harder to chew, like gnawing through a thick piece of tree bark knowing the fiber will at least fill your belly. After decades of tearing arms from shoulders and heads from necks, brutality is perfectly perfunctory, though I'll admit that it's strange to be fighting alongside humans instead of against them.

With a sweep of his arm, Bao knocks me away and I land with a yelp. My ribs are bruised, but mercifully unbroken. He wipes a hand over his skin, laughing at the tiny rivulets of black blood smeared against his palm.

"Stupid fox," he says with a deep laugh. "Weakling can never kill Bao."

I get back up on all fours, digging my claws into the dirt beneath my feet. I try again, circling around to attack at a different angle, but the boar once again throws me away.

Curses. He's too strong an opponent.

The boar demon lifts his axe-wielding arm and brings his weapon down. I jump out of the way, a narrow miss. He swings at me again and again, a flurry of manic attacks. There's nowhere to go, nowhere to escape.

"Fox!"

I hear him before I see him. The quick rumble of rushed footsteps, a grunt as he leaps, his hastily retrieved sword whistling as it slices through air. The wet *thunk* of Sonam's blade hits the back of the boar's neck, driving through hide and bone. It's not a clean cut, stopping only halfway through, the demon too hefty and Sonam without enough speed. The captain hangs there, jerking his legs forward to encourage tearing, but to no avail.

I get up hastily, running around while giving the demon a wide berth. Once I've put enough distance between us, I sprint forward, throwing all of my weight behind me as I come up from behind, snatch up the other side of Sonam's blade, clamping it tight between my teeth, and use my weight to drive us forward. We've turned his sword into a saw.

The boar's head falls to the ground, rolling a few feet before coming to a halt.

Quiet surrounds us, the stench of death filling my nose. I rise slowly, quickly replacing my mask as I sheepishly glance in Sonam's direction. I don't want anybody to look at me when I'm like this. Thankfully, he's distracted as he wipes his blade clean on a corner of his robes.

The Demon Hunter of Jian just saved my life, and I frankly don't know how to feel. A minutia of gratitude, certainly, but mostly bewilderment. Good manners dictate I should thank him, but my pride won't allow it.

"Idiots!" Lin wails, stomping her little feet as she approaches Bao's quickly cooling body. She kicks his head away. "Useless, all of you! Do you have any idea how long it's been since we've had fresh meat?"

I snatch Lin up by the scruff and rip the mask off her face. The magic falls away in the same manner it does when I remove my own. Standing before us isn't the innocent child she pretends to be, but a vicious, snarling, red-eyed boar demon. Smaller than Bao, but infinitely more clever.

"Tell me about the Jade Palace," I demand.

"I'm not telling you anything—"

I grab her up by the throat, applying just enough pressure to break skin with my nails. "Speak, or you'll end up like your friends. How do we get out of here?"

She *must* answer. "Ten courts," Lin huffs. "Each with its own trial. Only souls worthy of redemption can make their way through to the gate within."

"What's this nonesense about the stars?"

"The star gods. They serve as the judges of Hell. Pass their tests, and you'll be set free."

Sonam sheaths his sword. "But how do we get past the Sleeping City?"

Lin cackles. "You don't."

I frown steeply. "Speak plainly, swine. What do you mean?"

"You don't get past. You have to go *through*." The boar demon doesn't stop laughing. It's chilling, the sound echoing all around us as she grows more and more hysterical. The time for helpful answers has come and gone, but maybe I can pry one more truth from her wart-covered lips.

"The Maskmaker," I say harshly. "Where can I find him?"

"If I tell you, will you let me go free?"

This conniving brat, countering a question with a question. I weigh my options. I suppose it's a small price to pay. "That depends entirely on your answer."

Lin grits her teeth, no doubt weighing her options, too. "He hides within the walls," she answers, "or so I'm told. But believe me when I say you won't find him."

"Why not?"

"Because the Maskmaker doesn't wish to be found. Not until he's ready."

My nostrils flare. Ready for what, exactly? She couldn't have been less helpful even if she tried. There's nothing left to do now other than return to the Jade Palace and deal with what may come.

I tighten my hands around her throat. This whole thing has been a terrible waste of time.

"Let me go," the boar demon squeals. "Let me go!"

I never promised to do such a thing, and since her answer has proven less than satisfactory, I decide to feast. I bite through her hide and tear out her esophagus, black blood coating my lips. I wonder if I look terrifying, a human woman devouring flesh and sinew and bone. Lin's body falls to the ground with a *thud*, her legs still twitching as she slowly expires. I watch her eyes with morbid curiosity, wondering if this is how I'll look in death one day. There's no light to extinguish, no hint that anyone was even in there to begin with.

So much death. And to think we've only been here for an hour. As I inspect the carnage, I feel something sharp pressed up against my back. I turn slowly, my lip curling into a sneer when I see Wen behind me, the tip of an arrow in his drawn bow ready to fire at my spine. Even a poor archer is sure to meet his mark at this close a distance.

"Don't move," Wen warns. "Cap'n, we need to kill it, too. Before it decides to turn on us."

I shoot Sonam a withering glare. "We have a deal. Don't do anything foolish."

"You made a deal?" Wen asks, aghast.

"It was the only way," Sonam replies. "Stand down for now. She may prove useful to us."

"What if it eats us in our sleep? The moment our backs are turned—"

"If I wanted you dead," I snarl, "I would have let this horde hack you to bits and saved myself the trouble."

Sooah signs something with her hands, her movements nimble but sure.

"What did she say?" I ask.

"*Let's not fight among ourselves*," Sonam translates. "*We have bigger problems to worry about.*"

I force a grin to hide my unease. "Put your playthings away, children. We've got a lot of ground to cover."

Wen sneers. "You expect us to follow that thing, Cap'n?"

"That *thing* is our best shot at getting out of here alive," Sonam says bitterly.

"And don't you forget it," I reply with a devilish grin, deliberately allowing the black blood coating my teeth to drip freely down my chin.

The ugly one shudders. Good. I want them to fear me. Because if they fear me, they will keep their distance. And if they keep their distance, they won't be able to see how truly frightened of them I am.

12

Yue

Hunting Log #377:
The way it fights is . . . not unimpressive, I suppose.

H*ow did you two even* end up here?" Sonam asks his guards as we walk.

The Sleeping City is once again within sight, sitting upon the horizon of vast nothingness. Where once I found the glow of the Jade Palace foreboding, it now offers comfort amidst all the surrounding gloom.

Out of the corner of my eye, I notice Sooah signing something.

"You jumped in after me?" Sonam says, sounding almost flattered. "You really shouldn't have done that."

"Of course we should!" Wen replies with a boisterous laugh. "We swore an oath."

"But how did you survive the fall?"

"Landed right on top of that big, ugly boar demon. Broke our fall. He was right pissed about it."

I don't miss Wen's sideways glance, nor the way he and Sooah have placed themselves on either side of their captain. Human shields. One misstep on my part, and they won't hesitate to kill me. Their unshakable loyalty almost makes me a touch jealous, yearning for a sense of safety among kindred spirits. It reminds me of a time when I still had my sisters, when it was us against all who'd harm us.

Qin was the eldest and funniest, her jokes never failing to make me laugh. Even in weeks where food was scarce or hunts went wrong, Qin could lift our spirits as easily as the sun rose in the mornings—effortless because it was her nature.

Mihan was the most well-traveled, always ready with an enthralling tale to share. Stories were one of the few things I admired most about humans. So creative and inventive, painting pictures with their words—recounting our histories in the form of myths.

Ahn was the bravest of us, the first to throw herself at danger to protect the pack. She was the one who taught me to hunt, to always remain quick on my feet. She was exceptionally patient where I was concerned. Even though I was the runt of the litter, she took her time teaching me her ways even if it took me twice as long to learn.

Lu was the quiet one, preferring to spend her days dreaming rather than on the hunt. My fondest memories were of the summers we spent together foraging for roots and bugs, or swimming in streams. She liked watching the clouds, pointing out the shapes they made. And at night, she could name every single star in the sky. Not by the names humans had bequeathed, but ones we made up and were entirely our own.

Nuying was the smartest sister, who always had answers for my endless curiosity. She was the only one of us who knew how to read human script with any sense of fluency. Though I now know how to read, I still find it dizzying, a mishmash of random curves and strokes. Her gift for language proved useful from time to time, especially when hunters put up signs to warn of the presence of a nine-tailed fox. That's how we knew when it was time to move on to the next village, on to safety.

Chunhua was the one I got along least with, our personalities far too similar and therefore grating, but I still loved the way she'd curl up next to me to help soothe my nerves during particularly fierce thunderstorms. She was sweeter than she let on, even if she had a habit of hiding behind harsh words. She was never the type to apologize aloud, though she would always try to make up for her mistakes by gifting an extra portion of food.

Jiayi was the huntress. There wasn't a human she couldn't stalk. Men and women from across the land resorted to all sorts of weapons and traps, only to wind up in our bellies instead. She was good at hiding in the shadows, unseen to all until she chose to reveal herself.

And then there was Su, my favorite sister. It probably wasn't right to have a favorite among family, but it was the truth. I adored her dark sense of humor, the way she was always ready with a quip. As unserious as she was, I could always trust her to lend an ear and offer the sagest advice.

It feels almost a disgrace to describe them so simply. My sisters, my family. They were my whole world. Love is not an unknown concept to us demons; we are simply more guarded in the matters of the heart. In a realm that always let us know we were unwelcome, who could blame me for putting myself first once I no longer had anyone on whom to dote?

"Hey, dog!" Wen crows, snapping me from my thoughts. "Don't be getting too far ahead. I'm keeping my eye on you."

I take a deep breath. My patience is already at its limit, but I'll be damned if I let this imbecile with a toad-like face get the better of me.

We're roughly a li away from the outer walls of this hellish version of Longhao. The city sleeps on, unaware of our presence. I don't dare get any closer out of fear of waking it. All looks calm and unsuspecting, but now I know better.

"We need to make camp," Sonam says, not so much a suggestion as a strongly implied order. "We'll use the time to strategize. We won't get very far with that monster standing in the way."

For a brief moment, I wonder if he's talking about the Sleeping City or me. When I turn, I see Sonam has his back to me—which is either incredibly brave or incredibly stupid of him—directing his guards toward an area of relatively flat ground. I'm disgruntled at the thought of wasting time, though embarrassingly appreciative for a moment of respite. Weariness has seeped into my bones and muscles. My head is heavy upon my neck, weighed down by an endless stream of thoughts.

How do we get past the Sleeping City?

You don't. Lin's voice rings softly in my ear. *You don't.*

Sonam and Wen speak among themselves, casting me suspicious glimpses from time to time. Sooah busies herself by organizing a makeshift camp, a floating lantern taken from the demon horde serving as our dim source of light. The humans unstrap their leather armor and shrug off their outer robes, bundling them up into what I can only assume are sorry excuses for pillows.

I pay special attention to their weapons.

Sonam carefully removes several hidden daggers that I didn't realize he had on his person, a strap lined with darts, as well as his dao, and unties that impressive rope dart from around his waist. He keeps them close even as he sits cross-legged, facing in my direction. Even resting, he means to keep me in his sights, one hand settled a mere inch away from his cache.

He eventually pulls out that silly little book of his and begins to sketch again. The *scritch-scratch* of his charcoal against the paper makes my ears twitch, curiosity blooming in my chest. I resist the urge to circle around and see what he's working on. Which one of the creatures we slew will be immortalized on the page?

Wen attempts to rest, though he tosses and turns for a good twenty minutes before finding some semblance of comfortability. Sooah sits just off to the side, alert and vigilant. The first watch of the night. Not so much against unseen foes, but the nine-tailed fox pacing a stone's-throw's distance away.

I ignore them all, preferring my solitude at the edge of their camp. I won't dwell on my lack of invitation. I don't trust them not to kill me, either.

You don't.

You don't get past. You have to go through.

I stare at the Jade Palace for several hours, seated at the edge of the humans' camp, staring for so long that the shape of the glowing green palace burns into the back of my eyes. Lin's words echo around in my skull, taunting me. She has twisted her words expertly—I'm having difficulty deciphering their meaning.

Even if there was a way to make our way around and get to the palace, the Sleeping City would easily cut us off in its hulking form. We don't have the speed to outpace it, and we don't have the strength to fight it head on. Thinking back, our escape was nothing short of miraculous. I close my eyes and recall the details of its shifting mass, somehow fluid and impassable like a rockslide come to life, easily swallowing up the Jade Palace like a morsel.

A thought occurs to me. Perhaps I've been thinking about this all wrong. The Jade Palace is both a destination and a *part* of the monster. Lin was right. There's no getting past it. The only way in is through.

The voice in the back of my head tells me that it's madness. My fear pleads that I find another way. But my gut knows that this is the answer.

When souls arrive in Hell, they have two choices. They can

either accept their fate or wander the darkness. It's no small wonder there are so many ghosts lurking in our periphery. They're the ones who can't accept their place here, clinging to the memories of their mortal lives. The only way forward is to relinquish control, and that means willingly falling into the belly of the beast. To accept is to give in. My reluctant travel party may not be dead, but I'm sure the magic stalling our advance works much the same way.

I know what I have to do. Now it's a matter of whether I can convince Sonam and the rest to follow suit. Irritation simmers beneath the surface of my skin. I'd rather cut off my tails than suffer through that conversation. I can already hear them dismissing me, denouncing me for some devious trickster.

Which—fair.

But in this instance, I'm not trying to lead them astray. How in the nine suns am I going to convince them to let the city eat them alive?

Perhaps I don't have to say anything at all. Maybe what I need right now is to be reckless.

I press my lips together and whistle. One long, loud blast as high as I can manage. Sonam and Wen startle awake, while Sooah watches me with a frown.

"What do you think you're doing?" Sonam snaps, sitting up while quickly gathering his things.

"Has it lost its damn mind?" Wen grumbles, hopping to his feet.

I whistle again, this time a short blast. The sound echoes off the cobblestoned streets of Longhao, chirping back at me weakly.

Sonam steps up behind me and roughly grabs my shoulder. "Stop it. You're going to wake the—"

When the city releases a low, rumbling groan, I know that I've woken the beast. Wooden beams arrange themselves into a facsimile of a skeleton, roof tiles slotting together to create scalelike skin. Its gaping moon door eyes hone in on us, and I wonder if we look like mere bugs, easily squashed.

It lurches forward.

Before he can blink, I take Sonam by the wrist and run to meet it.

"Stop!" he shouts, but I ignore him, barreling at top speed toward the beast. Wen and Sooah aren't far behind, their thunderous footfalls giving chase.

The city opens its mouth—

And swallows the four of us whole.

I flinch despite the confidence of my theory. When I finally find the strength to pry my eyes open, my jaw gapes in astonishment.

We're surrounded by a beautiful garden full of golden peonies, white orchids, and drooping wisteria trees of soft violet. The footpaths beneath us are carved from jade, as are the walls penning us in, so tall and imposing that they reach the clouds above. If I didn't know any better, I'd say we'd found a way to sneak into Heaven.

The sea of listless souls staring at us proves otherwise.

We're caught in an inescapable net of eyes. Our scenery may be serene, but I notice the peculiar chill in the air. I smell the unnatural staleness of death all around us. These ghosts have a musty old scent despite the sweet young flowers in bloom. Like stepping into a long-forgotten memory, they're a suspension of blurry colors and sounds. The ghosts don't look at us so much as they do past. Aware enough of our presence to step out of the way as we walk, but too trapped within their own minds to give us any more focus.

"What is this place?" Wen asks breathlessly. It's the quietest I've ever heard him. "And who are all these people?"

"These are my flowers," a deep voice intones. "Aren't they beautiful? They keep me such good company."

The four of us whip around to find a man in ornate robes of golden silk, his sleeves so long and luxurious they glide upon the ground. His hair is a pale yellow, so soft and vibrant I could mistake it for twilight. A chill runs down my spine when I notice the disturbing crisp silver of his eyes. Everything about him seems to glow, radiating power and light even in the deepest pits of Hell.

A fallen star god from the legends of old.

"What do we have here?" the man muses. "Three warriors and . . . " He pauses when he gets to me, his lips pulling into a deviously wide grin. "If it isn't the Maskmaker's favorite. How wonderful to finally meet you in the flesh."

The hairs on my arm stand on end. "You know the Maskmaker? Who are you?"

"My name is of no importance to you," he says calmly. "Though if you survive my trial, I may be inclined to tell you." With a grand sweep of his hand, he gestures to his garden at large. "Welcome, dear friends, to the Court of Temptation."

13

Yue

Hunting Log #378:

Stay vigilant—this cursed place likes to play tricks.

With a snap of the star god's fingers, vines slither out from beneath the jade tiles and wrap around our calves and ankles, thorns needling our flesh. The vines creep up our bodies, squeezing ever tighter, trapping us in their viselike grip. We're lifted violently, suspending the four of us upside-down in the air. Wen cries out in surprise. Sooah struggles to free her legs. Sonam instinctively reaches for his blade to cut through his restraints, while I tear at the vines with my bare hands—until they, too, are bound and immobile at my sides.

"Release us at once!" Sonam demands.

The star god clicks his tongue in disappointment. "Worry not, human, I'll do exactly that. All you must do is answer one question each. If you are truthful, you may move on."

This sounds too simple. "Well?" I snap. "What are your questions? We don't have all day."

He throws his head back and laughs, deep and chesty. "A little patience, if you'd please. Works of art take time."

I'm lightheaded now that all my blood is pooling in my head. "What are you talking about?"

Behind us, I hear the snap of twigs and the rustle of leaves. The garden has come to life, rearranging itself into thick hedges so tall it blocks out the sky. A maze, I realize. A twisting puzzle of sharp, ominous bramble. It fills the entire outer ring of the Jade Palace, overgrown from wall to wall. With another snap of his fingers, the constricting vines pull back like slings and fling us to the earth below. Thorns and branches scrape my cheeks and claw at my limbs, bleeding black welts puffing up on my skin.

I clamber to my feet with a cough, a hand tracing over the back of my head. I can feel a small bump, but it doesn't appear that I've sustained any serious injuries.

Looking around, I find myself completely alone.

I sniff the air. The humans are somewhere nearby, but it's difficult to discern precisely how close. The heavy scent of magic fills my nose, so sweet it borders on pungent. The more I breathe it in, the dizzier I become. The more confused. There's a fork in the path ahead of me, but I can't decide if I want to go left or right. Or would it be smarter to turn back?

Just as I turn to glance behind me, the thick hedge walls grow and shift, sealing the way off. The message is loud and clear: going back isn't an option. I think I smell one of the humans ahead. Taking a gamble, I head right at the fork.

It's disturbingly cold in the Court of Temptation, so much so that I can see the silver of my breath. Twigs snap under foot. Leaves rustle, but I detect no movement. My heart hammers loudly in my ear.

I come across a strange sight deep within the maze. A part of the wall appears to jut out slightly, vines and leaves growing over some sort of obstruction. It isn't until I get closer, pushing past branches and thorns, that I see it isn't something—but *someone*.

It's a ghost. A human soul, lost for gods know how long in this wretched place. Her eyes remain open, unblinking, staring at something far off in the distance. So still and cold is she that I nearly mistake her for stone. Her translucent skin is the only hint of her incorporeal form. The star god's hedge maze has knitted her into its existence, leaching what little essence remains. What sin cast her down to the pits of Hell? How did she come to fail her trial?

These are my flowers, the star god had said. *Aren't they beautiful?*

I shudder. I'd loathe to be the latest addition to his collection. There seems little I can do for this particular soul—not that I'm inclined to help—so I carefully back away and keep walking.

I come up to several more turns, but I have the advantage of a keen nose. I pick up faint traces of leather and sweat. Left, then right, and then right again. The smell is getting stronger, getting closer. That's when I come across a small but open square of the maze, its walls still towering too high to entertain the thought of climbing over. At the center, I spot a familiar face. Sooah.

Except she isn't alone.

Kneeling before her are two people. They appear to be a man and a woman, both begging on their hands and knees as they look to Sooah with wide eyes. Their hands are bound with thick rope knots, sweat and tears dripping from their faces. I don't understand how they got here.

"I'm sorry, Sooah," the man says, trembling so hard that he's barely intelligible. He looks much like her. They share the same small mouth and square jaw. "I never should have done it! I've known nothing but regret."

"Sooah, my dear," the woman speaks loudly over the kneeling man beside her. She's dressed ornately, gold pins stuck in her hair. She, on the other hand, bears no resemblance to Sonam's soldier. "Forgive this foolish old woman. I never should have laid a hand on you, please—"

Sooah lifts a pair of iron-hot tongs I hadn't noticed before. Where did that come from? I could have sworn she was empty-handed mere moments ago. It's as though they were magically plucked from thin air.

The sickly sweet scent of magic is strong now. Overpowering. It burns the insides of my nose and makes my eyes water. The star god's manipulations are at work. To what end, however, I'm not yet sure.

"Take my tongue!" the man says. "That's what you want, isn't it?"

"Mine, too!" the woman adds frantically. "Don't you want your revenge?"

My skin breaks out into goosebumps, the fine hairs on the nape of my neck standing on end. Will Sooah do it? There's so much anger in her eyes, deep and dark and deadly.

Do it, I think fiendishly to myself. *Whatever their crimes, do it.*

I may not like seeing people suffer, but I also understand the need for vengeance. After all these years of searching for the Mask-maker, I know I won't hesitate to exact my revenge. There will be no begging for forgiveness, no second chances. I've already decided that when I find him, as soon as I can find a work-around to the oath we struck, I'm going to shred him apart with my teeth and leave nothing behind.

For the sake of my sisters. For me.

Much to my disappointment, Sooah drops the tongs. They're so hot the patch of earth they land upon begins to smolder. She looks at the man and woman, her brows knitted into a deep frown, and shakes her head.

Now denied, the two kneeling figures at Sooah's feet slowly disappear, crumbling away as nothing more than specks of dust. The tongs, too, suddenly evaporate from existence. The awful smell of magic dissipates into the air, and I'm finally able to draw a proper breath.

"I think it's safe to say you passed the test," I mutter.

Sooah turns rapidly, both her fists raised in alarm. She glares at me warily, her eyes flicking over toward a path opening to my left.

"You want me to go first, I take it?" I say dryly.

Sooah nods. I can't fault her. I wouldn't want something with obscenely sharp teeth following within biting distance, either. I suppose it's just as well. I'll better be able to sniff out the captain's location if she's standing downwind.

"Follow me at two arms' distance," I tell her. "If you try to strangle me from behind, you'll regret it."

Sooah huffs. I'm going to assume that was a reluctant *yes.*

It takes significantly less time to sniff out Wen, because he reeks of grease and week-old milk. I'm sure his human compatriots aren't offended by his smell, but my sensitive nose only amplifies the worst of his sour notes. After a right, another right, and then a long walk down a narrow straightaway, Sooah and I finally come across another open square in the hedge maze.

I'm not prepared for what I see. My eyes are assaulted by the sight of no less than two dozen beautiful young women.

Naked young women. I suppose temptation comes in many forms, but this is downright obscene.

Their long black hair flows freely over their shoulders, the smooth curves of their breasts and hips and thighs on full display. They fawn over Wen, who seems more corralled into his seat than a willing participant. The women giggle sweetly and offer to feed him fruit by hand.

"L-listen," Wen stammers. "I'm sure you're all l-lovely, but I have to get going—"

"Stay with us," the women coo. "Keep us company."

I don't know whether I want to stare or avert my gaze. There's something strangely impressive about how unabashed these women are. Where I can't stand to have anyone touch me, let alone look at me without my mask in place, they climb over Wen in their most vulnerable state with a confidence I doubt I could ever dare to master.

If the star god was going for subtlety, he's failed miserably where Wen's trial is concerned. It's obvious that this enticement is too strong for any man to deny—

"No!" Wen snaps, shoving one of the women away by the shoulders so that he can rise. There's a tremor in his left hand. "Whatever tricks you're playing, I won't fall for them. Now shove off, would you?"

"Don't you want to stay with us?" one of the women asks, clearly taken aback. "We'll love you for all eternity. Spoil you from sunrise to sunset. We can—"

"No means no, you harpies," he interrupts. "I've got important people waiting. My wife is a thousand times more beautiful than any of you!"

The putrid scent of the star god's magic dissipates, the mysterious women vanishing from view within a matter of seconds. Wen finally notices our presence when Sooah claps her hands together slowly in sarcastic applause. I don't think I've ever seen a human's face turn so red.

"How long were you standing there?" he grumbles sheepishly. He pivots his obvious embarrassment and sneers at me. "Where's the cap'n? What have you done to him?"

"Oh, nothing," I answer truthfully, but then I run my tongue over my front teeth and decide it would be fun to play. "All this walking around made me hungry. He made a delicious little snack." Wen and Sooah bristle, reaching for their weapons. I can't help but scoff. "Be at ease, I can smell him just up ahead."

Wen grits his yellow teeth. "You're not going anywhere. I say we kill you where you stand."

I clench my fists and will my heart to steady. I didn't think it possible to find a human more infuriating than Sonam. They really are full of surprises.

"I don't know how you managed to convince the cap'n to bring you along, but I won't be tricked," Wen continues. He trudges toward me, pulling a dagger from his belt. "Sooah, hold it steady so I can slit its throat."

"Come near me and die!" I hiss, preparing to unhinge my jaw.

But before either one of us can lay a finger on the other, a set of frantic cries cuts through the air. It sounds disturbingly close. With Sooah and Wen momentarily distracted, I race off before them. Wen shouts something obscene at me, but I can barely hear him past the shriek of wind in my ears and the whip of leaves against my sides. I run toward the smell of mangoes, rounding the corner with such speed I nearly collide into another one of the maze's entombed ghosts. I don't stop until I see him.

In the open area before me, Sonam stands at the top of a dais, inspecting a throne carved of pure jade. At the bottom of the steps, his seven brothers and father cry at his feet, bowing pathetically in full kowtow.

"We were wrong," they say in chorus. "Spare us, King Sonam."

14

Sonam

Hunting Log #379:
I am genuinely surprised the fox hasn't eaten us yet.

I might drown in all this silk.

Gone is my armor, missing are my weapons. Even the rock-like calluses upon my palms have somehow been erased from existence. I stand upon the dais in silk robes so smooth and beautiful it seems almost a sin to drape them over my unworthy shoulders. Even the mianguan that sits upon my head is ill-fitting, a little too large and heavy. Any sudden movements, and it will fall from its seat.

The throne room shines in all its brilliance. A forest of green, but without any of the same warmth and life. It's strangely empty, however. I count no guards, no palace advisors waiting at the ready. Intricately woven tapestries hang upon the walls, illuminated by the soft flickers of yellow lamplight. The lightest trace of cherry blossom oil lingers in the air, combining sweetly with the scent of burning sandalwood incense. Thick columns carved of smooth white jade hold up the heavy roof, a wide skylight carved out of the middle to let in the silver shine of the moon.

As magnificent as the throne room may be, I cannot be fooled. Never in my life have I been allowed to step foot in this place—which is how I know none of this is real.

"We never should have doubted you," Min says with a tremble.

"You are the most capable among us," adds my brother Han. He cannot bring himself to look me in the eye, and I can't help but wonder if it is out of fear or hatred.

"If anyone deserves to be my heir, it is you," Father says, lifting his head ever so slightly.

He doesn't look quite like himself. Upon closer inspection, none of them do. I know in my heart who each of them is supposed to be despite their faces existing in a state of blurriness. The finer details that would make each of them distinct are nonexistent, the result of an inexperienced painter using broad strokes to capture nothing more than an impression.

Could it be that this spell I'm under can only show me what I hold in my mind's eye? I have spent so little time with my family that they are but shadows of themselves. I have paid more attention to the faces of strangers than those of my own brothers. I suppose, in some twisted way, I should be grateful for being the forgotten son. This illusion's hold might have been too strong to break free from otherwise.

Now that I know this is some sort of ruse, how do I go about pulling myself from its clutches?

"What exactly are you praising me for?" I ask Father.

"You've rid the world of demonkind," he says, "an accomplishment only few could dream of."

"And you think I did it for the throne?"

"Only the strongest and most cunning of my children deserves to be king. You will have the entire kingdom at your command."

I ignore the ache in my chest. "I have no need for power."

"Of course you do. There is little else a man could desire."

I turn toward the throne. As with everything else in the Jade Palace, it has been cut from a large block of rich viridian, chiseled down into a wide chair with solid arms on either side. The crest of the royal family has been engraved into the center of its high back. A circular emblem showcasing a phoenix, its wings spread wide as it rises from a nest of many-petaled chrysanthemums.

I step closer and blink in confusion when I find that it boasts no phoenix, but a snarling fox. One with nine sweeping tails and six hideous eyes. How utterly vile. What fool thought to put this here?

"What say you, my son?" Father asks behind me. "Will you accept the throne?"

I run my fingers over the fox's etching, tugging at the hazy veil that has draped itself over my mind. Memories rush back to me with force. My fall into Hell. That blasted fox. Wen and Sooah, trapped down here with me in the Court of Temptation. The star god has tried to seduce me—with what he believed I craved—and failed.

"When my mother was sick, she wrote to you," I say quietly, ignoring his question.

"If she did, her letters never found their way to me."

"I find that hard to believe."

"Sonam—"

"All she wanted was to see you one last time. You couldn't even grant her that."

"My responsibilities kept me away."

"Responsibilities that will become mine if I accept the throne?"

"A necessary sacrifice."

I turn toward him and glare. "If that is the toll, I have no want of it. If the woman I loved needed me, I would gladly let the kingdom burn."

Father blinks up at me in confusion, as though he can't bring himself to understand something so simple. "You do not wish to rule?"

"I never wanted to rule, Father," I mutter. "All I ever wanted was your . . . " Attention. Approval. Acceptance.

I leave him without those final words. There is no point in speaking to a man who will never hear me.

15

Yue

Hunting Log #380:

Other cultures have their own names for the nine-tailed fox, as well as their own tales.

The main similarity between them is that they are signs of ill-boding.

Just as they did with Sooah and Wen, the illusions before us vanish into little more than dust. It makes sense that a man so stubborn and steadfast wouldn't fall for such a trick. Sonam turns and blinks at us incredulously.

"I'm glad to see you're well," he says evenly.

"You think a maze would get the better of me?" I reply.

Sonam sneers as he walks past, shoving my shoulder with his own. "I wasn't talking to you."

Ha. I should have known better.

Sooah signs something with her hands, frantic and quick. Wen wears a similar look of worry. Sonam is the only one with an air of calm—though I can detect his expertly veiled nerves from at least a li away. That maddeningly sweet mango scent he carries with him is noticeably sour now.

"I'm unharmed, Sooah, there's no need to worry," Sonam says, his tone firm, but not unkind. It's certainly a far cry from the bluntness he normally reserves for me. "How did you two fare? I assume you both met your own temptations."

"And succeeded," Wen boasts. "Getting through Hell is going to be a cinch if these're the sort of obstacles we're looking at."

Sooah puts her hands on her hips. Even *I* know what she means: Curb your overconfidence.

They speak to one another in hushed whispers, making no effort to check on me. Not that I expect them to. I take the opportunity to investigate our surroundings more thoroughly. Surely there has to be an easier way to get through this maze to the next Court of Hell. If we wander for too long, I fear the hedges may claim us as it's done to all the unfortunate souls who've come before. The humans have passed their test—so why is the way through not yet clear?

"The demon didn't give you any trouble, did it?" Sonam asks his guards, loud enough for me to hear. On purpose, no doubt.

"Said it'd eaten you," Wen grumbles. "Let me kill it. It'll save us all the trouble."

I glare at them over my shoulder, every muscle in my body tense. To lash out now would be a guaranteed death sentence, but I can't stand idly by and listen to Wen plot my murder—and all within earshot, no less.

Hate churns in the pit of my stomach. These humans will likely keep me alive only so long as I prove useful to them. I'm going to have to play along until an opportunity to escape presents itself. Then I'll flee and leave these wretches behind.

I sniff the air. "The exit is this way."

Wen glares at me. "It's lying. Mark my words, it's going to eat us when we least expect."

"If I wanted to eat you, I would have done it while you were busy writhing in that pit of sirens," I snap. Much to my delight,

Wen's face turns bright scarlet. "The air smells different down this way. Fresher. If it isn't the way out, I'll let you strike me down where I—"

The sound of a young woman's giggle interrupts us. It's soft and sweet like a springtime morning, radiating an almost welcoming sort of warmth. Sonam and I look ahead and find not just one woman, but eight. Sisters. They share the same pointed noses and alluring foxlike eyes, dressed in pretty white robes adorned with silky bits of silver ribbon. There's something familiar about them. I'm not sure how I hadn't noticed them before. It isn't until I take a few steps forward and look upon them that I realize why my heart aches so.

Qin, Mihan, Ahn, Lu, Nuying, Chunhua, Jiayi, and Su.

My most beloved sisters, here in the flesh.

This is my trial. I thought myself above it all. Without a soul to tempt, I was convinced that the Court of Temptation would have no sway over me.

Su spots me first. "Yue!"

My heart races at the sound of her voice. Her joy is contagious, the butterflies in my stomach fluttering up a storm. My sisters rush over to me, bombarding me with hugs and kisses. Qin lovingly runs her fingers through my hair while Lu holds my hand tight. They talk all at once, laughing and teasing the way they always used to. I bask in their love, the threat of tears stinging my eyes as I'm caught between joy and heartbreak. They've been dead for so long, and yet here they are, alive and well.

And I'm . . .

Confused.

My thoughts are overcome with a warm and persistent haze. This blasted *magic*. It twists at my mind, curling its fingers into the deepest recesses of my skull. It plucks at my consciousness like the strings of a zither, changing my tune to something that suits its vile intentions all the better.

"How are you here?" I ask. I can't . . . seem to remember anything.

"Have you been well?" Mihan asks, ignoring my question outright.

"Oh, how we've missed you!" Nuying cries while embracing me tight.

"My! Look how grown up you've become," Chunhua says, pinching at my cheeks.

I happily drown in their attention, my nerves both frazzled and somehow soothed. All those years I spent mourning and wallowing in my grief . . . None of that matters now. I don't understand how any of this is possible, or even how I wound up in this curious place, but I also don't question it. I have my family back. What more could I want?

"How are you all here?" I ask. "I thought when demons die, they—"

"Never mind that," Ahn interjects. "Tell us about you! What adventures have you been on without us?"

My brows pinch slightly. I can't shake the strange churn in the pit of my stomach. "I've been . . . "

I search my mind, but for some reason I find it blank. I scarcely recall anything that's happened in the last three decades, let alone the past five minutes. A heavy fog fills my head. The harder I reach for my memories, the more I try to grip them tight, they slip through my fingers like nothing more than smoke.

"The captain," I mumble under my breath, turning slowly to glance over my shoulder. He's the only one I can remember. Just the outline of him, the anger and distress he invokes whenever I look his way. But I find no one. Could I have hallucinated it all?

"Captain?" Jiayi giggles lightly. "There she goes again, making up her silly little stories."

"But I could have sworn—"

"Are you hungry, little sister?" Mihan asks. "We found something to eat. He's a big one, so there's plenty to share."

When I turn around again, we've been transported. I don't see a clearing, but the lush foliage of our old jungle den. The smell of the soil mixes with refreshing petrichor, the sound of distant songbirds chirping with glee. My sisters gather together and remove their masks, stretching out their tails and pawing the earth beneath sharpened claws. Feeling at home, I, too, remove my own. There's no need to hide what I am now that I'm with my family. I no longer remember how I got here, but I can't bring myself to care. For the first time in years, I'm finally at peace.

Qin nuzzles up beside me, inspecting my scars. "Your poor face!" she exclaims. "Does it hurt?"

"Sometimes," I reply quietly. "Not so much anymore."

"I'll go foraging for some gingerroot," Su offers. "Maybe I can make a salve for you."

I allow my sisters to fawn over me as we crawl into our den together. It's cozy, just big enough for the nine of us, the narrow tunnel connecting our home to the outside world wide enough to allow for an inch of space on either side. It's exactly how I remember it, not even a stone out of place.

"Come eat," Ahn calls, turning toward a wriggling mass in the center of our den.

A human male in mulberry red robes with beaten leather armor pulled over the top. They've bound and gagged him, so he can neither move nor plead for his life. The longer I study his face, the more I feel like I recognize him. There's something about the sharp line of his jaw and proud nose that's familiar to me. Or perhaps it's the scent of cinnamon, star anise, and mangoes that pulls at the strand of a memory tucked into the deepest part of my mind.

I think I had a travel companion once, one who looked and smelled exactly like him, but for the life of me I cannot recall his name. He tries screaming something against his gag, but his words are an incoherent jumble.

"Go on, little sister," Su urges. "You're nothing but skin and bones. Eat as much as you want."

I smack my lips, eyeing the human with great interest. Where to start? I could devour his whole left arm in three bites. Maybe I should put him out of his misery and eat his head so he doesn't endure any pain.

But those eyes . . . those honest axinite eyes. Why does the thought of eating this man bother me so? It isn't like me to pity my food, so why—

"Go on," Chunhua urges impatiently. "Don't you want a bite?"

I swallow hard, nearly succumbing to my hunger. "Yes, but—"

"Eat him," my eldest sister says firmly. "Eat him and we can be together again."

I stare at her in confusion, saliva nearly dripping from the corners of my lips. "'Together again'?"

"That's our question for you," Su says. "Do you want to stay with us forever?"

"Everything can go back to the way it was," Ahn adds. "All you have to do is eat him."

There's a pounding ache behind my eyes, the pressure threatening to make my skull shatter. Why wouldn't I want to be with my sisters?

The soldier screams something around his gag, managing to shove it partially out of the way with the tip of his tongue. "—temptation! Don't fall for it, Fox!" His voice sounds strange, not quite synced with the movement of his lips. It sounds as though someone is calling to me from behind, not from the soldier himself.

I stare at him, dazed. Temptation? What is he on about?

"Don't you want to stay with us forever?" my sisters ask again, this time in chorus. "Please say you'll stay."

My blood runs cold. My skin is suddenly feverish. A direct question requires a direct answer. I need to tell the truth. Of course I want to stay with them, but . . .

The Court of Temptation.

I look back at the man. Sonam. He watches with bloodshot eyes as he struggles against his bindings. This whole affair has been a test, some magical spell twisting my reality and making a mockery of my sisters' memories.

Unforgivable.

"No," I reply, ignoring the way my voice falters. My sisters' expressions fall, a mix of betrayal and sorrow. "This isn't real."

"It could be," Qin says. "We can make it real."

"I'm sorry, but . . . you're all gone."

Something shifts between us. The tension in the air so heavy that it's suffocating.

"And whose fault is that?" Jiayi hisses, her demeanor changing before my very eyes.

"If only you'd done what you were told," Su growls. "If only you'd done what the Maskmaker wanted, we would still be alive!"

I shrink back, guilt weighing heavily on my shoulders. "I didn't mean for it to happen. I just—I couldn't harm the boy."

My sisters circle me, flashing their fangs and tensing their shoulders as they prepare to pounce. They snarl and scream at me all at once, any semblance of sisterly affection melting away to reveal what they truly are. Monsters. Sonam used the term so often when referring to me, but I can understand now.

It horrifies me to see them this way, their faces warped in disgust and anger. How dare the star god use them against me. How dare he take what precious little I already had left of them and poison it.

"I've given you my answer," I say, loud and clear. "You've failed to tempt me."

My eldest sister, Qin, steps forward from the pack. She doesn't look at me, but the captain. "Are you sure, Yue? This is your only chance."

I remain perfectly still, waiting for any sign of movement. "As I said, I won't be tempted."

Where Sooah, Wen, and Sonam's illusions filtered away, the ghosts of my sisters don't leave in nearly as peaceful a manner. I watch, wide-eyed and slack-jawed as their thick fur catches flame.

The heat is so intense that it dries my eyes and burns the air in my lungs. I scream until my throat is raw and shredded. My sisters melt away to nothing more than bone and then dust while our surroundings trickle away like rain, returning me once more to the extravagant garden courtyard of the Jade Palace. There was never any jungle. None of this was real. Even the illusion of Captain Sonam fades away into nothing.

I can feel my pulse in the tips of my fingers, in my throat, my teeth. My legs are seconds from giving out. Sonam, Wen, and Sooah stand a few feet away, watching with expressions I can't hope to decipher. Shame and embarrassment heat my cheeks. They must have witnessed that whole sordid affair, as I did with their trials. With a shallow, shaking exhale, I pull on my mask, hating how naked I feel without it.

Exposed. I wish they'd stop bloody *staring.*

"Most entertaining!"

The voice of the star god reaches my ears. I look up to find him casually striding down the pathway, the winding vines and cutting leaves unfurling themselves to give him space. He claps his hands together with an amused laugh, clearly pleased with the grand finale of this wicked show.

"It's been at least a while since anyone's passed my test," he says, "but all four of you! I am most impressed."

"Spare me your speech," Sonam snaps. "We've conquered your trial. Now let us pass."

With an almost dismissive sigh, the star god waves his hand. The earth rumbles beneath our feet as the courtyard walls slide apart, revealing the next ring of small pavilions and gardens within the Jade Palace like the circles within the bark of a tree. A small temple lies ahead. A lone stone lantern sits before the arrival steps, though its light is no match for the constant green glow of the main building at its core.

"A pity," the star god says. "You would have made lovely additions to my garden. When you see my brother in the Court of Wrath, do give him my love."

I grind my teeth so hard that my molars squeak. My hands won't stop shaking. I can't seem to scream no matter how hard I try to find my voice. To witness my sisters die a second time . . . I'm used to being treated cruelly, but this is too much. Rage boils within my blood, threatening to consume me. God or no, he can't get away with this. I refuse to let anyone dishonor my sisters the way he's done.

I pounce, attacking with my bare fists, kicking and screaming and scratching with all my might. With the star god pinned beneath me, I pull at his hair and claw at his face. I want to hurt him the way he's hurt me.

"You bastard!"

Sonam grabs my shoulder. I nearly bite his arm off, surprised at the contact. He holds me with a stern look, pulling me onto my feet.

"Don't. There are consequences for killing a god."

"Curse the consequences!" I shriek. "He killed my sisters!"

"They weren't real, Fox." There's something close to pity in his tone. I hate it. I hate *him*. "You said it yourself, they're not real. Don't let him deceive you."

I force myself to breathe. Damn his calm head and cold logic. What am I supposed to do with all this anger? If I don't lash out, it may well destroy me. How dare Sonam look me in the eye and tell me to let things be?

I shove the captain away, utterly disgusted. "Don't touch me, human. Don't you ever fucking touch me!"

The star god rises with a chuckle, wiping a hand over his face. Seeing him now, I haven't left a mark on him. He's as radiant as he was before, not a cut on his cheeks or a wrinkle to sully his robes. The power of divinity flows through him with such force that it rendered my efforts wasted.

"You're full of surprises, little fox," the star god taunts. "Would you like to try again?"

To my surprise, it's Sooah who steps in between myself and the god, her imposing size casting a shadow over me. Her shoulders tremble ever so slightly, the hard edge to her expression ringing loud and clear—warning not to do anything foolish. She doesn't strike me as irritated or upset, merely uneasy. Her brow is covered in a light sheen of sweat. Sooah seems eager to move on from this place, eager to leave her memories behind. It's no small comfort to know I'm not the only one reeling from this horrid experience. If this is what we faced in the first Court of Hell, I shudder to think what awaits us.

I clench my fists. My nails dig into my palms hard enough to break skin, streaks of black dripping over my fingers. Taking a deep breath, I turn on my heels and trudge on, attempting to rid my mind of the faces of my sisters. Their ghosts are seared into my mind, haunting me even as we leave the first Court of Hell behind us.

16

The youngest star god clawed his way back up to the mortal coil, shocked to find the world above transformed into a paradise.

Luscious green trees grew ever taller. Sparkling blue rivers danced and curved across the lands to meet the oceans. Humans had crawled out of their mountain dwellings and begun to carve the earth to their will, breathing life into the soil in the form of golden wheat, vibrant rice paddies, and thriving bamboo forests.

He might have been able to appreciate the splendor, were he not burning with such terrible envy.

"Brother!" he called out to the Sun. "Brother, I beg of you, please help us!"

But the Sun did not heed his cries, unabashedly enjoying the attention and love of the world. As he was the sole solar deity, people prayed to him and him alone. They built shrines and temples in his name, bestowing upon him offerings of incense, ripe fruits, and mountains of gold. The Sun did not want to share in his newfound glory, and instead turned his back when his youngest brother called out his name.

Enraged, the ninth star cried out to the Heavens next. "Let me in!" he demanded. "I am a god as you all are! I belong neither in Hell, nor toiling away on this plane."

The Heavens, too, ignored his pleas. They looked upon him with disdain. A god felled by something as crude as a mortal arrow wished to rejoin their ranks? And now he was throwing a fit for all to see. How wholly undignified!

The only person to take pity was his mother, the goddess Xihe. She descended from the Kingdom of Heaven to meet with her youngest son in secret.

"I cannot bring you back with me," she said sorrowfully. "The best I can do is offer you a gift."

His mother produced a paintbrush with a quick flourish of her hand. Even though it was simply made—hollowed bamboo and a tip of coarse horsehair—and easily mistaken for any commoner's calligraphy brush, the magic within made the surrounding air spark and crackle. The sun mother plucked a large leaf from a nearby tree and demonstrated, painting a crude face upon its surface.

She pressed it to her face and was transformed. Once breathtaking, now she appeared a shriveled old woman.

"Use this to hide from Death," she said, raising a hand to cast a spell upon her son. "It is enchanted so that only those with a god's blessing may wield its power. Use it wisely, my child."

With paintbrush now begrudgingly in hand, the ninth star knew it was pointless to fight his fate. Perhaps, he thought, he could hide from it instead.

He picked a leaf just as his mother had done and drew himself a mask. It was crude and hideous . . . and the first of many to come.

If his brother the Sun and Heaven were both out of reach, there was yet one more person to whom he could direct his anger. Donning his newly crafted disguise, the star god went in search of the archer who shot him down all those years ago from his place in the sky, his thirst for revenge demanding to be quenched.

17

Yue

Hunting Log #381:
She has sad eyes. A trick, surely, to take advantage of my sympathy.

T***he four of us step*** into the waiting temple situated between the courts in silence. The building appears abandoned, not a soul in sight. The only reason I know others have been through before us is by the faint footprints left behind on the dusty floors, reminders that we aren't the first to attempt an escape. I wonder how far they got. Did they make it out of Hell in one piece, finally having burnt off their sins to once again step back into the circle of reincarnation?

Paper lanterns float of their own accord, suspending themselves a few feet in the air to illuminate the space in soft, flickering light. It's a welcome reprieve from the sickening green glow of the Jade Palace. It was starting to give me a headache.

"We should rest before we move on," Sonam says. His voice is low and hoarse, weighed down by obvious exhaustion.

Normally quick to fight him, I end up nodding along with Wen and Sooah. They seem as eager as I do to move on to the next trial. Which is to say—not at all. While they settle down near the center of the main room, I find a quiet, dark corner to sit down. With my back pressed to the wall and my knees tucked to my chest, I force myself to find calm.

I can't stop thinking about them. My sisters, dying. Burning. Right before my very eyes, all while the star god laughed.

Curse him. Curse him and all of Hell and these horrible humans who brought me here.

Mihan once told me a story about the star gods, all those years ago. They had always been cruel and uncaring, so much so that a human took it upon himself to end their tyranny. It seems almost fitting, in hindsight, that they should be tasked with running the Courts of Hell. They're certainly well suited for it.

My stomach grumbles, but I stifle the sound by hugging my knees tighter. It's impossible to tell how much time has passed since we arrived. A few days, perhaps? Though given my growing hunger, it could be closer to a week. This could prove troublesome. Eating Sonam while under a blood oath is out of the question, and killing his guards won't come without consequence. The more the seconds tick by, the more ravenous I become.

I bite my tongue and ignore my hunger pangs. This is no time to lose my head.

The humans shift out of their armor as they did before, clearly more at ease now that we've managed to escape the star god's torturous illusions. Nobody says a word as Sooah rifles through her pockets, pulling out a small package wrapped tightly in banana leaves. She unfurls them one by one, exposing a handful of rice balls. She's come prepared, it seems.

They look dry, and might have been sat on once or twice, but the scent of the salted salmon filling within makes my mouth water even at this distance. Sooah shares the three portions she has with Sonam and Wen without hesitation, though she does momentarily glance over her shoulder at me.

"Don't worry about feeding that thing," Wen says, already scarfing down his rice.

Sooah signs something with one hand. I don't understand a word, but I can tell by the tension in her shoulders and the frown she wears that she's agitated. Maybe she doesn't agree.

"We need to look out for ourselves," Wen continues with a huff. His voice is worse than nails screeching over porcelain. "Don't waste our food on that animal."

I don't suffer fools, but the usual anger that fuels me is nowhere to be found. I'm still too shaken, trapped in my own mind as I relive my sisters' demise again and again. What a cruel thing, to have your most horrifying memories used against you.

A shadow approaches, long and wide. I look up to find the captain a few paces away, hesitation knitting his brows together. We stare at each other distrustfully. Neither of us makes a move.

"Are demons even capable of eating human food?" he asks gruffly. As to the point as ever.

"We are," I reply, looking him up and down, "though there are certainly more nourishing things."

He huffs. After a moment, he settles for a simple nod and bends over slowly, portioning his food in half and setting it down on a banana leaf upon the floor. He looks like he's trying to appease a rabid dog, which I'll admit isn't as far from reality as it could be. Sonam backs away without a word, and I suppose it's better than sticking around awaiting thanks. I'm used to being cursed at, treated like filth.

This kindness is unsettling. No. Not a kindness, but an act of self-preservation. I shouldn't fool myself into thinking Sonam truly cares. This is but an attempt at pacifying me. It isn't an entirely foolish ploy. If I'm kept full, I am less likely to turn my teeth on them, though there's little to stop me from biting just for fun.

I momentarily entertain the thought of nipping off Wen's fingers, but what good is an archer who cannot nock his arrow?

Sonam returns to his little troupe, taking a seat with his back turned to me, and then pulls out that notebook of his and starts to write. The *scritch-scratch* of his charcoal against the surface sends a light shiver down my spine. He appears almost meditative, perfectly still save for his studious hand. I want to ask what thoughts he's committing to paper, but I decide against it. It's evident that none of us are in a particularly talkative mood.

Once the humans return to ignoring me outright, I reach for the offering of hardened rice and salted fish that Sonam left out for me. I give it a sniff. No poison. Not a trick. Ignoring the way my face heats, I finish it in two measly bites. It's dry going down, a grain or two stuck to the back of my throat, but at least it quiets my stomach. After I lick my teeth clean, I return to the safety of my corner of the temple and keep a watchful eye on all.

A rough hand claps over my mouth, cold metal biting the front of my throat. I made the mistake of nodding off. Something heavy drives itself into my chest—a pair of knees. Someone is on top of me.

Wen. Dagger in hand. The usual tremor that plagues him is gone.

He's going to kill me.

"Quiet," he hisses. "This'll be qui—"

I unhinge my jaw and bite off two of his fingers, the crunch of his bones echoing inside my skull. His flesh tastes foul, but I expect nothing less from this rat. Wen falls back in agony, clutching his hand to his chest as he cries bloody murder. My heart pounds and my lungs burn. I lunge at him, driving my knees to his chest just as he did to me.

"Attacking someone in their sleep?" I growl. "You're as cowardly as they come."

"Fox!" Sonam is on his feet, barreling toward me. He shoves me off of Wen with dizzying force. I can barely hear anything over the rush of blood in my ears.

"The demon attacked me!" Wen lies, groaning and whining as if he's suffered a fatal wound. He holds up his bloody, disfigured hand. "See? It was going to eat me!"

"He's lying!" I snap back. There's an unfamiliar sting in my eyes. "He was going to kill *me*."

"Like anyone would believe that," Wen huffs. "You saw how it was on top of me. Another second, and the beast would have taken my whole hand."

"I was defending myself. You had a blade to my throat!"

"You can't trust a blasted thing out of that monster's mouth. Everything it says is a lie!"

"But I'm not—" My throat chokes. I don't know what I want more badly: to convince Sonam that I'm not lying, or that I'm not a monster, because both are *true*.

I only eat humans because it's my nature. There's no choice in the matter. I don't take pleasure in killing—though there's an element of satisfaction in ridding the world of a particularly unkind soul. Would they call a tiger a monster for feasting upon a hare? What about a viper helping itself to the eggs in a bird's nest? And what of the dragons in the Far East who have been rumored to fly off with farmland ox? They blame me for what I am, hunt me for what I am, and even make sport of it. So it begs the question: Who is the real monster here?

"I've had enough of this," I say through gritted teeth, turning toward the temple's entrance.

"Where are you going?" Sonam calls after me. A direct question—I cannot lie.

"I'm going ahead. Worry not, *Your Highness*," I spit the title like a curse, "you don't have to worry about our deal. I'll clear the way, and you and your minions can follow."

Sooah stomps her foot, but no one heeds her.

"Fox, wait," Sonam says. "It's too dangerous to go alone."

"Maybe for you," I snap. "I've been on my own for a very long time. It won't make any difference now."

He attempts to grip my shoulder, but I'm twice as fast, my hands shooting out to grab him by the front of his shirt. I let loose a snarl, ready to sink my teeth into whatever foolish wolf stands in my way.

"What did I say about touching me?" I hiss.

"You need us."

"*You* need *me*. I don't need *anyone*—"

This time, Sooah presses her fingers to her lips and whistles. It's a sharp, high blast that bounces off the temple walls. All eyes turn to her—as well as to Wen, walking in from around the corner. He sleepily rubs his eyes and yawns. I glance back at my attacker standing directly next to the captain, seeing double. How can this be?

"What's going on?" the real Wen asks. "What's with all the shouting?" He notices his duplicate and frowns steeply. "Who the—"

The imposter smiles. It's eerie. A little too wide and unnatural for the proportions of Wen's slim face. His features almost seem to slip off—like a mask.

"Hello, Yue," he says. "It's good to see you've been doing well."

"You," I breathe, realization slapping me across the face.

After a tense beat, he runs.

I give chase.

We exit the temple together, barely an inch between us. The Maskmaker is within my grasp, but when I reach out—

He darts left. I follow, my momentum nearly causing me to careen into a jade divider. The muscles in my thighs burn, my human form unable to keep up with his speed. I refuse to give up, fueled by my rage. He leads me deeper and deeper into the Court of Wrath, and that's when I realize something.

What if this is another trap?

"Stop!" I scream at him. "Come back!"

But the Maskmaker keeps running. I lose him as I round a corner, nearly tripping over my own feet when I come up to a large courtyard with towering walls—a fortress within a fortress. The bitter taste of metal lingers in the air, along with distant battle cries and groans of agony. There are people fighting, but I know not who. Despite my growing trepidation, I venture in through the waiting arch, instantly greeted by the harsh sourness of sweat.

This is no courtyard, but an arena.

A frightening legion of men and women, fighting each other with their bare hands stand in my way. They come in all shapes and sizes, ranging from young to old. I wonder how long ago they abandoned their weapons, judging by the assortment of splintered shields, shattered swords, and snapped lances lying forgotten around us. One of them has had his eyes scratched out. The woman closest to me is missing an arm. But no matter the carnage, they continue the match, thoroughly absorbed in the senseless violence of it all.

Upon a throne of jade sits a man, his features strikingly similar to the first star god we encountered. He glows deep red, from his wine-flushed cheeks to his bloodshot eyes, to the wine staining his robes a dull maroon. The star god sits there, leaning to one side and breathing heavily as he watches the contenders with an almost sickening amusement. Through his drunken haze, he spots me.

"Enough," he says, voice low and hoarse. It carries throughout the arena like distant thunder. The ghosts stop what they're doing, looking at the god in confusion.

My heart rails against my rib cage. When will this nightmare end?

"Finally, some fresh meat." The star god settles into his throne with a chuckle. "Let's give our newcomer a warm welcome."

18

Yue

Hunting Log #382:
Gods, the way she fights is terrifying~~ly beautiful.~~

Their advantage: I'm outnumbered.

My advantage: seething fury.

These are human souls, I realize: thousands upon thousands of those unworthy of reincarnation without proper penance. They must have been lucky enough to pass through the first Court of Hell, only to end up trapped here.

I wonder what heinous crimes they committed in life to earn their place in Hell. Were they murderers? Thieves? Adulterers? In the end, it doesn't matter. I couldn't care less about their redemption now that they're in my way.

Instinct tells me to kill. I could easily slice them to ribbons with my claws or tear them asunder with my teeth. This could even be an opportunity to sate my hunger before it gets the better of me. They are nothing more than a field of souls ripe for the plucking.

The two closest souls to me charge, gnashing their teeth and raising their bloody fists. I brace for the assault, wincing in anticipation of pain—but it never comes. Before I have a chance to blink, my would-be assailants are on the ground, tackled by Wen and Sooah with startling force.

"On your feet, Fox," Sonam says, running up from behind. His dao is drawn and ready.

I'm surprised to see him. I was certain he'd let me run off ahead and leave me to my own devices. Now that he's standing before me, his body a sturdy shield against the impending onslaught, I feel . . . strange. Lightheaded and untethered. Likely the adrenaline of the fight.

The souls of the next circle of Hell storm us en masse, screaming and cursing all manner of vile slurs as they try to tear us apart. There's a crazed look in their eyes, so consumed with violence that they've been driven to madness. The star god has stripped them of their humanity, turned them into nothing more than ravenous beasts, all the while watching from atop his throne. He reminds me of a cruel child cutting off the tails of mice he's caught. He relishes in the pleasure of it, laughing simply because he can.

It's a matter of survival, but as the fight drags on, I realize just how slim our odds are. They must be under some sort of spell, because they never tire. No matter how many people I beat back, they keep coming.

I pin a man to the ground, my nails digging into his chest. There's bloodlust in his eyes, yes, but there's also a hint of something desperate. Anguish. Behind his anger, I can see his exhaustion. His helplessness. He doesn't want to fight any more than I do.

"Please," he rasps. "Just let me kill you."

His request confounds me. "Let you?"

"He won't let us sleep. Day in and day out, he has us fight." The man's voice breaks. "If I kill you, maybe he'll finally let me go."

I take in the violence surrounding us. Wen takes blow after blow, cracking his knuckles against jaws. Sooah is trapped in a corner, lashing out at those who draw too near. And the captain—I've lost sight of him. Panic grips my throat. What if he's hurt somewhere in the crowd? If anything were to happen to him . . .

"Human!" I cry out. "Dammit, where—"

"I'm here."

Sonam's behind me, kicking a man in the stomach with such force that the poor bastard crumples in half. The captain fends off a woman next, sweeping her legs out from under her before she can do me any harm. He fights off another, and then another, *protecting* me. The chaos unfolds around us. I could crush them all one by one, but not like this. Not against a seemingly endless horde.

"Take off your mask," the captain commands. "We need your fangs."

My insides churn. I don't want to take it off. He doesn't understand the true extent of the hatred I have for my own scarred face.

I spot the star god safe on his throne. Don't these people realize their efforts are wasted on each other? He is but one against the powerful many. They don't yet know the strength they hold in numbers.

"With me!" I shout over my shoulder, barging my way through the crowd.

Sonam follows without question, keeping pace as we charge toward the star god. The second judge of Hell seems unperturbed at first, but the closer we get, the more his concern begins to rise.

The star god stands abruptly, holding out a hand as if to stop us. "What do you think you're doing? That's far enough!"

Faster than I can blink, Sonam has his sword pressed to the god's throat. When he tries to squirm away, I stand my ground, flashing my teeth with a deep, rumbling growl. If I must, I will tear my mask off and give him something to fear. This god may thrive on chaos and torment, but I can smell his cowardice deep within.

"Command them to stop," Sonam orders. "Or I'll separate your head from your shoulders."

I glance at the captain. "I thought you said there are consequences to killing a god."

"Minds can change."

I don't know whether I want to laugh or groan, so it comes out as a short huff. "Typical. You change the rules whenever it suits you."

"A thousand humble pardons, Fox. I'll see to it that you get the next one."

"That best be a promise, Dinner."

A grin ghosts across his lips, though the glint in his eyes is undeniable.

The god sneers. "Unhand me at once, you filth."

"Let us all move on from this place," I say firmly. "Enough of this senseless violence."

His face twists up as he laughs, sharp and sinister. "You believe them trapped here?" he asks. "The doors are unlocked, as it were. There's nothing stopping these cretins from walking on through to the next court. They're here because they want to be."

Sonam frowns. "What do you mean?"

The star god presses his lips into a thin line, unimpressed. "Allow me to impart a little wisdom. Everything in Hell is about choices. If you wish to stop fighting, then stop fighting. These souls are here to redeem themselves, after all—to correct their wrongs before they're deemed ready for reincarnation—and what better way to purge their worldly sins than by giving them the chance to change? I'm not to blame for their violent tendencies. What they do is up to them—I just happen to enjoy watching mortals make fools of themselves."

Irritation simmers beneath the surface of my skin. "Maybe they weren't aware they had a choice."

"*Everyone* has a choice," he replies simply. "Everyone." The star god leans toward me and chuckles, evidently unafraid of Sonam's blade. "You made a choice once, too, didn't you? He told me all about you. What a pleasure to meet you in the flesh."

My stomach churns, a sudden chill gripping my spine. It does not bodes well that the Maskmaker has been talking about me. "Where is he?"

"He came running this way," the star god answers. "Didn't stay long. A shame, really. I would have loved to catch up. He has plans, or so he keeps telling me. They are far too important to stay for very long."

That coward—always running away. First he ruins my life, and now he's too frightened to face me for longer than a minute. He's always been keen to show off, but I thought he was above something as pathetic as taunting. If he knows I'm here, surely he knows his time is limited. After all these years of searching for him, I'm finally one step closer to taking my revenge.

"What is he doing down here?" I ask. "What's he planning?"

"Wouldn't you like to know."

"I would not ask otherwise, you snake—"

"Put the sword away, friend," the star god says to Sonam, ignoring me entirely. "The way to the Court of Hunger is just through there. Go on. I won't stop you." He gestures toward a moon gate, nearly identical to the one that saw us here.

The captain and I exchange a look. It's brief, but it's enough for a silent conversation to pass between us. I'm genuinely surprised when he takes a step back, gesturing with a subtle sweep of his hand. An invitation to take the lead. How uncharacteristically polite. He would have made quite the prince.

I snag the star god by the collar of his robes and toss him to the arena floor. He lands with an unceremonious yelp, surrounded by tortured souls. There's a beat of absolute stillness—before one of the human souls dares to put their hands on him. She's quickly joined by someone else now clawing at his robes. Within seconds, the star god is pulled this way and that; scratched, beaten, and maimed without remorse.

His cries go unheeded by all.

"Are you sure we should leave him here like this?" Wen asks as he rejoins us, Sooah in tow.

I bring a hand up to my mask, making sure that it's secured in place, before I shrug my shoulders. "Nothing wrong with a taste of your own medicine."

Sooah signs something quickly. A simple point in the direction of the nearest moon gate. I understand her meaning: *Let's get going.*

19

Yue

Hunting Log #383:
Time is impossible to track in Hell. Has it been weeks, or mere days?

D***espite leaving the arena behind,*** the stench of blood and sweat and aggression has seared itself into my nostrils. The fact that we have to survive eight more of these trials has me in a particularly foul mood, though I suppose progress is progress.

"The Court of Hunger," Wen mutters as we make our way up the steps of another pavilion. "You reckon they'll try to starve us to death?"

I snort. "How utterly imaginative."

Sooah points toward a small garden just past the pavilion, drawing my attention to the open space and drooping wisteria trees. They have no petals, their branches naked and thin. Despite its barren state, there's tranquility to be found here. Especially after witnessing the carnage of the Court of Wrath.

She gestures slowly, and I'm able to discern her simple signs. She presses her palms together and places them on the side of her cheek, like a pillow, before pointing at the ground.

Sleep here.

"Good idea," I reply. "You three need your rest."

"Someone needs to keep watch," Wen insists.

I take a deep breath. "I can do it. I don't need nearly as much sleep as your kind does."

Suspicion flits across Wen's face—which is, frankly, unsurprising—but the captain has the final say. Sonam nods, just once, before striding over to a jade bench. He sits with a heavy exhale, slouching forward, the weariness of all we've seen bearing down on his shoulders. He looks so much older like this. I wouldn't be surprised if his troubles lead him to an early grave.

Sooah is the next to follow suit, shrugging off her laminal armor to find a seat of her own. Wen stares at me for a while longer, but I don't detect his usual malice. I think he's beginning to tolerate me, though I'm not sure whether to feel grateful.

While the humans settle in for the night, I climb the garden wall and sit on top of the cold bricks, taking in the view of the Jade Palace from my new vantage point. It is a sight to behold, the heart of it all. Smaller palaces exist within larger ones, an intricate network of nesting districts and neat passageways cordoned off with ever taller walls. When I stare at the Jade Palace, I can't help but feel miniscule. Insignificant.

If I die with a scream in my throat, will anyone remember my piercing cry? If I go quietly, one final whisper of breath before the lights dim, will someone lay my body to rest? Picking at my fingernails, I think of my sisters. Even if I hadn't run that day, the Maskmaker ensured there was nothing left of them to mourn. They were burned beyond the point of ash, stolen by the passing breeze. If I die, I might have liked a grave marker and flowers. Wishful impossibilities, of course, but a demon can dream.

"It's even more beautiful in the light of day." Sonam's voice is calm as he hoists himself up onto the wall beside me. He keeps a generous distance, roughly five arms away. A smart, safe choice. "And the gardens are normally lush and vibrant. From what I remember as a boy, anyway."

I stare at him, my lips pressed into a thin line. "You should be resting."

"Couldn't sleep."

"Did Your Highness have bad dreams?" I mean to tease, but the way the words come out makes me sound sincere.

"Too anxious," he confesses. His honesty surprises me. After a long moment, he asks, "Who's the Maskmaker?"

I sigh. "He's none of—"

"Don't tell me he's none of my concern," he interjects. "This isn't the first time he's been mentioned. I think you can agree that his ability to wear our faces complicates matters. I need to know more, Yue."

The sound of my name makes my breath hitch. He pronounces it carefully, precisely. The low rumble of his voice is much too soothing. I don't trust it.

"When I was a pup, I found myself caught in a trap," I explain slowly. "Wound up falling into a tar pit that local hunters concealed with leaves. I was stuck there for three, maybe four moons. The more I struggled, the deeper I sank. It was only a matter of time before I'd suffocate. Or starve."

My jaw tightens as the memories unfurl in my mind. Not a day goes by where I don't think about the Maskmaker. I would have been better off if he had left me in that wretched pit. My sisters might still be here.

"Then what happened?" Sonam urges.

"Then he showed up." The back of my throat burns. "He was the one who pulled me free."

"And he was the one who made your mask?"

I nod slowly, bringing a hand to the burnt side of my face. With the mask's magic at work, it feels as though those scars don't exist at all, perfectly concealed to sight and touch. "He was."

"Can he make a mask of any face?"

"I believe so," I confirm. "Both the living and the dead, so long as he's seen it once before."

"If he helped you, why are you after him?"

I ball up my fists, studying the way my knuckles turn white and my nails bite into my palms. How much can I get away with telling him? I can't lie, but that doesn't mean I need to give him the whole truth. He's already pried more from my lips than I ever thought possible. Sonam's growing familiarity with me is jarring, to say the least. At this rate, there will be nothing left to hide—no distance left to keep me safe.

"Does this have something to do with those women we saw in the Court of Temptation?" he asks. "Your sisters, correct?"

"Yes," I murmur.

"He killed them?"

I chew on the inside of my cheek. "Yes. And for that, he must die."

A blanket of silence falls over us. Fragile and thin, but not as uncomfortable as it could be.

"Thank you," I mutter after a while. "For saving me from the boar demon. He might have killed me were it not for you."

Sonam stares at me as though I've grown a second head. He nods once. I don't think he was expecting words of gratitude, especially from me. "You held your own quite well," he replies. "Impressive."

"You, too."

"Good work figuring out how to get into the Jade Palace."

"Thank—"

"Though I'd appreciate a warning next time you have one of your little ideas. Damn near soiled myself."

I can't help but grin. "That's not a very princely thing to say."

"I'm no prince," he grumbles, though he doesn't seem wholly upset.

"Why is that?"

We fall into silence again. He very clearly doesn't want to tell me, so to change the subject entirely, I mumble, "Show me that notebook of yours."

If Sonam is irked by my request, he does an excellent job of hiding it. He produces his notebook and runs his fingers along the outer edges, almost bashful. It's a strange emotion to see on someone normally so stoic.

"They're not very good," he says while clearing his throat, but hands it to me all the same.

I flip it open to the first page, taking great care not to tear any of the pages or smudge the charcoal. The first entry is dated several decades ago, a detailed sketch of a water dragon so lifelike I'm convinced it could fly off the page. He's captured every single scale, every hair upon its flowing mane, and even the sharp hook of the creature's front and hind claws.

"You saw a dragon?" I ask, astounded.

"My brother, actually. Far out east in the uncharted lands. He told me he was only brave enough to observe them at a distance. Said they were a family of three—one blue, one red, and one green. Rare, to find a whole family. He drew that one before handing the book down to me."

I flip the page. Sure enough, there's a substantial difference in the art style. Where the dragon was constructed of confident lines, the next entry was clearly the result of shaky, inexperienced hands. Oddly enough, I find myself smiling at the thought of a young Sonam trying to illustrate with pudgy, childish fingers and the tip of his tongue poking out between his lips in concentration. It seems that the second creature he added to his hunting log was a forest spirit. I've encountered a fair few in my lifetime. Harmless little buggers, easily mistaken for a patch of weeds, though they have a nasty habit of trying to burrow into your ears and root themselves in place.

"Tell me more," I say, flipping the page again. Sonam's skills improve with each entry, his progress slow and steady. "About this brother of yours. The one who gifted you this book. None of the ones I met seemed particularly adventurous."

"I have eight brothers, actually," he says tightly. "Of which I am the youngest, all born to different mothers. The king has no shortage of concubines to sire his heirs." He offers a small, tight-lipped smile. "It would be accurate to call me one of the spares."

I look up from his book. "I only counted seven in the Court of Temptation."

"Han, Li, and Sang were all born days apart in different parts of the palace. Then came Sìzi and Zhong a year later. And then there are the twins, Nin and Min. They're both . . . Well." He makes a noise halfway between a grunt and a wretch. It's hard not to notice the way his expression grows more and more dour as he lists off the names of his siblings.

"I take it you're not particularly fond of them?"

"It would be . . . unbecoming to speak ill of people I hardly know. They are no better than strangers to me."

I snort. "I'll do it for you, then. Your brothers all seem like arrogant cocks."

Sonam presses his lips into a tight line, but it isn't out of irritation. If anything, I think he's doing his best to suppress a smile, though there's always a good chance I've misread him.

"Now," I say, "human arithmetic may not be my strong suit, but I'm fairly sure that counts seven."

Sonam is quiet for a moment, contemplatively watching the

Jade Palace with an almost weary calm. There's something amusing about the way he chooses his words as carefully as I do. It's one of the few things we have in common, I suppose.

"Jun," he answers finally. "He died roughly thirty years ago. He was the kindest of my siblings. So much so, I sometimes wondered how it was possible we were even related. He was the one who gave me the book."

I listen with rapt attention, unsure if it's the seriousness of the captain's voice or my natural curiosity that has me hanging on his every word.

"He was the eldest among us and therefore destined for the throne. But then he shocked everyone by joining the Order of the Albeion monks." Sonam shakes his head, as if in disbelief. "He gave up everything to live in a sun temple, of all things. Wrote to me often. He told me he was happy there. Father was furious, of course. All those years spent training Jun to be his successor, for naught."

"Good thing your father still has a selection to choose from, then."

Sonam huffs. "Yes, I suppose."

"And what, pray tell, became of this beloved brother?"

The captain swallows, his throat rising and falling heavily. "I was five when it happened. I'd already been sent away from the Jade Palace, so I didn't learn of his death until a letter came moons later. There was an attack."

I stiffen. "An attack?"

"Demons," he mumbles. "A whole pack of them, according to the reports." Sonam takes a deep breath, his gaze suddenly distant and cold. "They tore through the sun temple. Ripped him apart."

My heart does something it's never done—it sinks. I, too, know the pain of loss. It's brutal and unforgiving, an insidious kind of agony that lingers for years and years until it gives way to numbness. But I'm also wary.

"Is that why you decided to become a demon hunter?" I ask tightly.

"Not entirely."

"Care to elaborate? Or am I going to have to continue this game of questions?"

Sonam glares at me. "My mother was not an appointed concubine, but a scullery maid who happened to catch His Majesty's eye. It was . . . a bit of a scandal. I likely would have been worse off had it not been for her lineage."

I tilt my head to the side, curious. "What lineage?"

"Supposedly, my mother comes from a long line of accomplished archers. She had no proof, however. The family records only went back so far. Many within the Jade Palace who had my father's ear believed A-Ma to be a liar. Said she'd spun a tale to earn his favor."

I frown, deep in thought. "And this explains your lack of a title?"

The muscles in his jaw tick. I take his lack of an answer as confirmation.

"You humans are so strange, imposing all these rules on yourselves."

"You're hardly someone from whom I'll suffer a lecture, Fox."

A soft laugh escapes me, a wheezy little sound. I'll let the issue rest.

I absentmindedly continue to flip through his notebook, admiring the clear progression in artistic skill. Some creatures I'm able to put a name to, others I'm not. There are notes neatly scribbled in the margins, each stroke firm and confident. Sonam is a thorough huntsman. He's listed weaknesses, strengths. I'm convinced there isn't a beast in the entire world he hasn't encountered.

A fei beast with one frightening round eye in the middle of its face. A razor-toothed yayu. A flock of Zhenniao birds.

When I come up to the last entry, I freeze.

On the page is a nine-tailed fox, every detail immaculate. From my six obsidian eyes with gray pupils to my pointed ears and the matted sections of my fur that I have no time to groom. He's even captured my burns. I gingerly run the tips of my fingers over the image, careful not to smudge his work. It's strange seeing myself through someone else's eyes. He's even drawn me with my mask on, duplicating the slope of my nose and the voluminous waves of my shiny black hair.

I'm beautiful.

Or, more accurately, the mask is.

I want to admire his work. Truly, I do. But then I remember the purpose of his little notebook. His hunting log. There's a reason behind his study, and it leaves me unnerved.

"Of all the things you could have done," I murmur, "surely the king could have afforded you the life of a scholar, if not a proper title."

Sonam sets his jaw. "I vowed vengeance," he says. "When Jun died, I vowed to kill every demon on earth."

"And?" I prompt, sensing the way he hesitates.

"The Jade Palace will never recognize me," he says firmly. "Not the king, not my brothers, and not the advisors whispering in their ears. Not until I've proven my worth. Banishing you to Hell would have achieved that."

I bite my tongue, his words ringing loud and clear. There's a resoluteness in his tone that makes my stomach churn.

"When we first fell," I murmur. "You could have killed me."

"I'm aware."

"So why didn't you?"

Sonam is silent for a long while, his eyes cast down. "I don't know," he confesses softly. "But trust I won't make the same mistake twice."

I nearly forgot who I was talking to. No exceptions will be made, no more deals struck. Our reluctant alliance has kept me safe thus far, but sooner or later, Sonam will make his lethal move. Unless I come up with a plan, he will inflict hurt upon me just as everyone else has. I'd be a fool to expect anything less.

I close the book gently and hand it back to him, avoiding his gaze as I stare out toward the grounds of the Jade Palace. It looks so big and lonely. I don't understand why Sonam would want to return to a place like this.

"Get some rest, human," I murmur. "You need it more than I."

20

Sonam

Hunting Log #384:
She's surprisingly ~~funny and~~
She's rude and crass and I can't wait to be rid of her.

Sooah wakes me a few hours later for my turn on watch. She has a small fire burning, sparked to life using the shavings of what was once one of Wen's arrows. The flames are dim, flickering with its last sparks of life.

She brings her fingers up to poke at the space between my brows. *You frown even in sleep*, she tells me, teasing in a sisterly fashion. *Your face is going to get stuck.*

"We both know it already has," I say with a good-natured huff.

Warily, I glance over my shoulder. The fox appears sound asleep in the opposite corner of the pavilion. She lies on her side, knees tucked up to her chest. There's something upsetting about seeing her all by her lonesome, cast out like the reject of the herd. But most distressing of all . . .

Yue holds her own hand as she sleeps, held out just beside her weary head. She lies there with her fingers threaded, the gentle rise and fall of her chest barely perceptible. Every now and then, the muscles in her jaw twitch. Not once have I thought it possible for demons to dream. What haunts a monster's nightmares?

"Anything to report?" I ask Sooah in a hushed tone.

She shakes her head. *All quiet.*

"And how are provisions looking?"

Sooah checks the leather pouch attached to her belt. *Enough for one more day, I think. Maybe two, if we're careful.*

I set my jaw and ignore the tightness in my throat. This isn't ideal, though I can hardly blame her. It wasn't as if Sooah knew to pack for an indeterminate trek through Hell. If these trials don't kill us and we don't find ourselves in the fox's jaws by morning, starvation could quickly become our greatest concern.

What are we to do? I have a responsibility to see Wen and Sooah from this forsaken place. They are more than just my guards—they are my family. I am closer to them than I am my own blood, and I refuse to see them suffer. I could attempt to play this by ear, see what the next Court of Hell will present us, though its name might suggest we're in for trouble. Once the last morsel has passed our lips, what can I do to ensure our survival?

"Get some rest," I tell her.

Sooah nods, walking a short distance to lie down next to Wen. His mouth hangs open in a raucous snore, but we're used to it by now. Years spent around the campfire together have acclimated us to each other's greatest strengths and faults, Wen's mouth breathing included.

I scan the perimeter for any movement but find none. The fox hasn't left its corner. My friends sleep soundly, enjoying respite that's well deserved. As the minutes drag on, I find myself taking stock of my weapons once, twice, three times just to have something to do. All the while, my mind races, my thoughts too loud and my heart too skittish.

Without food or water, a human can last about a week, give or take a day. With just water, we may be able to survive a moon or two, but even now I'm aware of the dwindling weight of the canteen strapped to my belt. I'd heard old stories from my assigned tutors that, in times of war and extreme desperation, soldiers would turn to drinking their own blood in order to stave off their thirst. It was but a temporary solution, a small patch on a massive wound, yet if it comes down to it . . .

My chest grows painfully tight. I'm unable to draw a deep enough breath. My hand trembles when I bring it to my throat, powerless to loosen the invisible noose that's slipped itself over my head. It is far too early to succumb to this helplessness, yet my terror only grows—a monstrosity in and of itself. Hell is playing tricks on me, twisting my fear into outright panic. With the fire now reduced to little more than embers, I cannot help but wonder what horrors lie waiting in the dark.

With a deep breath, I reach for my hunting log. My fingers shake as I tear out a few pages from the back, ripping them into thin strips. I move slowly, setting the paper down to catch flame. My unease subsides as the fire grows, banishing my apprehension along with it.

When I look up, I find a pair of dark, fierce eyes watching me from across the way.

"You alright?" Yue asks, staring with unbroken concentration. It's disquieting, her stillness. It's impossible to tell what she's thinking. Will she remain, or will she pounce?

My cheeks burn. How much has she seen? "Fine," I reply gruffly, disregarding the way my heart rails against my chest.

Yue snorts. "Humans and your lies."

"I'm not lying."

"Fear has a smell, you know."

"I don't care—"

"It's sour," she interrupts. "Like curdled milk left out on a hot summer's day."

"That's disgusting."

"I'm glad we're in agreement. You're turning my air foul."

I shake my head slowly, as irritated as I am anxious. If there's one thing I can trust Yue to do, it's to put me in a worse mood. "You're not much of a conversationalist, Fox."

"You'll have to forgive me, Breakfast; I'm out of practice. This is the most anyone's spoken to me in years."

She stares at me, somehow both indignant and accusatory. The depth of her black eyes is haunting. I could drown in them, and she would laugh with delight at my suffering.

"What?" she snaps when I say nothing.

"Speaking of breakfast," I reply. "You told me you didn't eat that little girl. The seamstress's daughter."

Yue groans. "This nonsense again?"

"If you didn't eat her, who did?"

"What makes you so sure she was eaten? The brat probably ran off."

I shake my head. "It was a demon."

"Always so quick to blame."

"What other possibility is there?"

Her upper lip curls up into a sneer. I'm convinced she could cut me with a sharp enough glare. "Have you ever stopped to look inward? You humans are lesser demons yourselves."

"How dare you—"

"You hide hatred in your hearts for everyone and everything. You know for a fact I'm right."

I set my jaw, irritation simmering beneath the surface of my skin. "And you're an expert how, exactly?"

"Because I watch," she answers. "And I learn. Mankind hates what it does not understand and makes no effort to change its ways. Malice upon the man who speaks a different tongue, whose flesh is not a matching shade. Pity upon your women whose simple existence is an excuse to incur your wrath. Mercy for your children whose innocence will always be corrupted, either by time or by the hands of those they were taught to trust—"

"Be quiet," I snap.

"Or what?" Yue smiles then, wide and daring. "Will you show me firsthand what your hatred is capable of?"

Shame washes over me when I nearly give in to anger, my fingers itching to draw my sword. Damn her and her wicked tongue. I refuse to let her best me.

"We're not all like that."

"Enough of you are."

"You see what you want to see," I tell her coldly.

Yue huffs. "I see what is *there*."

It is strange to think that we've both walked the same green earth all this time, every step taken having led us to our unfortunate encounter. I do not believe in fate, only the possibilities we make for ourselves—yet I can't help but wonder if we were always meant to cross paths.

Yue is the first to break eye contact, rolling over to turn her back toward me. "Do me a favor and try not to panic again," she warns. "You smell atrocious."

"Are you always compelled to have the last word?"

"Yes."

I am a patient man, but she has a talent for wearing that patience thin. If I continue to challenge her, she'll meet me in force. And yet, if I say nothing, I will have no choice but to endure her conceited satisfaction.

In the end, I decide on silence. I'll be damned if I let the fox make a mockery of me. Ignoring her may be the only chance to keep my sanity. Flipping to a blank page at the back of my log, I allow my mind to wander, determined to fixate on the sound of charcoal gliding over paper.

My artistic ventures came reluctantly. As a child, I had no friends my age with whom I could play. While my brothers enjoyed the luxuries of the Jade Palace, I was raised far away in one of the king's many summer estates—an inconsequential son shunted to the side. Drawing was a simple pastime; one I could easily partake anywhere and in solitude. It's more meditative than enjoyable. A useful way to keep track of my hunts, yes, but also a way to quiet the mind.

I sketch what lies before me, calmed by the warm haze of the dwindling fire. I pay special attention to the point of Yue's chin. The way her hair falls neatly on either side of her face. I capture the sharp angle of her eyes—befittingly vulpine—as well as the fullness of her wicked lips.

Her beauty is ethereal. I have no doubts she could weaponize her allure to bring mankind to its knees. How many poor fools has she managed to beguile into becoming her dinner?

I will be the one to stop her. I have to.

It isn't until I run out of space to draw that I finally lift the charcoal off the paper, staring down at my work in horror. I've drawn her striking visage again and again, her aggravating gaze judging me at different angles. Frustration licks up the back of my neck. This must be some sort of demonic trick, unescapably worming her way into my mind.

You see what you want to see.

What the hell am I doing?

Gritting my teeth, I tear the page out and ball it up in my palm before tossing it on the fire, observing Yue from across the flames. She has fallen sound asleep—though I wouldn't put it past her to only be pretending.

The fox is far too clever for my liking.

I cannot let down my guard.

21

The star god found Houyi and his doting wife, Chang'e, in a scenic town by the sea. The sight of their children, happy and healthy, embittered him to his very core. How dare these mortals live in peace while he and his siblings were banished to Hell? The Heavens had even awarded Houyi an elixir of immortality for his righteous deed. The fool had accepted the gift, but had yet to drink it, for he could not stand the thought of trading his family for godly status.

"Such audacity!" the star god said to himself, thinking how best to punish the Legendary Archer.

He schemed for three days and four nights, concocting the perfect plan. He wanted the elixir for himself, but not for the purpose of immortality. He was an immortal god, after all, fallen as he may be. But if he presented such a divine treasure to Death himself, he could bargain for the return of his siblings and, with their help, take back what the Heavens had once refused.

Houyi and his children left for the day to collect firewood, leaving adoring Chang'e at home to prepare dinner. It was then that the star god broke in, surprising the poor woman.

"Who are you?" she cried. "What do you want?"

"I have no quarrel with you, mortal. Only your conniving

husband." He pulled off his mask and revealed his true face—as well as the puckered skin of his chest where Houyi's arrow had shot him clean through.

"You." Chang'e gasped. "How can this be?"

"Hand over the elixir," he demanded, looking upon her as though she were nothing more than a gnat. "Or I will burn everything you hold dear."

Although she was afraid, Chang'e bravely shook her head; proud and defiant. "I will give you nothing."

"Then die."

With a snap of his fingers, he set the bamboo hut aflame, trapping Chang'e within. No matter how loudly she screamed, no matter how she tried to claw her way to freedom, she understood that there was no escape.

Or was there?

It was a gambit, but it was one she had to take. As the smoke stung her eyes and ash filled her lungs, Chang'e pulled up the floorboards to reveal a hidden cache. This was where Houyi stored the elixir of immortality, far away from prying eyes and ne'er-do-wells. Chang'e could not allow it to fall into the star god's possession. It would only spell disaster. So, with little time and even fewer options, Chang'e uncorked the vial, brought the rim to her lips, and drank every last drop.

Houyi had seen the smoke upon the horizon and raced home to her aid, but all too late. The magic's effects were immediate—and irreversible. It spared her life, but it also spirited her away, carrying Chang'e from the wreckage of her burning home to the lonely surface of the moon.

"Bring her back!" Houyi demanded, gripping the star god by the throat. His eyes were red with rage, knuckles white with malice.

"No," the star god said with a laugh. "Suffer as I have suffered, archer. I want you to know the pain of watching your most loved waste away just as I have."

"I curse you, then," Houyi replied. "By my blood, I wish death upon you."

"Proud words for someone charred to a crisp," the star god said. He snapped his fingers, hoping to set the archer alight.

But nothing happened. For some strange reason, the star god's magic would not work. Upon closer inspection, he understood why. The archer had been blessed by none other than the Sun—yet another cruel betrayal by his eldest brother.

The star god threw Houyi to the ground and escaped into the night. Houyi gave chase, preparing his bow and arrow for one more hunt. Way up above, Chang'e watched in heartbroken dismay, for theirs was a story destined for tragedy.

The only aid the new goddess could offer her husband was the light of the moon to show him the way.

22

Yue

Hunting Log #385:
Demons are selfish beasts. They do nothing out of kindness.

There ***is only one path*** forward from the garden to the next court, the walls on either side of us making for a tight squeeze. We have no choice but to proceed in single file, Wen at the rear while I lead the charge up front. The passage between the second and third circle is so narrow that both my shoulders graze along the jade dividers.

"Can you see the exit?" Sonam asks directly behind me. I can feel the warmth of his breath tickle the nape of my neck. I'd normally be averse to having anyone this close, but there's little to be done given our cramped surroundings.

I look straight ahead and allow my eyes to focus in the dark. There's a slight curve to the path, rendering it impossible to discern anything past the bend. "Nothing yet."

The walls only grow tighter, more constricting. Panic doesn't come all at once. It's a slow build, a creeping sense of doom dripping down my back in a cold sweat. With the third trial nowhere in sight, the trek is starting to feel impossible. How much farther do we have to go? How much more of this must we endure? I'm being crushed from both sides, my shoulders now fully scraping against the walls, the friction caused by each step now shredding at my skin.

"W-we should turn back," Wen whimpers. "Are you sure there ain't another way?"

I can't blame him his mewling. Even I have half a mind to return the way we came. At this rate, the walls will squeeze the air from our lungs and crush our bones into powder. It's frankly a miracle that we've made it this far without getting stuck. If we continue, our chance of being wedged in place goes up exponentially. We'll have trapped ourselves, left to rot. No way forward, and certainly no way back.

A hand presses gently between my shoulder blades. Sonam's palm is warm, his touch neither forceful nor hurrying. The contact is brief, a gesture of assurance. "This is just another test," he says. "Like the Sleeping City. All there is to do is endure."

I think back to what the star god said. *Everyone has a choice.* We had a choice to give in to our deepest desires in the Court of Temptation. A choice to choose violence over peace in the Court of Wrath. And now, on the journey to the Court of Hunger, we have a choice to either be brave or cowardly. We could go back to the garden. It'd be leagues easier than suffering through the unknown. But how long would we remain there? We'd end up like all the other hopeless souls, too afraid to move on.

"Keep moving, Fox," the captain murmurs near my ear, the low bass of his voice sending a shiver trailing down my spine. "We will pass this trial, just as we did the ones before."

I heed his confident words and take a deep, slow inhale. My mind clears and my nerves soothe. For a moment, I can understand why Sonam is the leader of his little group. Always so steadfast and logical. The sort to keep his head when everything is on the verge of collapse. I suppose it's admirable, in a way. And once again, he's right.

Which only serves to irritate me further.

"Get your hot breath off my neck or I'll rip your throat out," I grumble.

The captain heeds my warning with an indignant scoff.

Ignoring the anxious twitch of my fingers, I force myself to continue, turning so that I'm better able to sidle between the two walls. If it's a tight fit for me, I can only imagine how suffocating it must be for the three trained soldiers behind me, with their stocky builds and bulky armor.

Each step becomes more difficult. We're being crushed. My skin chafes with the friction and my bones creak from the pressure, threatening to fracture. I don't know how much more of this I can take. The walls moan, as if taunting us, the Courts of Hell just as alive as the Sleeping City outside.

Just when all hope is lost, I see it. A light at the end of the tunnel.

Escape comes narrowly, and not in just the literal sense. With one final shove of my body, I free myself of the impossibly tight passageway, scraping a good chunk of my nose against the wall. Sonam and Sooah come tumbling after me, each of us panting with exertion and the dawning realization of how lucky we are to have made it out with our lives. I give them a once-over. They seem to be in good shape, all things considered. Except . . .

"We're missing one," I say. I look behind us at the narrow hall, barely wide enough to fit four tomes pressed together horizontally. Somewhere in the darkness, we must have left Wen behind.

"I'm going back for him," Sonam says without a second thought. But before he's able to take another step, the walls surge, expanding like a pair of lungs before squeezing tight all over again. I was right. The Jade Palace is indeed alive—and scheming. My sensitive ears pick up the sounds of Wen's rasping pleas.

"Help," he croaks. "Someone—"

Let him die, a voice whispers in the back of my mind.

All it would take is for me to stand here and allow the Jade Palace to crush Wen into nothing more than mangled pulp. Just as quick and effortless as a fly squashed beneath someone's palm. I don't know how far back Wen is wedged, but it certainly isn't worth putting my life at risk to save him. We might even make it through the Courts of Hell all the faster without a fourth slowing us down. I've never been particularly fond of that man, besides. All I need to do is turn a blind eye. It'll be over in seconds.

And yet.

My feet carry me forward. I have no control over my body. The only thought on my mind is to run, run, *run*. I'm between walls. There's no turning back. Not now that the walls are once again pressing together closer.

I find Wen lying on the ground, sweating profusely. His eyes widen and his mouth hangs open when he sees me. I don't give him a chance to speak, to protest. Stepping over him and snatching him up by the collar, I hoist him onto his feet and shove him toward the exit.

"Move," I hiss, flashing my teeth for extra motivation.

It's a race for survival. The walls shriek and groan as they give chase, spitting up dust and debris. We're only a few feet from the exit when the walls trap us, crushing our shoulders and smashing us flat. And to think we were seconds away from freedom.

Gritting my teeth, I let out a roar as I scrape my leg up and kick Wen in the back with all the force I can muster. He pops free, but I remain lodged in place, listening to the air rush out of my lungs and the pop of my joints.

"Fox!"

The sound of Sonam's voice is just barely noticeable over the sound of crushing bones. My vision blurs, swirls, an encroaching and ominous black seeping in around the edges. This is it. I've used up all of my rotten luck saving humans who hate me, and now I'm going to die.

"Give me your hand!" Sonam shouts. At least, I think he does. It's difficult to tell now that the walls have closed in over both my ears. I can hear the porcelain of my mask beginning to crack from the pressure. But I reach toward the sound of his voice.

The moment his fingers find mine, Sonam latches on and pulls me to safety. He nearly wrenches my arm from my shoulder. We fall together, crashing to the ground at top speed. The captain catches me, one arm braced around my back, using his own body to absorb most of the impact. It takes me a moment to catch my breath and will my heart to still.

"Are you alright?"

I blink up at Sonam in disbelief. I don't know what to say. He's so close. *Disgustingly* close. "I think so."

The captain tries to help me to my feet, but I won't have it, standing up on my own. Wen stands to the side, his face twisting with unease. If I didn't know better, I'd say he'd swallowed a toad. He certainly looks sick enough.

"You saved me," he mumbles, sounding like a chastised child.

"You call yourself the captain's guard?" I lash out.

"I just—"

"Don't expect me to do that ever again, human. Understand?"

Wen goes pale, but he nods all the same, taking his trembling right hand to rub at his flushed neck. Humility suits him as well as an oversize skirt.

Someone claps their hands in a small round of applause. Our attention is drawn to an old woman standing before a pair of sliding paper doors. They've been left ajar, allowing a glimpse of the interior. A kitchen, large enough to feed an entire army. What interests me most, however, is her smile.

Dazzling—like a star.

"That was thrilling!" she says with a giddy laugh. She sounds like a reed flute, sweet but raspy. "Oh, it's been so long since anyone has come this way."

Sonam's hand falls to his sword, hovering just over the pummel. "Who—"

The woman waves her hand dismissively. At first glance, she appears nothing more than a stout old lady. Her hair is as white as a scroll of parchment, and almost nearly as long. The corners of her bright white eyes wrinkle as she smiles ever wider.

"There's no need for that, boy," she says sweetly. "I mean you no harm." She gestures toward the kitchen. "Come inside the bathhouse and rest. I've prepared a feast in honor of you making it this far."

Sonam and I exchange a suspicious look.

"Who are you?" I ask.

She gives a delicate curtsy. "You may call me Kelai, keeper of the Court of Hunger."

23

Yue

Hunting Log #386:
How is it that the gods seem less trustworthy than the demon in my company?

I thought the star gods were all brothers," Wen says. "Like in the stories."

Kelai presses her lips into a thin line. "Disappointing, but unsurprising. It wouldn't be the first time your kind has written a woman out of her own story." She turns, silent as an owl gliding upon spread wings. The goddess enters the kitchen, wagging a single finger over her shoulder to beckon us follow. Whatever darkness once marred her brow disappears and is replaced with a grin. "Come along!" she all but sings.

The moment I step inside, my mouth waters uncontrollably.

Food. Mountains upon mountains of food.

I'm uncertain why I hadn't noticed it before, but now that I'm surrounded by sizzling meats, aromatic spices, and roasting vegetables, I'm left lightheaded. A long row of clay ovens lines one side of the kitchens, all of them blazing with iron woks placed on top.

Ladles stir soups and fry up sauces all on their own, enchanted to cook ceaselessly.

The kitchen opens up into a large atrium of glass, its domed ceiling dotted with winking stars. Suspended in the very center sits a chandelier in the shape of a glowing silver moon, so round and full it appears to have its own gravity, pulling me closer and closer like water at high tide.

"It's an illusion I've cast," Kelai explains with obvious pride. "After a millennium spent underground, I must say I dearly miss the sky. Come, friends. Sit and eat."

With a snap of her fingers, a circular table and five low chairs suddenly appear in the center of the room. A wide assortment of dishes appears from out of nowhere, glistening in oil and cradled in rising steam. The star goddess takes her seat without a fuss. She places a brown clay teapot over a small candle to warm the brew before helping herself to a little bit of everything.

Sooah is the first to sit, though not without hesitation. Wen follows, then Sonam, and finally myself. No one reaches for the food, so I volunteer, plucking a braised chicken leg from a nearby plate. I sniff at it.

"It's not poisoned," I murmur.

"Of course not," Kelai says with a laugh. "You have nothing to fear. I promise I'm nothing but a gracious host."

The first bites come cautiously. When none of us keel over or choke on our own tongues, we realize the star goddess is speaking the truth. The humans are hungry beyond words, digging in with rapt appreciation. Rice, pork dumplings, and garlic beans. Sweet buns, roasted beef, and sweet egg drop soup topped with minced green onion.

Sooah piles her bowl high. Wen stuffs his face. Sonam eats

with refined posture and all the manners one might expect from someone of his upbringing. And I . . .

I don't eat anything. Even though my stomach grumbles, I know the food set out before us will do little to sate my hunger. There's only one thing I crave, and human flesh is decidedly not on the menu. I keep my hands tucked away on my lap, chewing on my tongue in lieu of anything substantial. It would be like filling up on water. Enough to stop the stomach cramps and stave off starvation, but there would be no satisfaction in it.

Kelai watches me with a twinkle in her eyes. "You have questions," she says.

"Not really," I reply. "Just waiting for something to go terribly wrong."

"Goodness, my younger brothers must have done a number on you poor things." She leans back slightly, observing us with a graceful tilt of her head. "There's no need to fear. I'm nowhere near as spiteful as my siblings."

"You could be lying," Sonam points out.

"True, but if I wanted to harm any of you, I would have done it already."

"Why feed us?" Wen asks. "I thought this was the Court of Hunger."

"Precisely," Kelai says with a giggle. "I was tasked to oversee this place, but no one said I couldn't reinterpret the trial I set forth."

A scrumptious meal, the lovely scenery, a warm welcome, and easy conversation. All the elements of the perfectly safe and normal. And yet tension seizes my neck and shoulders, my jaw grinding my molars into a paste. Something's bound to go wrong. It has to. How else can I explain the unease churning deep within my gut? When things are too good to be true, I find that they are, in fact, just that.

"Are you really a star?" Wen asks around a mouthful. "I thought Houyi killed all of you—"

Sooah shoves her elbow into his rib, pinning him with a glare.

Kelai merely giggles. "It's alright, my dear. Yes, it's true the archer shot us down, but it takes more than an arrow to kill us."

"Is it even possible?" I mutter. "To kill a god."

"You sound keen to try." And then, after a moment, she says, "Where there's a will, as they say—though I have never witnessed such a feat."

Kelai studies me carefully. I feel her loneliness then. It washes off of her in a cold trickle, barely contained behind a crumbling dam of control. "What can I do to convince you to trust me?" she asks.

It's Sooah who answers, gesturing elaborately with both hands. I instinctively look to Sonam, who translates, "She wants to know what courts lie ahead. What challenges can we expect to face?"

"Well, next is the Court of Dreams—"

"That doesn't sound so bad," Wen mumbles.

"—where souls are tested against their heart's own paradise. To wake and see the truth that all is not as it could be leaves the soul shattered beyond repair."

"You spoke too early," I tell Wen with a bitter huff.

"And then?" Sonam prompts.

"Then comes the Court of Despair, which will test your resolve."

"In what way?"

"In *every* way," she replies vaguely. "And then there's the Court of Fear where most souls are haunted by their biggest regrets, the Court of Blades—"

Wen swallows thickly. "Blades?"

"Oh, yes. I hear that one's a fun one. You must find your courage and tread over a path made of knives that carve your feet down to the bone. And then comes the sea of maggots of the Court of

Rot, the Court of Beasts containing the venom of the world's most vicious creatures, and finally the Court of Fire, which I feel is self-explanatory. Once you've made it through, you'll find yourself at the Gates of Hell located at the very center."

Kelai's chipper tone has done little to soften the silence that follows. As determined as I am to escape Hell, there's no way all four of us are going to make it out alive at this rate. A soul doesn't have as much to worry about since they're already dead. But what about us?

Sooah signs something else, and Sonam translates. "She wants to know if there's a faster way out. A shortcut, perhaps. I don't know how we'll fare with all these courts standing in our way."

The goddess's face brightens. "Oh, but of course! I could probably draw you a map."

I squint at her. This is wrong. Something about the star goddess doesn't sit well with me. "You're willing to give it to us? Just like that?"

"Fox," Sonam warns.

"I don't believe you," I continue, on edge and queasy. "What do you get out of helping us?"

Kelai looks at me with genuine pity. "You poor child. When was the last time someone was kind to you?"

My face heats. It's a stupid question, but I can't help but wonder. When *was* the last time someone was kind to me? I've been on my own for so long that I've rarely had the opportunity for such a thing. And even if I did spend time surrounded by people, I'm sure their attitudes toward me would quickly change once they realize what I am.

Offering kindness to a demon? How absurd.

My jaw aches, my innate compulsion to answer direct questions forcing words into my mouth. "I don't recall," I mutter bitterly.

Kelai rises from the table, so graceful I'd mistake her for a cloud in all her pearly white robes. "Let me find some parchment so I can draw you that map. I'll return momentarily." She leaves swiftly, so light on her feet that I hear no footsteps. Kelai doesn't so much step as she does glide, disappearing beyond the doors of the kitchen to an adjacent room just out of sight.

Sonam plucks a bit of chicken between his chopsticks and places the morsel in my empty bowl. "Do you really think it's a trick?" he asks.

"Absolutely," I reply, reluctantly picking up my own utensils. I fumble with them awkwardly, unsure how to balance them between my fingers. "All this information, but at what cost? I don't trust a word out of her mouth."

"Neither do I," Sonam says with a heavy sigh. "The food isn't half bad, though."

"I would wait to see if Wen keels over first."

The guard in question looks up, his mouth stuffed full of rice and veggies. He swallows thickly. His face hasn't turned green, and his tongue has yet to swell. "Tastes fine."

"Stay vigilant," Sonam instructs. And then, quieter, so only I can hear, "Eat what you're able, Fox. Who knows how much longer we'll be down here."

His words are surprisingly gentle. I'd think it was sweet were it not for the fact that he probably wants to keep my belly as full as possible so I don't eat his compatriots instead. He must be nervous about upsetting me.

Running my tongue over my teeth, I risk a small bite of the food he's piled into my bowl. It's fine. The taste is pleasant enough, though it won't be long before I lose control. The countdown to ravenous, maddening hunger began the moment I finished with the drunkard back in Longhao. One wouldn't expect a tiger to subsist on a diet of vegetables, nor a demon on human meals. While not impossible, it goes against our better nature. I will need more than these few meager bites. All I have had is some stale rice, salted fish, and two fingers. I'm going to waste away at this rate.

Kelai returns with a giddy laugh, carrying an impressive collection of fabric in her arms. "Look what I found! You all look like you could use a hot bath and a change of clothes. Let's see what fits you."

She comes right for me and Sooah, ushering us to our feet. I take a step back, trying to avoid her excessive fawning. "A bath really isn't necessary," I say quickly.

"Nonsense! Believe me, you'll feel a lot better once you've washed off all this blood and grime."

"But—"

"This way, this way," she says, practically shoving us down a nearby hall.

I clench my fists, ready to strike. This could be her strategy. Lower our guard, separate us from the group, and then torture us until the end of time in some perverse, wretched way. There's a frenzied energy about her, I notice now, unstable and flitty like a hummingbird. Her old, feeble appearance won't fool me. I know all about using my looks to my advantage. Sooah seems just as alarmed.

I throw an urgent glance at Sonam, but the star goddess is surprisingly strong. She leads us away before I have the chance to do anything.

24

Yue

Hunting Log #387:
What must I have done in a previous life to deserve this one?

I ***pause when we step into*** a room full of steam. A bathhouse, built as an extension to the pavilion in its own standing structure. Moisture drips from the ceiling, coats the walls, puddles on the floors so that they're slick and treacherous. A deep pool sits in the corner, dotted by a border of large, coarse rocks. The water is shallow and clear, trickling over the edges from some unseen underground current. I taste salt in the air, the warmth of the steam filling my lungs and revitalizing my airways. How odd it is to find such a heavenly place in Hell.

"You . . . really only want us to bathe?" I mumble.

Kelai laughs, bright and bubbly. "Of course, my child. Set your clothes here, I'll leave new robes for you. Let me know if you need anything."

I furrow my brows. "What about the map—"

"Anything at all!" she interjects loudly, before skipping off the way she came.

Sooah and I glance at each other, unsure. Again, I smell no

poison in the water or magic in the air. The star goddess doesn't seem entirely sound of mind, but I'm finally starting to believe she means us no harm.

"I think the water's fine," I tell Sooah.

She gestures toward the pool, as if asking me if I'd like to bathe first.

I shake my head. "I can wait. To give you privacy."

The guard regards me carefully before moving toward the water's edge. Sooah signs something, but her meaning is lost on me. My sister, Nuying, was the linguist. I'm sure she'd have no trouble conversing with Sooah, were she here today. She had a knack for picking up languages within mere weeks, if not days.

I keep my eyes lowered until the gentle sound of parting water reaches my ears. Even though she's submerged to just below her shoulders, I can make out the frightening collection of scars upon her back from battles fought and won. Stab wounds, slices . . . burn marks. Just like mine.

Hers is not a classic beauty. Far from it, in fact, but I admire her all the same. Her body is lean and muscular—with a frame almost as large as Sonam's, even—no doubt the result of many years of arduous training. Appearance wise, I initially thought Sooah gruff and intimidating. The type who's quick to anger. Now that we've traveled with one another a while, I see how wrong I was. My more animal instincts can pick up on her calming presence—a soothing energy amidst all the chaos.

That is, of course, unless we're in the heat of battle.

"I wish to ask you a question," I say as she washes her hair with a provided bar of rice soap. "If you'll permit it."

She nods while patiently working up a lather.

"How did you come to be Sonam's guard?"

Sooah treads through the water and reaches over the edge of the pool, dragging her finger over the steamy jade tiles to write out her answer. Her script is wonky because she's writing upside down, but it's nonetheless legible.

I used to work in the pleasure district.

I blink at her, amazed. "As a woman of the night?"

A servant girl, she clarifies hastily. *When my father sold me, the madame said I was too ugly to train as a courtesan.*

I snort. "A blessing, then."

Sooah takes no offense, her grin growing wider. *Exactly.*

"How long were you there?"

Until I was seven and ten.

I lean back on the wooden bench, ignoring the heavy drops of sweat streaking down my forehead and cheeks. "Let me guess. You met the captain when he came for a night of pleasure? How scandalous."

Sooah shakes her head. *No. He came to investigate a murder.*

"Oh?" I sit a little straighter, intrigued. Of all the things she could have said, that wasn't what I was expecting.

She's run out of room to write, so I unfortunately have to wait for the tiles to fog up again. If Kelai hadn't hurried us away, we might have thought to bring something to write on. Perhaps we could have borrowed a few pages out of Sonam's hunting log.

The morning it happened, I mouthed off, Sooah explains. *So the madame cut off my tongue as an example.*

I bristle. "Were they the ones I saw in the Court of Temptation?"

She nods. *Surprised you never asked.*

I shrug my shoulders. "Your business is your own."

Sooah smiles even wider. *I rather like you, demon.*

A cackle rises out of me. What a strange thing to hear. "What happened after she took your tongue? Were you the one who murdered her?"

No, though everyone thought so. I would have hung if Captain Sonam hadn't shown up. Helped me prove I was elsewhere at the time of the madame's disappearance. Bedridden in the hospital as a result of her maiming. It couldn't have been me.

"Who killed her, then?"

Sooah shrugs. *We never found out. She simply vanished into thin air.*

"And afterward . . . was that when you asked to work for the captain?"

Didn't ask. He offered. Sooah combs her fingers through her hair, washing away the suds. *He knew I'd have a hard time finding a new job, so he gave me one. Served with him ever since.*

I allow her words to sink in, trying to imagine a younger Captain Sonam swooping in to save a poor servant girl. It's all rather fantastical, something out of an old, clichéd fairytale. The handsome and righteous Prince Sonam, slayer of demons and savior of damsels. The thought makes me laugh.

Sooah finishes with her bath and pulls herself out of the pool, wrapping herself up in a fluffy cotton towel Kelai left behind. She motions to the water, inviting me for my turn. I hesitate only a moment before shrugging off my dirty robes and quickly slipping beneath the surface. The hot water soaks into my skin—so hot it nearly stings—but it's a most welcome balm against the frigid weariness of my bones.

I startle when Sooah takes a seat behind me on the ledge of the pool and brings the rice soap to my hair. I jerk away for a moment, staring up at her in disbelief. She isn't afraid of me, and I can't decide whether she's brave or foolhardy—perhaps both. She holds my gaze, unflinching, before I finally understand. She's a gentle giant. Only looking to help. Normally, such a notion would disgust me. I am a strong, vicious, man-eating demon, for gods' sake. Has she forgotten this? I thought she had better sense.

But then her nails gently scrape my scalp, working up a lather. The calming sizzle of popping bubbles fills my ears. Something strange happens to me. My chest tightens and my throat burns. When I close my eyes, I'm able to remember my sisters. For a brief moment, I forget my clawing emptiness, reminiscing about the days when my family would fawn over me.

I miss them. More than anyone could ever know.

I take a deep breath and relent, letting Sooah wash my hair as a sister might. I allow myself this one rare indulgence and try not to fall asleep, lest the soapy water take me. I suppose this particular human isn't so bad. If it comes down to food, I can eat her last.

"I have one more question for you," I murmur. "Back in the Court of Temptation . . . if your father and the madame were so horrible to you, why didn't you take your revenge?"

I hear the squeak of Sooah's fingertip against the tile beside me. Turning my head to read, I fully expect some tired old idiom about how revenge is a two-headed snake, and how it will harm you as much as it will your victim. Instead, Sooah surprises me.

There is little time in the world, she says. *Why choose to hate when you can choose kindness?*

It occurs to me then, that out of all of us in Hell, Sooah might be the one person who doesn't truly deserve to be here.

I, on the other hand, do. Because I would never choose kindness where the Maskmaker is concerned. There isn't a mountain he can scale, nor the smallest crevice he can hide within—I *will* find him. Why choose hate over kindness?

Because it's all I have. If I give up on my quest for vengeance now, I may as well have let him kill me along with my sisters.

25

Houyi did not manage to catch the star god, for each time he came close, the god would don a new mask and disappear. The archer grew too old for the hunt, his justice unfulfilled. He spent the remainder of his days setting out cakes in offering to the moon goddess, the very same sweets she enjoyed when she still walked the earth.

"You must avenge her," he said to his son upon his deathbed. "And if you cannot, then the duty will fall to your own son, and then his in turn."

But revenge waxes and wanes, as does the moon. And eventually, it fades altogether.

The ninth star spent centuries exploring every corner of the world, slowly growing more dedicated to his craft. He found great pleasure in discovering new materials out of which to mold his growing collection of faces.

He had a distaste for marble, for it was a temperamental beast, oftentimes too difficult to handle. Crafting masks from paper was far too delicate a task. But clay . . . Clay was the perfect medium to hone his skills. Easily molded and cool to the touch, he painted the faces of all those he happened upon.

Beggars and kings, heathens and holy men, the local whores and ladies of chaste repute. With Death still on the hunt, he would don a human face and slip through the reaper's fingers. He'd change his mask as seamlessly as a leaf flowing along the current of a river. He vowed never to rest until he found a way back to his throne on high.

But as the years dragged on, with no end to his exile in sight, the star god grew embittered. While the humans worshipped his surviving brother, the rest of his family was trapped in Hell. He never stayed in one place too long for fear of Death, and thus grew sullen and miserable in his isolation.

Until, that is, he stumbled upon a pack of peculiar creatures.

White fur, nine tails, and six obsidian eyes. A family of nine-tailed foxes. Upon closer inspection, he saw that one of them—the smallest of the pack—had fallen into a pit, whimpering loudly as she clawed at the edges seeking purchase. Her sisters could only look on, much too large to reach in and grab hold.

The star god was just about to walk away, unbothered and uncaring, when the trapped beast cried out a low, desperate howl. He wasn't sure what compelled him to turn back. Demons were, after all, worse than the scum of the earth. Born from shadow, their powers could sometimes rival that of the gods, however. Their insatiable hunger, if left unchecked, could one day devour the world.

And yet, when he peered over the edge into the pit, he felt . . . compassion. How curious. Perhaps he needn't be so hasty to abandon the beasts. It might be nice to have a few pets.

"Allow me," he said, but was immediately met by a sea of sharp teeth.

"Stay away, human," one of the foxes snarled, "unless you want to lose your head."

He approached cautiously, reaching up to slide his porcelain mask to the side, revealing the bright flash of his startling white eyes and disarming smile. "No need to fear me. Stand aside, I am here to help."

With suspicious glares and claws at the ready, the family of fox demons watched with bated breath as this face-shifting stranger reached down to grab their sister by the scruff. The foxes yapped happily, their reunion sweet, but short. They regarded the stranger with wary appreciation.

"What do we call you?" one of the older foxes asked. "So that we may give proper thanks for the rescue of our dear sister."

The star god thought for a moment, readjusting his mask over his face. Few were around to use his true name anymore. The Heavens certainly wouldn't use it to call upon him. His siblings were unheard and forgotten. And what few worshippers who once knew his name were long dead.

"You may call me the Maskmaker," he said finally, foolishly believing he had nothing left to fear.

26

Yue

Hunting Log #388:
With her mask, her beauty is undeniable.

"You're back!" Kelai chirps, flitting about the main room with more enthusiasm than I have energy. She has an overwhelming essence, big and bright and all too much for so small a figure. "You must be feeling refreshed, yes? Here, some new dresses. Can't very well have you walking around in those uncomfortable, filthy rags, hmm?"

I don't argue when the star goddess tugs off my outer robe and shoves a new one onto my back, smoothing out any errant wrinkles she happens to find. Although the garment is beautiful, boasting a light-blue dye glittering with a pattern of delicate pearls along the edges, no doubt meant to mimic the foamy nature of waves washing upon the shore, I don't care much for her firm handling. Though I fear that if I say anything, she'll snap. Take a violent turn. Her frenzied state makes my skin prickle and my gut clench. Kelai may be outwardly friendly, but there's a stifling crackle in the air. Something unsound and jittery, like a bloodhound playing a little too rough.

"Where's Sonam?" is the first thing I ask.

Kelai adjusts my collar, brushing my damp hair out of the way. "Who?" she asks.

My heart stutters. "The captain," I say tightly, suddenly on edge. Sooah and I exchange a glance, our hackles raising. "What have you done with him?"

The star goddess blinks, not an apparent thought in her head, before something sparks. She slaps her own forehead and giggles wildly. "Oh, yes! Yes, of course. I sent the men off for their own baths. They should return shortly." Kelai steps back to appraise her work, fiddling with the silk of my sleeves. "My, you're a beauty. Isn't she a beauty?"

I'm not entirely sure who the goddess is speaking to until I hear the soft clap of shoes padding across the floor tiles. Sonam and Wen have returned, just as Kelai said they would, their hair damp and skin scrubbed clean to the point of pinkishness.

I find myself staring. There's something intriguing about seeing Sonam stripped down to his inner robes. Without his armor and the colors of the royal family, he appears almost unburdened. Relaxed, now that he's shed the appearance of both prince and hunter. He's let his top knot down, messy strands falling over his eyes. For some reason, the quick peek I take of his exposed neck and bare upper chest makes my face warm.

He's quite handsome, I suppose. For a loathsome human. I have no doubt that he'll make some princess very happy one day. Who wouldn't want to align themselves with the Demon Hunter of Jian, survivor of the Courts of Hell? When we escape this place, he will be the stuff of legends.

And I, no doubt, the villain of his story.

"Well?" Kelai urges when no one answers, batting her lashes as she twirls her fingers around a few locks of my hair.

"A demon in the robes of a goddess," Wen says wryly. "Now I've seen everything."

I sneer at his remark, biting back the avalanche of insults I could easily sling in his direction after having saved his life. Ingrate. I'm fully prepared for whatever jab Sonam has, as well, only . . .

He says nothing. The captain stares openly with a strange, heated intensity. What could he be thinking? Probably that I'm the vilest creature to ever walk the earth, or perhaps that I dishonor them all by simply existing in the same space as a goddess who once gazed upon the Kingdom of Heaven.

Sonam finally averts his gaze, the tips of his ears an unusual shade of pink. No doubt due to the heat of the bathwater. "A dress is a dress," he says bluntly, his voice unusually tight. It's not exactly an insult, but it's not a compliment, either.

"Show me your hands," I grumble. "Both of you."

There's a moment of confusion, but the captain and Wen do eventually raise their hands. They have all ten fingers. After our little scuffle, the Maskmaker will only have eight, his digits digesting nicely in the pit of my belly. Unless he knows the specific magic he needs to grow his fingers back, it's as foolproof a plan as we're going to get to ensure there isn't an imposter among us.

Kelai is the first to speak, wringing her fingers together. I also count ten there, though it's unlikely she's the Maskmaker in hiding. "Well, I'm sure you're all very tired after the long journey you've had," she says. "I think a good night's sleep is in order."

With a simple snap of her fingers, the table full of food shoves to one side, making room for four bedrolls of soft goose down to unfurl beneath the moon chandelier. It's waning now, a crescent shadow stretching across its surface.

"What about the map?" Wen asks bluntly, not that I can blame him.

The star goddess rubs her temples with the tips of her long fingers and hums. "Ah, yes, the map, the map . . . I will have it for you very soon. The ink is drying. Wouldn't want to smudge all the details and have you lose your way." She laughs brightly, but I can't help but notice how strained the sound is in my ears.

"How long will it take?" Sonam presses on. "We appreciate what you've done for us, but we're in a hurry."

Kelai's hands start to shake as she nervously combs her hair. "In a hurry? But don't you want to stay for breakfast? I'll make sweet egg tarts. You'll love them!"

I take a cautious step forward, fearful now of her manic energy. "Kelai, we just—"

"Go to sleep now," she says with a dismissive wave of her hand. "Sleep, everyone. Rest is important."

"But we need to—"

"SLEEP!" Kelai's face darkens, her eyes flashing bright red. It takes her a moment to regain her composure, a friendly smile quickly plastering itself upon her lips as though nothing ever happened. She returns to her usual singsong manner and says, "Good night, my friends. I hope you have the most pleasant dreams."

She all but glides out of the room, sealing the doors behind her. The four of us are speechless. My palms are clammy as I step toward the door and reach for the handle.

Locked.

I turn to face the humans with a grimace. "I have bad news."

Wen lets out an angry roar as he charges toward the door, kicking the frame with all the strength he can muster. It doesn't budge. Doesn't even creak. The fool falls onto his back like an overturned beetle and groans. One sniff is all I need to know that the door's been enchanted, sealed until Kelai decides otherwise.

"Should I give it another try?" Wen grunts.

"Please do," I reply. "I would love to watch that again."

"Spread out," Sonam orders, taking the helm. "Look for windows and other doors."

It takes us less than a minute to realize we're completely trapped in. Kelai has left us all the comforts of the steam room and main atrium, but there's no point in denying this place for what it is—a prison. I knew her generosity was too good to be true. Like flies to sugared water, she's lured us into her trap. We should have left while we had a chance.

Sooah gestures as if to say, *Now what?*

Wen looks at me with a shiver. "How thick do you reckon these walls are? Could you dig your way through in your other form?"

I crinkle my nose, my breath appearing in the form of silvery clouds. "I can't smell the earth. The jade around us is too thick. Doubt I'll be able to make a dent."

Sooah rubs her arms for warmth, looking around in confusion as unmistakable traces of frost are slowly crawling up the walls, across the ceiling, and over the floors. My teeth chatter, the tips of my fingers and toes already swelling with the sudden drop in temperature. We're going to freeze. Was this Kelai's plan the entire time?

Sonam is quick to act. He gathers up sitting cushions and shoving them into a corner, beckoning Wen and Sooah to him. "Gather in close. We need to stay warm. We'll ambush the goddess when she comes to check on us." Sonam looks to me next, something close to a question behind his eyes. "You, too, Fox," he says, slowly holding out his hand.

I hold my breath, taken aback by the invitation. My insides squirm. This is merely a matter of survival, nothing more.

Then an idea occurs to me. It isn't a pleasant one, but given the circumstances, it is necessary. The chill is already eating away at my skin, but I doubt this strange magic will bother me as much if I'm concealed in warm fur.

Slowly, I lower my head, relinquishing control as Sonam steps forth. I pry my disguise off. The magic drips away and I crouch down on all fours, scraping my claws against the tile.

"Don't break it," I tell him, allowing him to hold my mask.

He nods. "I won't."

This mask is my most prized possession—arguably my *only* possession. Yet I know it will be safest with him. I'll simply have to take him at his word.

A strange wave of insecurity washes over me. I'm so terribly exposed without my mask. Willingly allowing Sonam, Wen, and Sooah to watch me in my true form goes against every fiber of my being. I've spent so many years hiding from humans, my survival instincts having taken precedence. Yet here I am, my truest self, helping these three where I normally never would have spared them a second thought.

Ignoring the sensation of their eyes raking over my hideous form, I make my way over to the corner and sit down first. The sourness of their trepidation curdles the air. If I were in their shoes, I wouldn't want to curl up with a man-eating demon, either. Without another escape plan, however, they have no choice.

Sooah is the first to sit at my side, tucking her knees to her chest. Wen is next, so cold that he practically buries his face against my fur, any disgust reserved toward me momentarily shelved now that he finds me useful. Finally, Sonam, who holds my mask close to his chest like it's something precious. He likely wants to keep his arms near his body for warmth, that's all. Once they're all seated, I curl my nine tails around them, wrapping the humans up in a cocoon of fur. Far from a perfect solution, but I should be able to see us through the worst of it.

The temperature plummets until it grows unbearable. The moisture from the steam baths only makes things that much more precarious, ice droplets clinging to the fine hair around my eyes and on the humans' skin. Sooah's teeth won't stop chattering. The tip of Wen's nose has turned an alarming purple. And Sonam . . .

His eyes are open, tirelessly darting around the room in search of something. An exit, perhaps. Even in our dire situation, he hasn't stopped trying to formulate a plan. Plotting. Ever alert and looking for solutions. I'd be impressed if I wasn't so preoccupied with freezing to death.

"Rest," I whisper, the thin skin of my lips so brittle it's begun to split. "Save your strength for when she returns."

Sonam shivers. "What about you?"

I appreciate that he sounds so concerned. Humans are such clever little liars.

"I'll be fine," I answer him truthfully. "I'm always fine."

27

Yue

Hunting Log #389:
Without her mask, she's somehow more beautiful still.

"Yue?"

Tentative fingers brush over the scars along the right side of my face, trailing back to settle just behind my ear. Someone gives my fur a light scratch, but I can't say that I mind. It's quite . . . comforting.

"Yue, wake up," comes a deep voice.

My joints are stiff and creaky. I fear my eyelids are frozen shut. It takes an alarming amount of effort to pry them open.

Even more alarming is the angry growl of my stomach.

It grumbles with such ferocity that I can feel it reverberating in my chest. It's as though someone's reached inside, digging their nails into the empty cavern of my belly as they squeeze without remorse. My head is light, the room around us spinning uncontrollably.

"Hungry," I rasp. Lick my lips. Saliva fills my mouth, turning cold against my teeth. I find Sonam crouched beside me, surprisingly alert despite our troubled sleep. He smells good. Too good.

Where's the harm in a little bite? "So hungry," I say again, but this time, it comes out as a whimper. It hurts too damn much.

What am I thinking? I can't eat him. Nor can I eat Wen or Sooah. They will execute me before I can even open my jaws wide enough.

The sharp twist of blood suddenly fills the air, catching me off guard. I look up at Sonam, alarmed to see that he's dragged the tip of one of his daggers across the surface of his palm. Blood pools within the cup of his hand, the tips of his fingers blue from the cold.

"Here," he says, teeth chattering. "Hurry up. I hear movement outside. I think Kelai's coming back."

"But I—"

"It is freely given, Fox. Just don't overdo it."

He holds his hand out to me and I can no longer help myself. I'm not allowed to raise a hand to him so long as our blood oath remains in effect, but that doesn't mean he cannot offer himself to me. As long as I keep his heart beating, I think it should be fine.

Emphasis on *I think*.

I slowly dip my head down toward his palm, keeping my eyes on the humans—as bleary as my vision may be. With a hesitant final inhale, I swipe my tongue over his palm.

His blood tastes divine. I knew it would. From the moment I smelled him, I knew Sonam would be a feast like none I've ever had before. Sweeter than nectar, more refreshing than crisp water on a scorching summer's day. I drink greedily, forgetting at times what it is to breathe. My mind grows more alert with each drop that finds its way past my lips.

I am so lost in the taste of Sonam's blood that all my thoughts seem to tumble out of my head. For a moment, I forget where we are. Gone are my worries, my anxieties, my fears. There's nothing but the satisfying weight filling my belly and the taste of iron on my tongue. It doesn't occur to me until I've licked his palm clean that I've forgotten precisely who it is I'm drinking from.

Pulling away, I ignore the nervous pounding of my heart.

The blood of my enemy. And fed by his very hand, no less. I don't know whether I should feel grateful or ashamed. I have half a mind to keep going. To chew off his fingers, his hand, maybe even his whole arm, but I push the craving aside. My hunger has been assuaged, so there's no need to push my luck. It's enough for now.

Sonam watches me with a strange look in his eye. I have to assume that it's disgust, but there's something else, too. Something I can't quite put my finger on. It's difficult to tell given his ever-present scowl.

"You're . . . " He hesitates, clears his throat. Sonam's eyes drift from my scars to my tails.

"I know, I know," I grumble. "I'm wretched. Stop staring."

The captain bristles. "No, I didn't mean—"

Whatever Sonam has to say dies on his tongue with the sound of soft padding of footsteps and the hum of a gentle tune. Kelai. She sounds to be in particularly high spirits considering how she locked us in to freeze to death.

With nowhere to hide, our only option is to attack.

Sooah and Wen have already risen, their sights set on the large doors into the room. Their weapons are drawn and ready. Wen's fingers are a troubling shade of purple, and Sooah's breathing comes in shallow puffs. All things considered, they're in impressive shape. It seems I was able to shield them from the worst of the cold—but to my own detriment. I struggle to my feet, shifting uncomfortably beneath the matted, frozen sections of my fur.

I push through the numbness. They need my fangs, my size, and my strength if they want to stand any chance against Kelai. Three humans against a goddess is nothing short of a joke. But with a demon on their side, it might be enough to tip the scale in their favor.

I throw myself at the star goddess the moment she steps through the heavy doors. It's not as graceful a landing, nor as accurate a launch. Every inch of my body is too numb, out of control. Thankfully, I'm able to use my weight and tackle Kelai to the ground. She shrieks in surprise, struggling to free herself from beneath me, but Sonam, Wen, and Sooah swarm with a level of precision and coordination one can only expect from years of working closely together.

They pull out familiar strips of yellow parchment. Binding talismans—the very same that they used to immobilize me that fateful night in Longhao. They press them to Kelai's wrists, ankles, and her chest. Her body goes as rigid as stone.

"No!" she wails. "No, let go of me!"

None of us listen. We run past her, leaving her flat on her back, struggling with all her might. We barrel down the hall, leaving the despairing cold behind us. It's a relief to feel the chill melt from my bones.

"We have to hurry," Sonam says as we round a corner. "Those bindings won't hold long. They're designed to keep demons at bay, not one of the gods."

"Where's the damn exit?" Wen rasps.

I can't blame him for his exasperation. We're all turned around and shaken. To make matters worse, I'm pretty sure I can hear Kelai's stomping feet growing louder from down the hall. She must have broken out of her bindings. That certainly didn't take long.

"In here," I say hurriedly, stepping through a set of wooden doors. We've managed to find our way back to the kitchens.

I sniff the air, searching for any hint of fresh air or earth. If I can find a fault in the foundation or a minor crack in the walls, I might stand a better chance of digging our way out. I catch a whiff of something sweet. Soil. It's faint, but there's no denying its rich wetness. I scrape at the jade tiles beneath my feet, but to no avail. The surface is too smooth to leave a mark. There's nothing for my claws to catch on, to peel away.

"The foundation is thinnest here," I tell Sonam.

He nods, looking to Sooah. "Help her."

She moves quickly, eyeing a large wooden barrel placed by the woodstoves. Sooah wraps her arms around the middle of the barrel, lifts with her legs, and with a loud grunt, throws it to the ground with impressive force. The tile cracks where it landed.

"Wen," Sonam says. "Barricade the door."

Wen moves swiftly, dragging over a heavy kitchen table to press up against the door. It's a smart call on Sonam's part, because Sooah raises the barrel over her head and brings it down with all her might, the harsh crack like a lightning strike. She picks it up again and slams it against the tiles, hammering until a section of the floor finally gives way. There's a wide enough fracture that I'm able to get my claws underneath, digging up as much dirt as I can.

"NO!" Kelai's voice shakes the room. Something slams against the other side of the door, but Wen's hastily built barricade keeps them from swinging open. Wen and Sonam throw their weight against it for added protection, practically toppling over when the star goddess attempts to ram her way in. "What are you doing? Let me in!"

"Hurry!" Sonam exclaims.

He doesn't have to tell me twice.

I dig and dig and dig, kicking up dirt and small stones and shards of broken jade. I don't know the first thing about tunneling. For all I know, the floor is seconds away from caving in on us. Being buried alive would be a terrible way to go. Even worse, I could be digging in the wrong direction, leading farther beneath the bathhouse where we'll be trapped for all eternity.

The first hint of fresh air nearly has me gasping for joy. I haven't doomed us. I claw my way forward and breach the surface, coming up on the outside of Kelai's bathhouse. I never thought I'd see the day when I was happy to lay my eyes upon the cold, indifferent green glow of the Jade Palace.

I clamber out, turning to help Sooah to her feet. I grab Wen by the collar of his shirt between my teeth and yank him out with great force, letting him huff indignantly as he falls flat. Sonam is next. He reaches out blindly and I don't hesitate to bite down on his gauntlet. He's just about escaped when—

"No!" Kelai shrieks. She's crawled after us, her hair a mess and her eyes red with fury. She snatches Sonam by the ankle, digging her nails into his flesh. "You can't leave me. You can't, you can't!"

I tighten my bite on the captain's wrist. Sooah and Wen are at my side, grabbing hold of Sonam's arm and pulling with all their might. The star goddess is too strong. I should have suspected as much from a divine being. It's an unfortunate game of tug-of-war, and Sonam is the strained rope pulled taut between us. With a pained roar, Sonam jerks his leg up and manages to kick himself free.

The four of us fall together, landing in a messy heap. There's no time to let our guard down. My sensitive ears can hear Kelai's nails scraping against the earth as she climbs out.

At least, she tries to.

Sonam lifts his leg and stomps as hard as he's able, the sudden force causing the mouth of the tunnel to cave in. Kelai screams, falling back, the lower half of her body buried beneath the weight of the earth and pinned by sharp stones. Her wretched cries no doubt heard from every corner of the Jade Palace. It will take ages to dig herself out.

"Come on," Wen urges impatiently. I'm of like mind. We've wasted enough time as it is, and the longer we leave Kelai trapped in that pit, the angrier she'll get. I'd rather not be around to suffer her wrath.

The star goddess weeps as though in mourning. "No one ever stays," she sobs.

It's then that I realize that this Court of Hunger has nothing to do with food or starvation. It has to do with her hunger—for companionship. For someone to call a friend. Someone to love and keep and dote upon.

As I stare down at her, I can't help but think about the time I fell into a hunter's pit, left down there for moons with no hope in sight. There was nothing so torturous as the cloying realization that I might never get out. But at least my sisters tried their best to rescue me. Kelai has no one at all.

Sonam silently offers me my mask, holding it out so that I can press my face into the cup of his palms. The magic takes hold and I stand tall, taking a deep breath as I crane my neck over the edge of the hole. My fingers are red, almost raw from digging. I clench my fists just to feel the sting. Sonam notices, his brows knitted together, but he makes no comment.

"We should go," he says softly. Too softly. It makes my heart flutter.

"Right," I whisper.

Kelai's wails decrescendo into nothing more than sniffles and whimpers. She's fallen far from her seat in Heaven.

"W-won't you come back?" she asks weakly. "Please, just—will you come back to at least visit?"

My chest seizes. I'm not sure if Kelai is aware of what she's doing, or if it's merely an accident. Either way, I'm compelled to answer. No one in their right mind would want to deliberately spend time in Hell. I have to get back to the surface, to see Sonam safely back to the mortal coil. But if I tell her no, I may as well strike

Kelai across the face. It would certainly hurt her less. One thing is certain, however—whatever my answer, it must be the truth.

"I'll come back," Sonam answers before I have a chance. "Once I've guided them from this place, I'll come back to see you."

I'm surprised by his response, but I'm grateful all the same. The burning compulsion I feel to answer quickly fades into nothing more than a spark. There's no need for me to tell the truth now that Sonam has spoken on my behalf.

Kelai's face brightens, beautiful even despite her tears and puffy cheeks. She glows bright at his words, offering a glimpse of the radiant star she once was. "R-really?" she stammers. "Oh, bless you, my child. Bless you—"

"*If* you give me that map you spoke of."

I ignore the bitter taste of guilt coating my tongue. I should have known Sonam would have conditions. It doesn't feel good or fair to lord anything over Kelai's head when her defeat is so clear.

After a moment, Kelai nods, lifting her arm toward us. "Give me your hand," she says. "I'll draw it on your palm."

"Wait," I interrupt. "If you know the way out, why haven't you attempted to leave Hell after all this time?"

"This map is only a spell," she explains. "It will guide you to what your heart most desires. And the way out is what you seek, is it not?"

The air is thick and heavy, the stench of mistrust—bitter like bile.

"Let me do it," I say. I manage a single step forward before Sonam outstretches his arm, stopping me from going any farther.

"It could be another trick," he warns.

"All the more reason for me to handle it."

"You've done enough, Fox."

I hover warily, watching for any sign of treachery as Sonam

steps forward and reaches down toward Kelai. She grasps onto his hand so tight I fear she might try to drag him back down. I'm directly beside him, prepared to wrench him back, but the exchange is so quick that I nearly miss it. Sonam pulls back with a hiss as if burned, and upon closer inspection I notice—he *has* been.

Bright red welts run the length of his palm lines, the smell of cooked flesh searing the inside of my nose. It's a crude rendition, as far as maps go, our path laid out across Sonam's hand with a few blisters serving as landmarks.

"You'll have a few more courts to endure, I'm afraid," Kelai explains tiredly, "but after the Court of Despair, you'll find a servant's corridor. It will save a lot of time." And then, in a much smaller voice, "That way you can come back and see me again sooner."

The humans turn away first, but I linger. I listen to Kelai sobbing softly and feel nothing but pity.

"Yue," Sonam calls gently. His hand hovers over the small of my back, too far for contact, but close enough that I can feel the warmth of his skin through the fabric of my dress. I wonder if his refusal to follow through is out of fear or respect.

"Were you telling the truth?" I whisper. "Will you really come back?"

There's a hardness in his eyes that makes my heart stutter. I can smell his guilt, tangy like citrus peels. But I can smell his resolve, too, like copper left to bake in the sun.

"No," he answers, also in a whisper. "I said what had to be said."

He is the first to turn and leave, followed quickly by Wen and Sooah. I have no choice but to follow, the star goddess left behind alone in the darkness.

28

Yue

Hunting Log #390:
Her presence is oddly calming.

We walk in silence, save for Sonam's occasional direction. Our exhaustion translates into a general air of bitterness. Were it not for Kelai's map, our last shreds of hope would have faded ages ago. The burns on Sonam's hand heal as we walk, the guiding line erasing itself as we make progress through the wide passage of yet another empty gardenscape. Any semblance of awe I had for the Jade Palace has long since left me.

"I need a break," Wen complains.

Sonam grunts his agreement. As do I. None of us have the energy to carry full sentences.

Sooah helps herself to a jade bench while I look around the garden. There are no plants whatsoever, only a collection of tall statues carved with incredible detail. There are twelve of them in total, arranged in a perfect circle, all facing inward. A similar arrangement can be found at the corner of Sonam's palm, just above his wrist bone, in the form of heat blisters. I inspect the carvings carefully, noticing that each statue represents a different animal.

A rat, an ox, a tiger, a rabbit, a dragon, snake, horse, goat, monkey, rooster, dog, and boar. I'm particularly intrigued by the dragon. Its lifelike eyes seem to follow me as I walk around the circle, its lips pulled back into a fearsome snarl.

"It's a calendar," Sonam explains.

I jump slightly at the sound of his voice. Everything here in Hell has me on edge. I'm afraid the concept is completely foreign to me. "A what?"

"It's how humans keep track of the years."

I arch a brow. "By using . . . animals?"

Sonam laughs softly, standing at my side as we study the dragon statue together. It's a sound I've never heard him make before. Light and easy, as though we're out for a perfectly normal stroll through the palace gardens, not a single horror in sight. "It's an old story among my people. A fairytale."

When I continue to look at him expectantly, he begins.

"Many millennia ago, the Jade Emperor, ruler of the Heavens, wanted to keep better track of the days, moons, and years. He invited all of the world's earthly creatures to a race for the chance to join the twelve-year cycle he'd devised. The rat, knowing that he was far smaller and would therefore be slower, persuaded the ox to carry him across the river. When they arrived upon the opposite bank, he jumped off first and won the race, earning his spot at the beginning of the calendar. The ox, rather begrudgingly, came in second.

"The tiger and the rabbit came one after the other, the latter of whom kept a safe distance behind his friend's sharp teeth. The noble red dragon of the east was the fifth to arrive despite his ability to soar through the skies, having stopped to help a few villagers in need. Sixth was the snake, and then the horse not long after. Then came the goat, the monkey, and the rooster on a raft built of lotus petals. The dog unfortunately found himself distracted, wasting most of the race playing in the river, though he managed to arrive just before the boar, who slept the day away before finally waking hours later, finishing off the race."

I find myself smiling, thoroughly enjoying the captain's tale. "Do you think the fox was invited, too?"

His smile grows wider, eyes crinkling as he does. It leaves me breathless. "It's possible. Jun was the one who told me the story. He said that there were versions where the cat was invited, as well, but the rat tricked him and said the race was, in fact, the day after. If I had to venture a guess, I'd say the fox was too clever to be tricked into working for someone else. Without proper reward, at least."

I reflect his smile, amused. "That sounds about right."

I don't know what to make of it when he lingers, his gaze drifting over the details of my mask. It's strange, having him so close. My heart beats faster when he's near, surely because of my more primal instincts to hunt and kill. That must be it. There's no other way to explain why, when he slowly reaches down to take my hands in his, the voice in the back of my head screams at me to flee.

Sonam inspects my bloodied nails, carefully running the pad of his thumb over the tip of my index. It isn't enough pressure to hurt. In fact, there's no pressure at all; a mere ghost of a touch. Neither of us breathe. I'm wound up tight, though I'm unsure whether I want to run or give in to his peculiar gravity.

"Are you in pain?" he whispers, almost as if he doesn't trust his voice to carry the question.

My lips part as I suck in a shaky breath. "A little. But you don't have to worry about me."

Sonam looks like he wants to argue, but before he has a chance, I take his hands in turn and study the burn lines of Kelai's map. I gently trace the path she's laid out before us, less concerned with our destination than I am the red swelling of his skin. His palms are calloused and rough, his long fingers easily, but almost bashfully, knitting with mine.

"Are *you* in any pain?" I murmur back. I'm worried that if I speak too loudly, too quickly—too brashly, as is my nature—I might shatter this delightfully warm haze that's fallen between us.

In this rare moment of tranquility, this little slice of Hell, I indulge myself in the finer details of his face. I've never noticed the tiny scar running diagonally along his left temple to the innermost corner of his ear. The skin has faded to a light silver, barely perceptible to a passerby's glance. I can appreciate the strong, high bridge of his nose and the seemingly permanent slant of his ever-serious brows. I'll admit there's something intriguing about the firmness of his lips. Now that I know they're capable of the gargantuan task of smiling, a part of me is eager to see it again.

Out of general curiosity, of course. Nothing more.

"What other silly human stories do you know?" I ask.

"Only a few," he confesses. "'The Legend of the White Snake.' Or perhaps 'The Butterfly Lovers.' Or maybe you've heard of 'The Cowherd and the Weaver Girl'?"

I scrunch my nose, trying to recall the little snippets I'd overhear when I stalked the streets of Longhao. I don't think I've ever heard the tales in their entirety, too concerned about being caught to stay in one place for too long. Frankly, most human stories sound the same—what with their beginnings, middles, and ends. All highly predictable, though there's admittedly something comforting about their structure.

"Those are all love stories," I say.

"Not to your taste?"

"I just wouldn't expect someone like you to enjoy romantic tales."

"Someone like me?" he echoes, the corner of his lip ticking up into a grin.

I shrug. "No-nonsense. Tough. Brave."

Sonam's grin stretches into a full smile. I am both mesmerized and horrified by it. I don't understand the skip of my heart or the unease gripping my throat. The only explanation I can muster is that I must be falling ill.

"You think I'm brave?"

"More than most humans, I'll give you that. But what you have in bravery, you sorely lack in humor."

"But Wen tells me I'm the funniest man he knows."

I can't help but snort. "He's obviously trying to spare your feelings."

"Very likely," he muses, still inspecting my hands. He holds me gently, as though he's happened upon a baby bird with clipped wings. I . . . don't mind it.

"So why *does* a man like you know so many love stories?" I ask, a warm haze blanketing my thoughts.

Sonam shrugs slightly, contemplatively tracing my knuckles with his thumb. "All stories are love stories, if you think about it."

"What about tales of war?" I challenge skeptically.

"Fought for love of land and family."

"Tales of murder?"

"Crimes stemmed from passion."

"And tales of revenge?"

Sonam looks deeply into my eyes. I cannot for the life of me begin to read them. "Revenge is only born when you or your loved ones have been wronged. We seek justice for them—our friends, our family, who we once were—no matter the cost, because—"

"Because we loved them," I finish quietly.

Wen clears his throat behind us. I withdraw my hand from Sonam's as if his is made of molten iron.

"What?" the captain and I snap in unison. Sonam's face is as bright and red as a bride's wedding dress. Judging by the heat emanating from my cheeks, I'm no better off.

"I wanted a moment with the—with Yue," Wen corrects himself. "If you don't mind."

I squint at him suspiciously. As a matter of fact, I mind a great deal, but for the sake of peace, I give Sonam a tight nod. He walks off and joins Sooah on the other side of the statue garden. Chewing on the inside of my cheek, I wait for Wen to speak.

"I wanted to thank you," he says, avoiding my gaze.

"What for?" I ask.

He takes a deep breath and shifts his weight from foot to foot. I don't understand the delay. Wen was the one who wanted to talk. "For saving me," he answers, speaking so quickly that his words run together. "If it hadn't been for your quick thinking, I'd probably have been crushed by those walls. You didn't have to come back for me."

"I know."

"Then why did you?"

My mouth opens only to close again, an explanation eluding even me. There's no logical answer. It would have been so easy to let him die. Yet another casualty of Hell. And one less human to worry about. Fewer moving parts, fewer annoyances—especially where Wen is concerned.

"Because being crushed to death is a terrible way to go," I answer honestly. And then, after a deep breath, "And no one deserves that. Not even you."

I'm keenly aware of how his body language changes, melting into something slightly more comfortable. There's a flash behind his eyes. Not admiration—I wouldn't expect that of him—but there's an undeniable inkling of respect.

"Well, I guess I owe you," Wen mumbles. "If you hadn't saved me, I would've left my wife and kids all by their lonesome."

I gape. "You have *spawn*?"

"Is that really so hard to believe?"

"Yes."

Wen sighs, hands on hips. "Sooah says the same thing. '*Really lucked out*.'"

"Because your wife agreed?"

"'Cause the man she was supposed to marry disappeared the day before the wedding." He shakes his head. "Ling and I were best mates since we were tots. I've loved her since forever. And she, me. Problem was I come from nothing. Piss-poor family. A few crooks in my line, you see. There wasn't any hope of her parents giving me their blessing. So they wanted to marry her off to some wealthy bastard. A jewel merchant. He could probably take care of her alright, but there were rumors."

I lean in, intrigued by his story. "What rumors?"

Wen's face darkens. "Word around the teahouse was that he was a mean drunk, and just as mean sober. The type to talk with his fists. Ling would've been his second wife."

"Do I dare ask what happened to the first?"

He kicks at a loose pebble next to his shoe. "Authorities found her dead in the canal a few moons before he and Ling were arranged. Shrugged it off as an accident. Reckoned she must've slipped and drowned. But I happened to be passing by when they fished her out of the water." Wen looks me directly in the eye, so stone-cold and serious it sends a shiver down my spine. "Drowning don't leave bruises like that."

"What wound up happening to this merchant?" I ask.

"Haven't the faintest," Wen admits. "Ling asked me to run away with her right before the wedding. It would've been easy to load up the carriage and make off, but then the news broke. The merchant went missing overnight. Not a trace left, except for one of his silver rings. Ling wasn't too heartbroken about it, if you can imagine, but . . ."

"They suspected you," I say knowingly.

"Course they did. Wasn't exactly a secret that I was willing to do anything for her. They would've had my head, were it not for the captain."

"What does the captain have to do with any of this?"

"He'd been chasing after something. A demon known for prowling our little corner of Longhao. He vouched for my innocence and saved my neck. Helped me prove I was out drinking away my sorrows at the teahouse. Got into a fight that night. It's how I wound up with this." Wen holds up his right hand, displaying the slight tremor he carries with him. "Broke my arm in four places. Doctor didn't set it right."

"Why would you choose the bow, of all things?"

"Not strong enough to lift a sword. Can't fight with my fists. The cap'n knew I'd have trouble finding work after, so he asked me to join him. Had me practicing day in and day out. I ain't that bad of a shot."

"He did the same thing for Sooah," I realize with a light laugh. "Always playing hero."

"Not playing," Wen says sternly. "I owe the cap'n a debt. If he hadn't come along . . . I made an oath to him that day. He protected my life, so I'll protect his."

I'm silent for a moment, allowing Wen's words to sink in. There's something endearing about the concept of human loyalty. Wen could have easily thanked Sonam for his kindness and been done with it. Why he feels the need to go above and beyond baffles me, in fact.

But it's surprisingly nice, how they've banded together. A banished prince, a pauper, and a servant girl. Such an unlikely trio. Throw me into the mix, and I could be their rabid pet.

I quickly push the thought away. How ridiculous. Once we leave this place, that's it. I don't suspect we'll remain in each other's company. We'll write this whole experience off as the terrible misadventure it was. I'll run back to the jungle until the next time I need to feed, and Sonam, Wen, and Sooah will return to their sport of hunting me down. It's the natural order of things.

I glance at Sonam over my shoulder, and an awful tightness burdens my chest. What a shame. I think I've rather come to tolerate him.

"I would ask something of you," I say quietly.

Wen frowns, mildly suspicious. "What is it?"

I take a deep breath and sigh. "That captain of yours is too noble for his own good. When the time comes, and I'm sure it will—don't let him do anything foolish."

He nods. "That was always the plan."

29

Sonam

Hunting Log # 391:
She smells of the jungle—of rich earth and petrichor . . .
Though it's hardly an important detail.

W***en sacrifices another one of*** his arrows, handing it to Sooah so that she can slowly carve away at the bamboo shaft to make a feather stick—the thin peeled wood perfect for fire kindling. There is little else here in this statue garden for us to use.

"Only seven arrows left," he mutters to himself as our campfire grows. Wen smirks at Yue, who has yet to sit down. She seems to have taken a particular interest in the dragon statue. "Can't you find us some sticks? Dogs love to fetch, don't they?"

"Don't antagonize her." My words come out in such a rush that I surprise myself. Wen has always enjoyed a good jest, but for some reason I can't allow this one to slide. Perhaps it's because I feel indebted. If not for her, we might have frozen to death or befallen some other horror at the hands of the star goddess.

"It's fine," Yue says breezily, flashing a grin at us over her shoulder. "I could, and they do. But I'm not fool enough to do you a kindness for free."

Sooah huffs a laugh and gestures at Yue to come closer. Once Yue takes a seat across the fire, Sooah demonstrates a short series of hand signs. I can't help but chuckle. Wen snorts and rolls his eyes. When Yue shoots me with a quizzical glance, I say, "She's teaching you how to sign."

"And what did she say?"

"'*If he ever pisses you off, tell him to go fuck a hungry tiger.*'"

Her lips break into a gleeful smile as she copies Sooah. Once to learn the words, and a second to get a sense of flow. She has the phrase memorized and perfected by the third. Yue giggles when Sooah teaches her another string of insults, the sound so light and giddy that, for a moment, I find myself speechless.

She has no right to look like that. No right to sound so sweet. I remind myself that it's the magic of her mask and nothing more. Not to mention I'm exhausted and growing more irritable with every passing minute here in Hell. The only reason my palms are clammy and my breaths come thin is because I'm eager to leave this place as soon as possible.

The sound of Yue's laugh startles me from my thoughts. It's a cackle from deep in her belly. Orange flickers against the smooth planes of her face, the fire's light glimmering against the severe cut of her obsidian eyes. What terrible blasphemy makes it possible for a demon to appear so angelic?

"What else can you teach me?" she asks excitedly. "How do I call him an idiot?"

Wen groans. "The first thing you want to learn is how to cuss me out?"

"Of course. That's where the fun is."

"Good luck," he replies dryly. "Took me years to learn—"

Idiot, Yue signs after Sooah demonstrates. "It's not that hard."

"Shut up," Wen grumbles. "Course it's easier for you. We had the hard job of coming up with it."

Yue tilts her head to the side. "You made it up?"

"The cap'n did. Hand speak ain't all that common, and we needed a way to talk to each other, so he helped come up with a lot of it."

All eyes find me now, but it's the heat of her stare that I can't stand. Her usual malice and disgust are nowhere to be found. Instead, I see admiration.

It makes me squirm. Yue has no right to look at me this way. Not after everything I've done.

"Hunter, artist, and linguist," she muses. "So full of surprises."

I'm the one to avert my gaze, glancing down at my own palm. The line that I cut in order to feed the fox has started to scab, the surrounding skin red and irritated. It takes a great deal to make me uneasy, but the rapid thudding of my heart against my rib cage is enough to see me rise.

"Where are you going?" Yue asks as I move away.

"To see if I can find anything to make arrows out of. Short of that, more fuel for the fire."

"I'll come with you," Wen offers, but I shake my head.

"Stay and rest. I won't be far."

I keep to my word and only venture as far as the high wall cordoning off the garden. The gardens of previous courts were lush and beautiful, full of flowers enchanted with the brightest of hues. This one can only boast a few shrubs and a neat stone pathway, as well as a patch of silky white sand resting in the corner hosting a meditative pattern of lines. All it would take is a sweep of my hand to disturb the canvas and blot the sand with my presence. Would it even matter if I did? After we've long ventured into the next court, will a wandering soul come across the marks I've left behind?

"If I knew a single compliment would send you running, I could have spared myself all this trouble when we first met."

I turn abruptly, startled to find Yue standing not an arm's length away. I am both impressed and troubled by her featherlight footing. "I wasn't running."

"No?" Yue grins coyly. "Panicking, then."

"I'm not—"

"Don't lie." She taps her nose. "Sour scent, remember?"

A deep sigh escapes me, my shoulders slumping with the release. "You're welcome to keep your distance, Fox. I'm sure Sooah and Wen would be happy to continue with your lessons."

Yue presses her lips into a thin line. "Have I offended you?"

Yes, I nearly say. *Everything about you offends me*. Yet the words never leave the tip of my tongue. I cannot bring myself to say them because I cannot decipher this strange sensation brewing beneath the surface of my skin.

Perhaps it is the way she moves like the wind, effortless and haunting. I hate it, yet I find myself yearning to feel her breeze ghost across my skin, craving the reminder that I'm still alive. I see the way she watches me; those large, alert eyes betraying her thirsty curiosity. Does she still view me as prey, I wonder? Or will I only ever be a threat to her?

I don't know that I want to be.

"My mind is restless, is all," I finally answer.

"The only cure for a restless mind is to keep it busy." Yue tilts her chin toward my rope dart, which I've tied securely around my middle. "Since I'm already in the mood for lessons."

I arch a brow. "It wouldn't be wise."

"Because you're an incapable teacher?"

"Because this is not a novice's weapon."

"If a fool like you can learn to master it, how hard can it be?"

"*You're* the fool if you think you can rile me."

"Am I?" she murmurs. She takes a step forward, her head tilted back to look up at me. My blood hums with exhilaration. There's a fire in her gaze, a challenge. "Teach me, Sonam. I want to learn."

A spark crackles its way down my spine. She has never said my name before. Who does she think she is, taking a bland name like mine and making it sound like music?

"Fine," I bite out, pulling on the rope to loosen it from around my waist. "Don't blame me if you end up hurting yourself."

Yue gives me that blasted smile—too wide, too triumphant. "My failings are that of my teacher's."

If her aim was to get under my skin, it's working.

I sigh. "Turn around and give me your hand."

She does so, but at an infuriatingly slow pace. Once she extends her palm, I step forward and give her the tail of the rope to hold, careful to let the dagger on the opposite end down slowly.

"The key isn't speed or strength, but balance and timing," I say, taking my place behind her. With a guiding hand braced against her wrist, I help her swing the dagger as if it were a pendulum. "You must acquaint yourself with its weight, its momentum. Release only when the dagger is out and away."

"Not unlike a whip," she says as the dagger makes a full rotation in her hand.

"I suppose. Though this is far more flexible. Mistime the release, and you may well stab yourself." Gently, I grasp Yue by the hips and turn her slightly. "Aim for that rock over there."

She releases the rope to disappointing results. The dagger flails through the air, landing with a clatter at least a foot from the intended target. Yue frowns. "I want to try again."

She tries again and again with a determination that is . . . admirable, but to no avail.

"You're not so terrible," I tell her when she huffs in frustration.

"You haven't lost a finger or the tip of your nose yet, so that's worth some praise."

Yue turns and pins me with a skeptical glare. "How long did it take you?"

"My whole life."

"And who was your teacher? I might be better served learning with them."

A grin tugs at the corners of my lips. "Trial and error were my teachers, Yue. Proficiency isn't a garden that blooms overnight."

She snorts. "How poetic."

"Here," I offer with a low chuckle.

Continuing to stand behind her, I take up her wrists, using the length of my arms as a frame for her to balance against. I correct her hold around the rope, adjusting her fingers so that the dagger's end can slip free of her grip. I am close enough to smell her hair, my lips grazing the curve of her ear. I move her hand as though it were my own, swinging the rope with a controlled rhythm.

When we let go, the dagger flies true, striking the rock with such force that the tip leaves a noticeable mark against its jagged surface. The clang that follows echoes into the expanse of the garden, a gong announcing our success.

"I did it!" Yue exclaims, laughing softly as she turns toward me. "With help, of course."

A low chuckle rumbles in my chest as I yank the dart rope back. I'm alarmed to realize I am studying her enchanting visage, now that I can do so unhindered in close proximity. Why am I intrigued by the curl of her long lashes? Why do I find the shape of her lips so beguiling?

She is a monster of monsters. A beast who feeds on those far more wretched. At any moment, she could unhinge her jaw and rip my throat out if she felt so inclined. I have foolishly allowed myself to be alone with her. If Yue decided to attack, Wen and Sooah would be helpless to stop her. I should put distance between us.

Yet all I can focus on is the whisper of her breath hitting my cheeks. The way I could tilt my head down, easily capture her mouth with my own and—

"CAP'N!"

The panic in Wen's voice lances through my chest. The hairs on my arms stand on end. There's something bitter in the air, the undeniable stench of rot. The jade statues creak and groan, craning their necks as they step down from their column pedestals. I realize then that these aren't statues at all. One by one, they step down and expose themselves for what they truly are: demons hiding in plain sight.

"Bring the woman," the dragon statue growls.

"And the rest?" asks the rat.

"Eat them. The Maskmaker doesn't care so long as we bring her alive."

I reach for my sword. "Keep your hands off of—"

It's too late. They move with startling swiftness, attacking us in full force. Caught by surprise, we have no choice but to fight. I make it to Wen and Sooah, but the mistake has already been made. I thought Yue was right behind me. I shouldn't have taken my eyes off her.

I turn, all too late, to see one of the beasts strike her over the back of the head.

30

Yue

Hunting Log #392:

The element of surprise is a tactic demons know all too well.

My joints creak. *There's a* terrible pressure threatening to burst through my skull like a hammer nailing a spike outward. I can feel my pulse thudding in the tips of my fingers, causing them to swell. I pry open my eyes, but see nothing. I've either gone blind or I've awoken in the dark. I'm not sure which is more terrifying.

"Little thief, awake at last," a familiar voice claws into my ear. A chill runs down my spine. "My, you've grown into a fearsome thing."

Someone snatches me up by the chin, fingernails digging into my cheeks. I struggle against my restraints, which I realize is the stone body of the snake statue. The demon has wrapped itself around me, pinning my arms at my sides in a vise. I try to free myself, but the more I struggle, the harder it squeezes, forcing the breath from my lungs and crushing my bones. My vision comes into focus just enough to reveal the Maskmaker's face—he's wearing Sonam's. Though they look perfectly identical, the Maskmaker's cruelty seeps through the captain's features like ink blotting fine linen. Even at his worst, Sonam lacks this harsh a coldness.

"How dare you wear his face," I hiss. "You're still the same old coward hiding in fear."

The Maskmaker scoffs, gripping my chin that much harder. "Hypocrite." With a harsh yank, he rips my mask off my face. "I've missed this beautiful mask of mine. Did you really think you could steal it from me?"

"Give it back!" I snarl.

He ignores me, turning the porcelain over in his hands. He inspects it, clicking his tongue when he notices a few scratches along its left cheek. "Look what you've done. One of my best works, and you've gone and scuffed it."

I grit my teeth. "Where are they?"

"Who?"

"My humans."

"Does it matter?" There's a conniving glint in his eyes. Sonam's eyes. I hate how he's managed to twist them into something malicious. The Maskmaker grins that much wider. "I presume your little friends are dead by now. My army has been hungry for a very long time. Who am I to deny them?"

My rage almost gets the better of me, but then I think carefully. He's lying. If Sonam is dead, then the magic binding me to my vows would have struck me down, too. He is alive somewhere. For how much longer, I cannot say, but at least not all hope is lost. I never thought I'd see the day when the deal I struck with Sonam would prove more help than hindrance.

There's movement behind the Maskmaker. We're not alone. There are too many demons to count—maybe a hundred, if I had to venture a guess—milling about the empty room of the pavilion they've dragged me into. An army, as he called it, flitting about in silence as they organize a massive pile of shining porcelain disks in the middle of the floor.

Masks. Thousands of them. Faces of men and women, young and old. It seems the Maskmaker has crafted quite the collection since we parted ways.

But to what end?

"Where are we? Let me go." My words burn, my throat too tight. I can hardly breathe now that I'm trapped in the snake's crushing embrace.

"No."

"What do you want with me?"

"What do I want?" The Maskmaker laughs. "You, of course. I've been so worried about my little runaway. Let's let bygones be bygones, and I'll promise to take you back."

I snarl. "Why would I ever want you to take me back?"

"My spies tell me that you've searched high and low for me. I'm sure you're eager to apologize."

"Apologize?" I shriek. "You had my sisters killed!" My six obsidian eyes sting with the threat of tears. There's so much pressure inside my skull I fear they'll burst from their sockets like grapes crushed in one's fist.

"Yes, I did," he replies matter-of-factly, not a trace of remorse to be found.

"But why?" I rasp. "Why did you—"

"You disobeyed me, Yue. I had to punish you."

I may be a demon, born of shadows and an eater of flesh, but there's nothing more terrifying than a god without feeling. I tremble beneath his dead stare, hating his use of Sonam's face against me.

"All you had to do was listen," the Maskmaker continues. "The blame falls on you."

"No, that's—"

He leans in close, just out of reach of my powerful jaws. "Was I not good to you? I masked you. Fed you. Loved you. And how did you repay me? By stealing my most prized mask and running off into the night. *You* made me do it."

Errant tears streak my face, soaking into my fur. No matter how hard I try to shrink from his gaze, there's no escape. Doubt creeps into my mind. It's true that the Maskmaker once cared for me. He saved my life. Protected me from those who would do me harm. All he asked was that I eat. That I do what demons do best. What if I did bring this upon myself? What if my sisters are dead because of my own stubbornness?

"There's no need to cry," he says. "As I said, I'm willing to forgive you." He chuckles to himself. "I thank fate for sending you after me."

I bite my tongue. "You do?"

"I have use for your teeth when we finally return to the surface."

His words pull me from my thoughts. I stare at him in confusion. The mortal realm? What could he possibly . . .

I look around and take in all the ingredients of the Maskmaker's recipe. An army of starving demons with an arsenal of faces to conceal their true nature would spell disaster for mankind. There's no telling how many thousands that they'll consume while disguised, and by the time the humans and even the Heavens above realize what's come to pass, it will be too late. They'll be overrun. Not even the formidable Demon Hunter of Jian will be able to put a stop to it.

I eat humans, yes. But only ever enough to ensure my survival. The Maskmaker hopes to orchestrate a mass extinction.

I shake my head slightly, restricted by the snake's punishing grip. "I won't have any part in it."

"Don't be hasty. Take a moment to think it through."

"There's nothing to think about," I snarl. "What you're suggesting is madness."

The Maskmaker laughs. There's an unhinged glint in his eyes. "Was I not the one who taught you never to pity your food? You've gone soft."

I wince when he reaches out and strokes the burn scars upon the side of my face. I resist the urge to bite at his fingers. "*Don't* touch me."

"You really won't apologize?" he asks.

"I'd rather die."

"How disappointing. I suppose I could feed you to the other demons. Beggars can't be choosers, after all. Unless . . . " He clicks his tongue and looks around the sparse landscape of the pavilion.

It's by far one of the most underwhelming Courts of Hell I've seen. The furniture sits shoved aside. The delicate floral wallpaper is faded and peeling. I wonder if the star god tasked with running this place abandoned it long ago.

Then a thought occurs to me.

"This was your court," I realize aloud. "Before you managed to escape Hell."

"I never took kindly to being told what to do," he says thoughtfully, stepping away to inspect the high ceiling. A thick layer of dust powders the lanterns fixed to the walls. "We have that in common, you and I. Do you have any idea how long Death had me trapped down here? Centuries upon centuries, tasked to torture all those filthy, disgusting human souls." Disdain etches into Sonam's regal features. "I was a *god*. How dare he sully our hands."

I cough, failing to ignore the distinctive *snap* and *pop* of one of my ribs. "If you hate it so much here, why did you come back?"

The Maskmaker shakes his head. "You won't be around long enough to know, little fox."

"You mean to kill me?"

"No," he says finally. "Killing you is too merciful a punishment. I have something far better in mind." The Maskmaker stalks toward me, bending over so that we're face-to-face. I freeze beneath his gaze, as terrified and helpless as I was in that pit all those years ago. "I don't have to lift a finger to hurt you, Yue. Your dreams will do it for me."

A bone-deep exhaustion suddenly crushes me from head to toe. I can't keep my eyes open. The more I struggle, the more it grips my mind. There's no telling what horrors the Maskmaker might inflict while I'm asleep. But try as I might, there's no fighting the spell he's cast.

My head drops forward and sleep claims me roughly in its arms.

31

Yue

Hunting Log #393:
Daggers over swords, and poison over daggers.
To kill a demon, death and subtlety must go hand in hand.

Songbirds, sweet and lovely, sing their morning tunes. The warmth of the rising sun peeks through the woven bamboo curtains and kisses my cheeks, painting the skies a soft orange hue. I tuck my knees up against my chest, curled up beneath my blanket of soft linen, determined to sleep the day away in peace.

That is, until someone throws a cushion at me.

"Yue," one of my sisters calls out. My eyes are too bleary to see. She rushes over and all but rips my blanket off. "Honestly, Yue, I've been trying to call you downstairs for ages. How long are you going to stay in bed?"

I blink up at her in confusion. She's . . . human. Her silky black hair is pulled up into a neat bun, her vibrant robes of floral-patterned silk hugging her slender shoulders. She has a pointed nose and rosebud lips, but her eyes are soft and bright, contrasting against the sharp edges of her jawline and high cheekbones.

"Qin?" I croak, my voice heavy with sleep.

She laughs good-naturedly. "Goodness, look at your hair! Did a bird decide to make itself a nest?" My sister takes a seat on the edge of my bed and starts to pick and prod, combing her fingers through my locks. I can't help but stare at her in disbelief. She smells of jasmine tea and summertime grass.

Curious, I bring a hand up to my face, dragging my fingers along the corner of my jaw to peel off my mask. I sit up in alarm when I find nothing but soft and supple skin.

"Is this . . . real?" I whisper in amazement.

Qin gives me a strange look. "Are you feeling alright?"

I furrow my brows and concentrate. My mind is strangely blank. I look down at my hands and find my fingertips red and swollen. They smell faintly of dirt and blood. How strange. I don't remember how I managed to scrape them.

"I think I had a nightmare," I confess. "A very bad one. I dreamt I was a nine-tailed fox. And there was this man—a hunter. He banished me to Hell."

"Goodness, that sounds terrible." Qin smiles sweetly. "Not to worry. What's in your head can't harm you. Now, get dressed quickly. He's just arrived."

"Who?" I ask.

"The painter, silly," she replies with a mischievous grin. "We have to save the poor man from Jiayi's clutches. I'm convinced she has half a mind to whisk him away for herself."

I move as though wading through honey. Climbing out of bed is a trial. The air is thick and humid, my muscles sore and stiff. Clothes have been laid out for me, silks folded neatly upon a low table, an assortment of glimmering hair ornaments to choose from set before a watery silver mirror. I shuffle over and kneel before the table, running my fingers along the patterned silk, admiring the dye work and details of the embroidered flowers along the hems.

Unsure what to do with my hair, I decide to wear it down. I'm too preoccupied with my reflection. My cheeks are rosy, my eyes sparkle with life. I feel . . . happy. Good. Like everything is right with the world. Reaching for a small jar made of porcelain, I remove the lid and discover red paste within. After dabbing a light layer of rouge on my lips, I smile at my reflection. I giggle at the pretty woman I see.

By the time I get dressed and descend the steep wooden stairs of our home, I find my other sisters crowded around the low table in the parlor room, all of them giggling and chatting with a guest who's just out of view. A freshly brewed pot of tea sits between them, though it goes ignored, silver clouds of steam lifting lazily into the cool morning air.

"Is today the day you're finally going to ask her?" Su asks, sounding quite serious.

"It better be," comments Ahn. "You'll answer to us if we find out you've been stringing her along."

A low chuckle reaches my ear. The deep, rich voice belongs to a man, who, now that I've descended the steps, I see has a strikingly sharp jaw and mesmerizingly dark eyes.

"I wouldn't dream of it," he answers as he looks up at me with a growing smile. He rises from the table and bows his head respectfully. "Yue."

"Sonam?" His name rolls off my tongue with ease, failing to fully capture my surprise.

He wears a faded brown tunic and dark linen pants, the canvas of his shoes worn down around the edges. His hair is shorn down to the scalp, not a royal insignia or piece of jade jewelry to signify his status. To the naked eye, Sonam is nothing but a common man. And it's strange. Not because I dreamt of him as a prince, but because the simple life suits him well. It carries in the way he smiles, the corners of his eyes crinkling. There's an air of ease and contentment about him.

When my sisters stare at us with all the subtlety of a pouncing tiger, Sonam clears his throat and says, “Perhaps we should take some air. It’s a lovely day for a walk.”

He offers me his hand and I hesitate, noting the way his skin is stained with dried black ink. I think I dreamt of him doing something similar last night, though I can only make out the barest shadows of my nightmare now. I place my hand in his, flooded with a sudden sense of ease.

“Behave, you two,” Jiayi teases us as we make our way out the door.

“And be sure to come back with good news!” Su cackles shamelessly.

Ignoring the embarrassment burning the tips of my ears, I allow Sonam to lead me down the worn dirt path toward the rolling hills of soft green grass behind my family’s quaint farmland home. He was right. It truly is a lovely day for a walk.

The sky stretches as far as the eye can see, the serpentine mountain pass appearing dark blue from this distance. Wide steps have been carved into the hillsides, each of them hosting a shallow pool of water to nurture the season’s rice harvest, each row stacked one on top of the other like the scales upon a dragon’s back. Farmers work tirelessly, their shoulders hunched over as they plant new beds, the sweat dripping from their brows worth every grain of rice they’ll one day reap.

Sonam guides me to the gentle bed of a nearby stream, long cattails swaying along the water’s edge. Dragonflies hover above the surface, tending to their eggs cradled in the gathered droplets floating atop lotus leaves. Beneath the shade of an arching wisteria tree, I’m delightfully surprised to find a picnic spread. It seems Sonam has gone out of his way to lay out a soft blanket and prepare a basket full of pastries to share. It’s all so wonderful.

So what is this sinking feeling?

"Yue?" he calls gently, sweetly. Like he's said it a thousand times before but will never tire of the sound. "Are you feeling alright?"

I swallow hard. That's the second time today someone's asked me that question. I take a deep, slow inhale with the passing breeze, listening to the steady beat of my heart and the hum of distant work tunes as the farmers go about their day. I can't recall if I've ever known such peace, but despite the unease rumbling in my stomach, I want to hold on to this feeling for as long as I'm able. Forever, if the gods will permit me this one wish.

Sonam lifts my hand to his lips, pressing the softest of kisses to my knuckles. "You're not yourself today, my moonlight. Is something troubling you?"

Again, I don't answer. I lack the words. The world of my nightmare truly shook me to my core. My greatest fear is to say the wrong thing and destroy whatever strange paradise I've somehow awoken to.

"I had a dream last night," I say slowly. "You were a captain. A prince, actually."

"Oh?" Sonam smiles wide, amused. Even the sun couldn't rival such magnificence. "Were you the princess I was tasked to save?"

The harder I reach for the memories, the faster they slip through my fingers. Tiny grains of sand flowing through a sieve, draining until nothing remains. A soft laugh pulls from my lips. "I can't remember anymore," I confess.

He gingerly brushes a few loose strands of hair away from my face and tucks them behind my ear. "I'm sorry I'm no prince," he says with a chuckle. "Were I as wealthy as one, I would have asked for your hand ages ago."

My cheeks warm at his words. "That doesn't matter to me."

"But it matters to me." He gestures, offering me a seat upon the picnic blanket. "I want to be able to give you a good life. One that you deserve. I have one last commission to paint for my patron in

Longhao, but then we'll finally have enough to buy that house up on the hill."

I follow the direction of his gaze and spot the house in question. At this distance, it looks no larger than a bronze coin. It's a cozy wooden structure with a roof of neatly laid terra-cotta tiles, the perimeter surrounded by tall grass and wildflowers, all of it resting beneath the swaying shade of the nearby ginkgo trees.

Sonam shrugs his shoulders. "Of course, if my patron decides he doesn't like my work, I'd build you a house with my bare hands if I had to."

I shift awkwardly. "I don't think I deserve such kindness."

"Of course you do," he states firmly, as if what I've just said is egregious enough to offend the gods. "You've always looked down on yourself, and I won't stand for it. When we're married—and even now—I will make sure you want for nothing." He takes my hands again and kisses my palms, my wrist; so sweet and loving that it brings tears to my eyes. "Let me make you happy. Let me keep you safe. Would you allow me, Yue?"

Excitement floods my veins, setting my heart aflutter. The sinking feeling I had earlier this morning is long gone, replaced with a rising hope that I want to cling to for the rest of my days. I lean forward and press my lips to his, melting against his chest as he circles his strong arms around my waist. He tastes of mangoes, the warmth of his embrace as soothing as the lazy summer sun.

Our kiss is tender. Soft and sweet and unhurried. It almost feels like a secret, one shared and closely guarded between the two of us. I think I might lose myself in the taste of his lips, could abandon the rest of the world for the promise of another. The heat between us grows, a fire left unchecked and burning wilder with every passing second, the two of us grabbing and caressing and kissing ravenously.

It's when Sonam brings a hand up to stroke my right cheek with his thumb that I pause.

"Be mindful of my scars," I murmur.

"What scars?"

I pull back and stare at him, perplexed. My scars, my greatest insecurities—does he not hate them as much as I do? I bring a hand to my face and allow my fingers to rest on the skin, confused and a little alarmed to find my cheek smooth. Why did I say that? My complexion has always been pristine.

Something isn't right. I knew it from the moment I woke up this morning, yet now I'm more convinced than ever. Everything's too wonderful, too perfect. And to make matters worse, I feel safe and loved—impossibilities, given what I am. I exist as though suspended in thick honey, every movement and thought doused in a sweetness that's too good to be true.

"This is a dream," I whisper, the realization dawning quickly. "None of this is real."

Sonam stares at me, confused at first, before his expression goes blank. "A dream? You're not making any sense."

My stomach lurches, my skin suddenly feverish as a wave of nausea grips my mind. There's magic at work here, I'm sure of it now. I was too wrapped up in the splendor of it all to notice it before, but now there's no denying the sour twist of an illusionary spell—and a strong one, at that.

"I need to go," I say, the words so desperate and heavy I nearly gag around them. "I have to wake up."

Sonam takes my hands. "Stay with me, Yue. Don't you understand? I *love* you."

Those three simple words are colder than a sea of ice water. Tears sting my eyes, and my heart twists mercilessly in my chest. "You could never love me, Sonam. No one can. Especially not you."

32

"We want masks of our own," Qin, the eldest fox demon said. "They'll help us on our next hunt."

"I can make them for you," the Maskmaker replied, "but my work does not come free."

"Is it fortune or flesh you seek?"

"I have need for neither."

"Then, is there something you would have us do?"

The question inspired a most devious thought in the Maskmaker's mind. He looked up at his loathsome brother, the Sun. He glared up at the Heavens with his blackened heart.

Alone, he never would have stood a chance. But with a small army of indebted demons at his side . . . He would have to play this carefully, to be sure, but if everything went according to plan, the Maskmaker would finally have his revenge—nearly a millennium in the making.

He cursed the Heavens and the Sun and mankind who betrayed him. He would blanket the world with these beasts leading the helm and take back what should have been rightly his. It was not enough to be a god, for clearly one ill-placed arrow could strip him of his power. The Maskmaker would not find satisfaction until he was the *god, reigning supreme over a world built in his image.*

"Nothing comes to mind at the moment," he lied smoothly, "but I propose we make a deal. I will create masks for you, and when the day comes, you must vow to uphold my word."

The sisters whispered among themselves. They were no strangers to making deals. They did not see the Maskmaker as a threat, for how could anyone, let alone this curious painter, hope to swindle a pack of nine-tailed foxes and live to tell the tale?

"Very well," the fox sisters said together. "You have yourself a deal."

The Maskmaker held back his smile. "I need more than just your promise. I must have your vow in blood."

33

Sonam

Hunting Log #394:
Demons are stronger, prouder, more lethal–
but lack any semblance of creativity.

"K*eep your hands off of–"*

I barely have time to get the words out. One of the demons hits her over the back of the head. Yue crumples like a paper doll, threatening to rip as they drag her away by the hair. Black trickles down her forehead.

There's no time to go after her. We're surrounded with no escape in sight. The only way to get to her is by going through.

Sword in hand, I prepare for the onslaught. I've been at a loss up until this point, confused by all these trials and tests of character. But this—tearing demons limb from limb—*this* I can do.

The possessed statues charge us all at once with no plan, only bloodlust. Their attacks come in a blind rage: intimidating at first, but easily countered if I can keep a clear head. Their jade bodies make it difficult to hack and slice. They'll blunt and dent my sword at this rate. Sweat drips from my brow. Victory will not come easily.

The tiger demon pounces, its fierce claws and teeth ready to maul. Its movements remind me of Yue's. Wound tight and overflowing with aggression. That's where the similarities end, however, for this beast lacks Yue's cunning. It's capable of nothing more than biting and swiping, easily avoidable given its lack of precision. When it charges, I rear my leg back and kick with all my might, decapitating the tiger's carved head from its rigid shoulders. The monster crumbles into a pile of dust and rubble.

That's one down, but there's no time to rest. I keep a watchful eye on Sooah out of habit. She won't be able to call for help if she needs it, so I make sure to keep her in my line of sight. Wen is somewhere behind me. Fine for now, judging by his stream of colorful insults that would make even the most hardened of sailors blush. I'm within an arm's reach if he needs me. Even in the heat of battle, protecting my family is top of mind.

The jade dragon is next to strike. A fearsome foe thrice as long as I am tall, it whips the jagged interlocking pieces of its tail and hits me square in the chest. I lose my footing, tumbling backward, the air knocked from my lungs. The beast rears back, preparing to swing again.

I'm not delusional enough to believe I can overpower it. If there's one thing I've learned in all my years hunting, it's that there's no such thing as an honorable fight. The rules of a duel, the structure of war—they serve no purpose when going toe-to-toe with a demon. They don't fight fair to begin with, slinking around in the shadows and using all manner of tricks to defeat their victims.

The only way to level the playing field is to cheat.

I reach for my belt, retrieving a set of throwing needles from a leather pouch. I'm mindful not to prick myself on the ends. Such a mistake would be costly, for they are thinly covered in Zhenniao poison. A single drop is enough to stop my heart in an instant and kill a demon within minutes. Now that I have them in hand, it's simply a question of administration. Sooah and Wen like to charge in headfirst, and that's all well and good, but I prefer to fight with more finesse.

I scramble back onto my feet and dig my heels into the ground. The jade dragon hurtles toward me, but I make no attempt to dodge. It hits me again, this time ramming its head against my stomach. I use its own momentum to drive one of my needles straight into its eye. The dragon pulls back, bellowing in agony, the poison already working wonders to destroy it from within. Life drains from its eyes. I'm on to the next demon before it even hits the ground; jamming needles into arms, necks, and between ribs. Whatever I can get my hands on.

Save for the rat caught beneath Wen's foot and the snake—who has disappeared from sight—they're all dead.

Wen applies pressure, the rat's eyes bulging from its sockets. It shrieks and it claws, but it does little more than scratch at the thick leather of Wen's boot. It seems the little demon gave my brother a hard time, however, for he's covered in all manner of scrapes and bites.

"Slippery bastard," Wen huffs, sweat dripping from his brow. His cheeks are a blotchy red.

"S-spare me!" the rat squeaks.

Sooah gestures angrily, slamming a clenched fist into the opposite open palm. She cracks her knuckles, the sound of popping joints reverberating off the smooth courtyard walls. Her stance on the matter is clear.

"I'll tell you where they took that fox of yours," the rat continues, growing desperate with every ounce of weight Wen applies.

"Why should we believe anything you have to say?" I demand.

"Because we can't lie."

Wen snarls. "What a load of—"

"It's true, I swear! It's a rule all demons must abide by." The rat squirms uncomfortably, under so much pressure that its eyes seem ready to pop out of their sockets. "Demons can't lie when you ask us questions. Just as humans can't live without air or fish without water—that's how the gods deemed us made. Believe me, please."

I set my jaw. A single poisoned needle remains, pinched between my fingers. I'm ready to use it if I must.

The rat could be deceiving us. I'd expect nothing less. But I think back to all the times I've asked Yue questions. She's always answered truthfully. At least, I believed her to be truthful. It didn't go unnoticed, the way Yue grew quiet as she chose her words carefully, oftentimes begrudgingly. Perhaps there's some merit to what the rat is saying, though I'd prefer to err on the side of caution.

"Fine," I say. "Where's Yue?"

"In the Court of Dreams."

"What does the Maskmaker want with her?"

"To have her join us, I suspect. Another pair of fangs for his army."

I frown steeply. "What— Ease up, Wen. What army?"

"There's more of us," the rat croaks. "Thousands and thousands and thousands. He promised to take us to the surface. We've been waiting in the shadows for his signal."

"Why?" I say through gritted teeth. "What is he planning?"

"I'm not sure. But I know that we want to eat."

The hairs on my arms stand on end. I imagine it, the chaos that would ensue if even a handful of demons managed to make their way to the surface. An entire army's worth of demonic hunger is all but guaranteed to wipe humanity from the land. My goals are shifting. Yue wanted the Maskmaker dead.

And now, so do I.

Sooah signs. *What do we do now?*

I look down at the map Kelai seared into my palm. We have two options. The logical thing to do is head straight for the exit and leave this blasted place behind. I've seen enough of Hell to last my next three lifetimes. I feel especially bad for dragging Sooah and Wen down here with me. We've managed to survive each new horror, but there's no telling when our luck will run out. I want to leave and never look back.

Yet the thought of leaving Yue behind fills me with guilt. Before, I wouldn't have thought twice about abandoning her. Just another demon, another shadow in the night. I've killed thousands of her kind without batting an eye. Grown numb to it, in fact. Killing monsters comes as easily to me as breathing.

But Yue is not quite so monstrous as I once believed.

She's frustrating, yes. Rude and distrustful and sulky. In the beginning, I was worried that she'd eat us in our sleep or betray us at the first possible opportunity. Not to mention I've never met anyone with such an irritating need to have the last word. Yet, for all her glaring faults, there's good in her, too.

She saved Wen at risk of her own life. She never once treated Sooah poorly nor differently for her lack of speech. And when she looks at me, I swear she reminds me of an old friend—one I can't quite recall, though their impression still lives with me.

I have my doubts, of course. She's still a demon. I vowed all those years ago to rid the world of her kind. If she escapes from Hell with us, I'll be condemning my people to her hunger.

But it's as the old Albeion monks used to teach: there is good in evil, and evil in good. We've come this far, and in no small part thanks to Yue. To leave her behind would be to doom the sliver of goodness I see in her.

"Kill him," I say, pocketing my last poisoned needle. "We have to go after her."

34

Sonam

Hunting Log #395:
Morality is a human affliction.

We climb the carved steps of the pavilion and approach the heavy main doors easily. Too easily. For someone with a supposed army at his beck and call, there doesn't appear to be anyone around. It isn't until I hear something whimper, heartbroken and weak, that I realize this place is anything but abandoned.

Over here, Sooah says, crouching down low beneath the sill of a latticed window.

The three of us peer inside and find Yue, constricted and bound in the vise of the jade snake from the garden. Her mask is gone, revealing the truth beneath.

Yue is horrifically mesmerizing. The first time I laid eyes upon her in Longhao, I was frightened. In all my years of hunting, I'd never seen a creature more nightmarish. I care not for the sweeping length of her nine tails or the overgrown curl of her yellowed claws. What unsettles me most are her six obsidian eyes and those haunting gray pupils that remind me of crumbling midnight moons.

And then there are her burns, hideous and cruel. I can't help the ache in my heart each time I catch sight of them. I wonder what happened. I caught myself wanting to ask a handful of times but thought better of it. When I'm on the hunt, I always aim for the quickest, cleanest kill. Even I am not hateful enough to torture a beast so. What, or perhaps who, could have done such a thing?

"Killing you is too merciful a punishment," comes the sound of a familiar voice. Far too familiar. I hold my breath, staring at the back of a familiar silhouette. A man stands before Yue, her mask in hand. He wears my clothes, carries my weight, and even the manner in which he speaks perfectly replicates my own.

The Maskmaker. He's wearing *my* face.

My heart seizes.

Any face at all, Yue once told me. *Both the living and the dead, so long as he's seen it once before.*

I don't know whether I'm more enraged or bewildered. To compare it to looking in a mirror would be a gross understatement, for at least my reflection doesn't have a mind of its own. Just think of all the damage he could do if he returned to the mortal realm, masquerading as one of the princes of the Southern Kingdom of Jian. No one would be the wiser. He could commit unspeakable acts in my name. The only discernible difference between us is the fact that he's missing two of his fingers, courtesy of Yue's powerful jaws.

"I have something far better in mind." The Maskmaker stalks toward her, staring deep into her eyes. "I don't have to lift a finger to hurt you, Yue. Your dreams will do it for me."

Yue slumps forward, her head dropping so suddenly I fear it will snap off her neck. My breath catches in my throat. For a moment, I fear he's killed her. I nearly leap out from our hiding spot, my trusty dao halfway drawn, when I notice the subtle rise and fall of her chest. Not dead, merely a deep slumber. There are no words to describe my relief, and there are fewer words still to explain why I feel this way.

It was always my intention to kill her. To rid the world of demons would be a feat unlike any other. Just one more hunt, indistinguishable from all the others, and yet . . . The thought of harming her now leaves a bitterness on my tongue.

The Maskmaker turns away, Yue's porcelain mask in hand. He runs his fingers—my fingers—over a small scratch. He clicks his tongue disapprovingly. "Gone and ruined it," he says before tossing it to the floor. The Maskmaker lifts his foot and crushes the mask beneath his heel, shattering it into several sizable pieces.

Anger simmers in my veins. I've seen how protective Yue is of her mask. There was no reason for him to destroy it except out of pure spite.

It's then that I notice the Maskmaker isn't alone. There's movement from the shadows of the pavilion's main room. Demons. Were it not for the Jade Palace's ominous green glow reflecting in their dark, beady eyes, I might not have noticed them until it was too late. They all appear transfixed with a tall pile of porcelain gathered near the center of the room. A collection of masks stacked tall enough to touch the ceiling.

The Maskmaker sits before the pile and reaches into the long, drooping sleeve of his robe, retrieving something long and slender. I have to squint against the dim lighting to get a better look. It takes me a moment to place the slim bamboo handle and black-stained tip.

"A paintbrush?" Wen murmurs.

I shush him. We'll be damned if we give away our position.

The three of us crouch low when a demon rounds one of the inner corners and approaches the Maskmaker with a set of fine porcelain discs in hand. "That's all of it, master," the demon croaks. "If I may, my lord, how much longer do you suspect we'll be here?"

"Not much longer now," the Maskmaker replies, sounding annoyed as he picks up one of the discs. "I'll craft a few more and then we'll make our way to the main gate. No harm in having spares."

The demon bows deeply, hinging at the hips. "Very wise, my lord."

"The handful of demons I've sent ahead have made excellent progress. Their masks have been working perfectly."

A chill passes through my veins. If what he's saying is true, that means there are more demons lurking in the dark corners of Longhao than I first believed. I think back to the seamstress's daughter, to all the reports I'd received about those who'd vanished without a trace. I was wrong to think Yue was behind all of those disappearances. It was the Maskmaker all along—how many of his minions lie in wait up above? What catastrophes will they rain down upon my people?

With a wave of his hand, the Maskmaker sends the demon away and returns to his work, picking up his brush to paint even strokes against the porcelain surface. I spot no ink stick nor bottles. The end of his brush is completely dry, yet the details of the mask magically appear.

I stare in fascination. So this is how the masks are made. But does the magic come from the Maskmaker, or the brush itself? Can he only create masks of human faces?

Sooah nudges me with the tip of her elbow.

How are we going to get past them? she asks.

I grit my teeth. The last time we took on a horde this size, we barely escaped with our lives. Were it not for Yue's strength and ferocity, we'd be digesting in the pit of some forsaken beast's stomach. It would be foolish to bet on the three of us taking on a thousand starving demons, which means we have two options: wait for them to leave, or—

"We need a distraction," I whisper. "To draw them off. We'll grab Yue and make a break for it before they can follow us to the surface."

Wen frowns. "But—how?"

I take inventory of the weapons I have left at my disposal. Only a handful of hidden daggers, one last needle, a few jars of poultice in case of any cuts and bruises. My sword is looking worse for wear, the tip blunted and the edges dented. An idea occurs to me as I eye Wen's bow and nearly empty quiver strapped to his back.

"Hand me an arrow," I instruct. He does so without any fuss, only squawking with disapproval when I move to drag the tip across my palm. I hand it back, the arrowhead now coated in my blood. "Through this window and out the one across the way," I tell him. "This should be enough."

Wen nods, but I sense his hesitance. "But my tremor . . . "

"You can do it," I say. "You *will* do it. I have faith."

I sidle out of the way, giving Wen enough room to draw his bow and nock the blood-soaked arrow. It's possible for him to kill the Maskmaker while his back is turned, but that will only draw the horde's attention. We need to thin out the herd, and the best way to do that is by using their hunger against them.

Wen releases the arrow, the precisely cut eagle feathers that form the fletch slicing past his cheek. It's a near-impossible shot—in through one window, past the writhing mass of shadows, and then out through the opposite side of the room into the pavilion's private gardens. Drops of blood splatter across the floor. Wen sucks in a breath, triumphant. I never had any doubt.

"Food." One of the demons gasps. "I smell food!"

A sudden eruption of sound. It's a cacophony of howling, slobbering, hissing. They trample over one another, clawing and biting their way forward to follow the scent trail—lost to their insatiable appetites. Even the snake demon tasked with binding Yue in place moves to follow, dropping her carelessly to the floor. Yue doesn't stir.

"What is the meaning of this?" the Maskmaker snaps, but his voice is drowned out by the mayhem.

The moment the crowd dissipates is the moment we strike.

Sooah is first through the latticed window, the thin paper and wood tearing away beneath her bulky momentum. She goes straight for Yue, leaving the Maskmaker to us.

I draw my sword and swing in my run up, slicing straight through the mask he wears. He drops his paintbrush in stunned horror. It's terrible, watching my own visage fall apart. Skin, muscle, bone, and all. I can almost feel it on my own cheek, a truly strange form of self-inflicted harm. The mask falls away and shatters upon the floor, and I find myself staring into a set of bloodshot eyes.

For the first time, I'm able to look upon his pathetic face. There's no hiding. Not anymore. There are bits and pieces of him I recognize. The first star god's ears; the second star god's wide mouth; the goddess Kelai's nose—features shared among siblings.

The Maskmaker is a fallen star god. Did Yue know? Surely not. She is too smart to willingly make such a powerful enemy.

He drags a hand over his bleeding face and snarls. "How dare y—"

I have no time for speeches. I bring my sword up in one swift motion and attempt to run the star god through the chest, but he stops my blade with unspeakable strength, gripping the sharp metal with his bare hand. My first attack was a fluke.

The Maskmaker throws my sword away as if it were a used toothpick. He snatches me up by the throat and squeezes hard enough for his nails to break skin. I rear a hand back and attempt to strike him, but he blocks that, too, snatching me by the wrist and twisting to get a better look at my palm.

"My dear sister gave you a map?" he says, surprised. "Yes, I recognize her magic. This would have come in handy the last time I escaped. How did you trick her into giving it to you?"

The Maskmaker tries to wrench my arm from its socket. The pain explodes through my shoulder and my chest, so dreadful I fear my heart will burst. I choke on a scream, but he doesn't stop there. The deranged star god keeps wrenching. He means to tear my arm clean off in hopes of taking the map.

"Don't struggle," he says darkly. "This will be over soon."

And yet, nothing happens. He attempts to break my arm, but for some curious reason, he is unable to do so. The Maskmaker glares at me in disbelief, something akin to recognition causing his eyes to widen.

"You," he seethes. "The Sun's magic flows through your veins."

I frown in confusion. "What are you talking about?"

"Houyi . . . Even after all these years, you're still a thorn in my side. Now your descendant has come to finish what you started."

Descendant? I can't make sense of what he's saying. My mother often spoke of how she came from a long line of accomplished archers—but I never expected one of them to be *the* archer. I should dismiss his ramblings as a mistake, but what reason does the Maskmaker have to lie?

"Release him!" Wen shouts from across the room.

He's readied another arrow, the drawn bowstring slipping from his fingers, but this time the arrow hits the Maskmaker in the thigh. The vengeful star god releases me and I drop to the floor, landing harshly on my bad shoulder. It pops loudly, dislocated once more. Gods, what terrible luck. I struggle to breathe past the pain. There's a ringing in my ears. I can feel my erratic, panicked pulse in my *teeth*.

A woman's scream. Sooah. It's a sound from deep in the back of her throat—a wail as much as a war cry as she charges the Maskmaker at full speed like a bull. He manages to step out of the way at the last possible moment.

"Pathetic," he scoffs. "You'll have to do better than that."

I use his distraction to my advantage. I lunge for my sword, grip it by its handle, and launch it with all my might. The blade goes tumbling through the air, sawing its way through the Maskmaker just below the elbow. His severed arm falls to the floor with a wet splat, his fingers still twitching as he bellows.

Looks like Yue won't be the only one who gets the privilege of maiming him.

"In here!" the Maskmaker shouts, retreating toward the doors leading into the courtyard. "You stupid beasts, they're in here!"

"We have to go!" Wen snaps, pulling my good arm over his shoulder. He drags me to my feet.

"Yue," I croak. "We can't leave her."

"She's too big to carry," Wen protests.

He's right. In her fox form, Yue is nearly three times Sooah's height and no doubt quintuple the weight. If only her mask hadn't been destroyed. Were she human, we'd be able to carry her out with ease. The mountain of masks sitting before us is our only solution.

"Grab one," I order Sooah. "Any one. Put it on for her."

Despite her size, Sooah is quick and nimble on her feet. She snatches the first mask within reach and races back to Yue, pressing the porcelain to her face. The magic takes quickly, almost instantaneous. The nine tails of the fox shrink away, as do her ears and snout and claws. Yue transforms into a little human boy. Barely five, and plenty small to carry. Sooah scoops Yue up in her arms and starts toward the exit. Wen and I aren't far behind.

Before we manage to leave, I spot something.

The Maskmaker's paintbrush lying forgotten on the floor. I reach for it with a wheeze. The demons are coming. I can hear them, snarling and drooling and barking. Wen realizes what I'm trying to do and huffs in exasperation.

"Now really ain't the time, Cap'n."

"We need it."

With an agitated groan, Wen stoops down and picks it up in one fluid motion. Our enemies are almost upon us, the shadows they cast eclipsing our own as they grow near. We won't be able to lose them at this rate.

In one final, desperate attempt, I kick the star god's severed hand toward them. The demons swarm like starved vipers, feeding on the flesh of their own master. It's the morbid distraction we need to make our escape.

35

Sonam

Hunting Log #396:

We are made of sharp edges, she and I.
Perhaps that's why I'm beginning to understand her.

W*e find solace in a* dark, quiet corner, safely hidden within the shadow of an abandoned outpost. On the surface, this building might have served as a storage unit, though it's clear that it rarely sees any use down here in Hell.

Wen works quickly. I'm on my back against the ground, drenched in cold sweat.

"Not a sound," Wen warns.

I bite down hard and take a deep breath. If he doesn't snap my shoulder back into place, I won't be much use in a fight. I don't think I'll ever be ready for what's about to come, but I give Wen a tentative nod all the same. He hesitates for only a moment before yanking my arm backward, effectively shifting my limb back into its socket.

I don't scream. Can't. To do so would be to put us in further danger. I have no choice but to endure in agonized silence. A part of me prays for unconsciousness. At least then I wouldn't have to be aware of the screaming agony in every one of my nerve endings. My mind is stubborn, however. Too strong and proud to do something as merciful as faint.

I keep my eyes on Yue, who's still fast asleep, cradled in Sooah's arms like a babe. It's strange to see her in the form of a boy, but perhaps it's a testament to the Maskmaker's undeniable artistry. Yet while I marvel, I can't help but wonder where and when he stole this face.

The revelation that the Maskmaker is a fallen star god unsettles me greatly, but the fact that he and Yue have a history disturbs me even more. How did they come to cross paths? And when did things take a turn for the worse?

The Sun's magic flows through your veins.

Whether from the adrenaline or the subsequent shock, my thoughts are a jumbled cacophony within my skull. There was recognition behind the Maskmaker's cruel eyes. A burning hatred that I could smell searing into my very soul. He called me the descendant of the Legendary Archer, and for whatever reason, he could not strike me down despite having ample opportunity. If I am truly of Houyi's bloodline, I fear it will only place a larger target on my back.

But for now, I have more pressing concerns.

"How is she?" I ask, my voice weak and small in my own ears.

I don't know, Sooah replies with one hand. *She won't wake.*

Wen helps me sit up. An intense vertigo knocks the wind from my lungs. It takes all of my strength not to keel over and wretch up the contents of my stomach. By some miracle, I manage to make it onto my feet. My sense of balance is skewed. Everything is off-kilter.

I tell myself that I'll be fine. After all, I'm only a spare. I'm the least favorite son of His Majesty the King. Where my brothers took up philosophy, mathematics, the zither, or even the arts, I dedicated myself to the hunt. I was aware of the dangers, always knew the risks—severe maiming and death are both part of the path I've chosen.

Every step is a struggle, my body in shock. The only reason I'm able to move is out of the pure need for survival. I manage to kneel before Sooah and Yue, taking great care as I lift the mask off of Yue's face. It was ill-fitting, anyway, so loose that it sat crooked. The magic melts away, revealing her head resting gingerly against Sooah's lap. I don't sense any distress or pain, only a deep, undisturbed slumber. Whatever spell the Maskmaker cast upon her has an impressive hold.

"Fox," I say, a gentle whisper at first. When she doesn't rouse, I try again. "You need to wake up."

Her ears twitch, but her eyes remain closed. Yue's breathing is deep and slow. I detect the faintest trace of movement beneath her eyelids. I think she can hear me, but she can't seem to push through.

"What did that bastard do to you?" I hiss under my breath. I look to Sooah and say, "Leave her with me. Stand guard with Wen. I'll wake her."

What if she doesn't?

"She will."

Sooah gives me a hard look. I wonder if she thinks my confidence foolish. Nevertheless, she gently cradles Yue's head and transfers her onto my lap before standing. I reach out slowly, shakily, stroking the fur behind the fox's ear. It's surprisingly soft and warm.

"Yue." I say her name slowly. If I startle her, she might attack me in surprise. I really can't afford to lose a limb. "We need to get out of here."

When she fails to stir, cold, genuine panic begins to fill my chest. What if she's lost to us? It's nothing short of cruel—to come this far only to fail.

Exhaustion seeps into my marrow, too, almost encouraged by Yue's peaceful breathing. I fight the urge to close my eyes, tempted to give up the struggle. How easy it would be.

But I try again, short of breath and sweating profusely. I gingerly run my fingers over her old burns. They don't seem to cause her any pain, for which I find myself grateful.

"I don't think I can make it out of here without you, Fox. Whatever spell the Maskmaker has you under, I know you're strong enough to fight it. Come back to me, Yue. Please."

The next few seconds may as well last hours, the air around us so thick and heavy I feel as though I'm being crushed. I can't imagine abandoning Yue in Hell. No one deserves this twisted, torturous place—not even a man-eating nine-tailed fox.

She sniffs. Once, twice. Her ears press down flat against her head. Her six eyes crack open one by one, blinking slowly as her tails sweep lazily behind her. She's not fully alert, her movements sluggish. Yue stares up at me, blinking.

"Sonam?" she murmurs, rising onto four unsteady legs. "Where are . . ."

Yue looks around, her delirium quickly fading into something far more horrified. Her gaze snaps back to me, to the walls of the Jade Palace, to her claws now digging into the ground.

"No," she wheezes. The look she gives me is one of utter betrayal. I see heartbreak in them, too. "Why did you wake me? You shouldn't have woken me."

I frown in confusion. "Of course I should have. The Maskmaker was—"

Yue scrapes her claws over her face as if to hide. Or perhaps peel it off. She whimpers, pathetic and helpless, muttering nonsense. "Don't look at me! I can't stand it. You shouldn't have—you shouldn't have!"

Instinctively, I attempt to pry her claws away before she hurts herself. "Calm down. Now isn't the time to lose your head."

She doesn't listen. She instead curls up tightly, using her long tails to sweep around and hide her face. I didn't think it was possible for Yue to look so small. It isn't often that I find myself at a loss, yet I don't know what to do.

Souls are tested against their heart's own paradise, Kelai had said. *To wake and see the truth that all is not as it could be leaves the soul shattered beyond repair.*

"What did he do to you?" I ask, barely above a whisper.

Yue is silent for a long time. For a moment, I wonder if what that rat said earlier about demons being unable to lie was indeed a farce. But then Yue slowly pulls her tails away, her chin resting upon the ground as tears bead down the sides of her face.

"He showed me a life that will never be mine," she replies, her voice breaking into a soft sob. "A life I can never have."

"What was it?" I ask before I can realize how selfish I'm being. What right do I have to the details of her most intimate dreams?

She hesitates, though the answer eventually escapes her lips. "One full of love," she answers bitterly. I've never heard anyone sound more ashamed. Embarrassed, even, for wanting something so simple. So freely given.

Just not for her.

"The Maskmaker is taking his army to the surface," I pivot, unsure what else to say. "We need to get to the gate before them. We can use the shortcut Kelai spoke of. If we're quick, we might be able to beat them there."

Yue says nothing.

"We must seal the gate behind us," I continue, hoping for

something—any reaction. "If his army is released upon the earth, it could be the end of life as we know it."

Even as I say this, I don't expect her to care. What can she do—what can any of us do—in the face of such great evil? Yue has no stake in this fight, only a vow to keep, but maybe that's enough. I need allies wherever I can find them, and I'd rather not have Yue as an enemy.

She stands slowly on all fours, claws digging into the ground. There's a blankness in her eyes, no spark of life.

I'm tempted to reach out. I'm used to patting Wen on the shoulder, giving Sooah's elbow a pinch. Little gestures we've adopted over the years to ease each other's worries. But I don't know what to do when it comes to Yue. I know she's unbelievably strong and fierce—but I can't help but worry that right now, something as small as an act of kindness may break her.

I want to comb my fingers through her fur but resist the impulse. I stand straighter and clear my throat.

"We should get going," I tell her.

Yet again, Yue says nothing.

Before we leave, I stoop down to pick up her discarded mask and tie its fastening strings to my belt. It may be of use, or at the very least, it will make for a fascinating study in my hunting log.

36

Sonam

Hunting Log #397:
She possesses more good than I gave her credit for.

T***he fifth Court of Hell*** has no signs of anyone present. The Court of Despair, Kelai had called it.

There isn't even a star god here to oversee our trial. Instead, we find ourselves standing at the edge of a wide moat, its waters dark and eerie. I can't make out the bottom. It must be deeper than it looks. But the other side is only about half a li out, the high walls of the sixth court standing there as if to goad us into coming over.

"A swim in the waters of Hell, this'll turn out *great*," Wen mumbles, sticking his foot out so that the sole of his boot just barely grazes the water's surface.

"Wait," I tell him.

I reach for one of the small daggers attached to my belt. One of my last. It's taken a lot of damage—the edge is now blunt, and the leather wrapping around the handle is coming loose. It might not hold up during our next battle, but it can at the very least serve me one last time. I toss the dagger as far as I'm able, watching as it sinks into the inky water, leaving ripples in its wake.

Nothing happens. No monsters creep up from the depths, the water doesn't somehow come to life on its own. I should be relieved—but the fact that we're not met with chaos leaves me wholly unsettled.

I glare down at the crude map burned into my palm. The shortcut we're looking for is somewhere on the other side of this moat. All we have to do is get across. I turn to Yue, who is staring blankly into the distance with a slight downward curl to the corners of her lips. Where once she was an inferno threatening to burn me to a crisp, now she's nothing more than a candle flickering at the last of its wick.

My chest tightens.

"Do you know how to swim, Fox?" I ask, my voice so gentle that I sound foreign to my own ears.

"Yes," she murmurs. "Don't worry about me."

But I do worry.

I don't know when it began, this . . . fondness for her. All my life, I've trained to kill her kind. No hesitation, no remorse. Demons are nothing short of a plague; the damage they can cause is immeasurable. I've studied them for years. They're cruel, driven only by an incessant need to devour human souls, and therefore simple-minded and easily felled.

But Yue is far from that. Hungry, yes—I can see it in the way she tracks my movements and discreetly licks the corner of her lips—but there's something soft beneath her jagged, protective layers. Behind her rows of teeth and matted fur and the woman's face she so desperately hides beneath. Her curiosities, her insecurities, her delights, and her displeasures. She lashes out in anger because it's the only response she has in a world that's made her unwelcome.

In a world where *I* have made her unwelcome.

I take a careful step toward Yue, drawn to her like the tide to the moon for which she was named. When she finally looks up at me, there's but a foot of space between us. The dark circles under her six eyes are concerning, the heavy slouch of her shoulders so severe I can feel my own muscles ache in sympathy. My hand moves of its own accord, reaching out so that my fingertips ghost along her muzzle.

Yue doesn't recoil, which I take as a good sign, but I don't miss the way her breath catches and her eyes widen, vulnerable and unsure. She could tear out my heart for this.

Instead, she turns into my palm, the warmth of her fur soaking into mine.

"We're almost there," I whisper. "And then you can be free of me."

I mean it as a jest to ease her tension, but Yue's lip curls before she pulls away completely. "Right," she answers tightly.

Yue advances without us, sinking her front paw into the moat. The embankment's slope is subtle at first, rising to her ankles and then her calves. Sooah and Wen step in after her, and then I follow to bring up the rear, shivering against the obscene chill of the water. Even the harshest winters of the Southern Kingdom couldn't have prepared me for the cold that bites through my skin and freezes my joints.

It isn't until we're all chest deep and treading the surface that I realize this is no ordinary water. Of course it isn't. A simple swim across the fifth Court of Hell would have been far too easy. Even though I kick with all my might, do everything I can to keep my head above water, something strange happens to the moat.

The more we swim, the farther the distant shore appears, the space between us and safety growing with every stroke. Where once the moat was only half a li, now it's grown to two, three—five. The currents turn violent, dragging us beneath tumultuous waves as the water expands into what can only be described as an endless sea.

Wen chokes on foam. I grab onto Sooah's arm to help her stay afloat. And Yue—

My heart plummets.

I've lost sight of her.

Calling her name proves disastrous. Water rushes into my lungs, the heavy taste of salt burning my tongue and throat. I'm dizzy, breathless. *Drowning.* The longer we spend in the icy sea, the more the colors of the world begin to drain away. It's my duty to see my friends to safety, but how am I supposed to do that when I can barely save myself?

So this is why it's called the Court of Despair. A man only has so much fight in him. And neither strength nor bravery is any match for the wrath of the open sea. At the whims of the powerful current, defeat finally claims my heart, drowning out the final inklings of my hope.

Something below grips my ankle.

It yanks with so much force I fear it will tear my whole leg from my hip. There isn't time to take a full breath before my head is completely submerged, water rushing into my nose, clogging my ears, stinging my eyes.

Despite my blurry vision, I can see them—thousands of souls lost to the bottom of the sea, doomed to a perpetual drowning. Their arms reach upward like floating weeds, latching on to us as would starved parasites. They claw at my arms, snatch my hair, wrap their elbows around my throat; all in the hopes of pulling themselves up to the surface.

Instinctively, I reach for one of my remaining weapons. The current is too strong, however, washing them away before I can grasp it. I'm running out of time. Out of air.

There's something peculiar in the water with us. It isn't like any of the other desperate souls trying to use me as a stepping stone to the surface. Only a few feet away, I see the figure of a young man who seems strangely . . . at peace. He makes no effort to swim or struggle. He has given in to his sorrows, allowed his despair to swallow him whole. When I catch sight of his bright white eyes, I suddenly understand who he is.

A star god. The one tasked with governing this forsaken place. It seems he's resigned himself to his seat in Hell.

Something grabs me by the collar. At first, I fear it's yet another one of the damned and forgotten souls, but then comes a sharp scrape along the nape of my neck. I twist just enough to see a pair of fangs, along with six obsidian eyes staring back at me. Yue's managed to nab Wen, Sooah, and I with her teeth. With incredible strength, she kicks and bats at those standing between us and air.

The four of us breach the surface with bone-rattling gasps. It's as much a relief as it is painful, burning all the way down my throat and into my searing lungs. The current is still strong, our muscles cramping with the frigidity of the water. The souls of Hell continue to try to drag us down with them, but Yue fights—against our enemies, against the sea itself. She turns her head and throws us onto her back, freeing up her mouth to bite and maul.

"Hang on!" she yells.

I cling to her fur despite my swollen fingers and water-logged muscles. The distant shore is still several li out, and this wretched trial shows no sign of ending. But Yue doesn't give up. She swims and swims and swims, her head tilted up awkwardly to keep her snout in the air. Sooah, Wen, and I beat back any stray soul who attempts to touch her, combat reduced to nothing more than our fists. We won't let them harm her.

There are moments when I think we might be done for. Yue's pace slows, her breathing frantic and shallow. But the seconds drag into minutes, and minutes into a near hour. I'm impressed by her endurance, but my heart twists knowing she can't possibly last much longer. I stroke her fur, though whether it's for my own reassurance or hers, I cannot say.

Blessedly, and not a second too soon, I finally see the shore and the imposing red walls of the sixth Court of Hell.

Yue hauls us onto dry land with slow, arduous steps, collapsing onto her side with a wheezing cough. I'm quick to kneel at her side, water dripping from my hair and clothes. She trembles violently, the rapid rise and fall of her rib cage alarming.

"Easy, Fox," I say hurriedly, pressing my ear to her chest to listen to her heart. It drums so hard and fast that I can hardly distinguish each individual beat. It's going to give out at this rate. "You have to calm down."

She makes a noise, almost like she's trying to say *can't*, but the word doesn't fully form.

Not knowing what else to do, I lie down next to her, placing Yue's head so that it rests upon my arm. I gingerly stroke the fur behind her ear, press my nose lightly to her muzzle. I don't mind the sight of her jagged teeth.

"It's okay," I whisper, staring into her strikingly deep eyes. "You were magnificent, Yue. Everything's going to be alright. Just *breathe*."

It's no small relief when I feel her pulse begin to slow, her ragged breaths eventually coming under control. Yue's shivering, however, does not stop—I fear she'll succumb to exposure.

Sooah lowers herself onto her knees and lies down behind Yue's arched back. With a cautious stroke of her hand over Yue's fur, Sooah settles in with a sigh. Wen sits next to Yue in a similar fashion, his back pressed up against her matted belly.

When I shoot them a questioning look, Sooah answers, *She kept us warm once. We'll return the favor.*

It's unclear how long the four of us lie there together, exhaustion having carved away at what little we have left. The calm that blankets us is more soothing than sunshine after weeks of earth-moving storms. But I keep an eye on Yue's condition. Her eyelids droop heavily until she can keep them open no more.

"We can't stay here," Wen says, breaking the silence. "The Maskmaker's army's well on the way."

I glance down at my palm. The shortcut Kelai spoke of is close, a servant's corridor somewhere near the outer perimeter of the sixth Court of Hell. Nothing short of a miracle, frankly. Even if the Maskmaker knows his way through Hell, we should be able to beat him to the gates.

I look back at Yue, sound asleep at last. We'll be cutting it close, but I'm sure we can spare at least an hour for her sake. Wen is right, of course, that we can't stay here out in the open. We need to find shelter, stay out of sight until we're ready to move. It's simply a question of how to move Yue without disturbing her. Even with our combined strength, Sooah, Wen, and I can't carry Yue in her fox form.

An idea occurs to me.

With a heavy exhale, I reach for the boy's mask tied to my belt, setting it down on my lap so that I can smear the painted surface. Using my sleeve, I wipe the porcelain clean, surprised at how easily the ink falls away. I reach for the Maskmaker's brush next, unsure how to wield the magic within.

Will it reject me, I wonder? Only a fool would be so brazen as to think they could wield a tool crafted for the gods. Yet I am out of options and desperate enough to try.

It feels like any other calligraphy brush, but when I bring the coarse hairs to the surface of the mask, I'm surprised at the marks it leaves behind. It produces ink all on its own, easily changing color with a mere shift of my intentions. The process is perfectly intuitive, enchanted to bring what I see in my mind's eye to life. I can feel the magic flowing through me, a river of warmth rushing through my veins and into the brush. I feel *blessed*—by the spell, by the paintbrush itself—as if chosen by some higher power to wield it as the gods would.

I'd find enjoyment in the process, were I not so worn down and fearing for our safety.

I refer to the sketches in my notebook. Who knew such a thing would be so handy? I've already made careful study of her, having captured her at various angles, but when I put brush to porcelain, I work from memory, too.

It's not perfect. A copy of a copy. The Maskmaker's rendition was without a single blemish or fault, cold and otherworldly in its appearance. My artistry offers a touch more warmth. Soft curves where once there were hard edges. The palace scholars had an old saying that an artist gives a piece of their soul to each of their works, be it writing, music, or the fine arts. I like to think that by making Yue a new mask, I'm giving her a sliver of what it means to be human.

Once finished, I place the mask upon her face. The magic seeps into her skin, transforming her almost instantaneously into a young woman.

Before, her beauty was arresting. Ethereal. All-consuming.

Now, she casts a soft but undeniable radiance. Her lips are plusher, her nose not as sharp. Her cheeks are full and a sweet pink, her long black hair as smooth as silk.

I'm quick to lift her, one arm bracing her back with the other tucked under her knees. Yue's head settles against my chest, her lips parted just so as she continues to sleep.

I nod to Sooah and Wen. "Scout ahead. I'll carry her."

37

The Maskmaker set them loose on every sun temple they came across—a way to not only feed his new army of foxes, but to disrespect his brother's good name.

Men, women, children—all fell victim to the nine-tailed foxes and the magic of their masks. They were too beautiful for men to deny, so beguiling that women let down their guard, so sweet that children came to them willingly. The foxes would return to him with their bellies full, entire sects and their neighboring villages thoroughly emptied of souls.

The Maskmaker was pleased with his foxes—

Save for one.

The youngest was a curious little beast. She was the runt of the litter: smaller, weaker, and slower than her elder sisters, she had a propensity for watching humans rather than devouring them on sight. He would need to train this strange behavior out of her. If she didn't eat, she would never grow strong.

"Come with me, Yue," he told her one sunny afternoon. Her elder sisters were out on yet another hunt, but the little fox, claiming not to be particularly hungry, declined to join them.

"Where are we going?" she asked as he placed a newly crafted

mask upon her face. The magic took hold and turned her into a beautiful young woman with raven hair and plump red lips.

The Maskmaker, however, did not answer.

He brought her to the outskirts of a small village. It could only boast a few wooden buildings and one main road. The only impressive thing about it was the sea of golden grass that surrounded it, a narrow river winding through like a blue silk ribbon. There were a handful of humans out and about, but Yue's attention was drawn to one in particular: a boy, playing by his lonesome next to the water.

"Your sisters are excellent hunters," the Maskmaker said. "And I would have you be the same."

"He's a child," Yue protested. "I don't like eating children."

"Why not?"

"Because they are small. It's not fair."

"Fair?" the Maskmaker scoffed. "Believe me when I say this world doesn't care about fairness. It doesn't care about those who are weak. Whatever you want, you must take. Remember this, Yue: never pity your food."

The fox eyed the little boy apprehensively. It struck her as odd that his parents were nowhere in sight, nor did he seem to have any friends to play with. Isolated and alone, there was no denying that he would make the perfect meal.

And yet it didn't sit right with her, eating someone so defenseless.

"Don't come back until you've eaten," the Maskmaker said firmly as he turned away to leave. "Or I will tell your sisters."

Yue shifted uncomfortably. She certainly didn't want that. Her sisters teased her often. Told her that a soft heart would one day be her undoing. She didn't want to be the shame of her family. What she needed was to prove herself, to make her sisters proud.

She approached the boy slowly, placing her mask onto her face. It aged her into a beautiful human woman. She forced an unassuming smile upon her lips. "Hello, little one. What are you doing all the way out here?"

The boy looked up at her with large, innocent eyes the same color as axinite. Although he seemed surprised to see her, he didn't appear to be alarmed. "I'm playing," he said.

"All alone?"

"My brothers don't like me, and A-Ma is sick."

Yue tilted her head to the side, amused by the boy's unfiltered honesty. Weren't human children taught not to speak with strangers? "I can play with you, if you'd like."

His face brightened. "Really?"

"What's your name, little one?"

The boy beamed proudly. "You can call me Sonam."

38

Sonam

Hunting Log #398:
What is this pain in my chest when I look upon her?
Why does my heart race when she draws near?

Demons ahead, ***Sooah informs us.***

We've got our backs pressed up against the outer wall of the sixth Court of Hell, peeking out from around the corner to get a better view of what lies ahead. Unexpectedly for the pits of hell, only row after row of stone houses sit before us, their windows and doors all boarded shut with planks of wood. A ghost town. I wonder where the path we seek is within these empty houses.

"Are you sure this is the way?" a snake demon hisses, a porcelain mask of a young man's face tied to the side of his head. "How did we lose the others?"

"It's because this moron thought he smelled a human," grumbles the ox demon standing just beside, snorting angrily at the monkey rounding out the group. The strap of his mask, one of a little girl, is tied around his thick forearm.

The monkey, whose mask of a feeble old man hangs from around his neck, scratches his head, turning around to inspect the area. We duck out of the way before he can catch sight of us. "But I could have sworn—"

"We have to catch up," the snake insists, already slithering its way down one of the rows. "Who cares if there are stray humans around? There will be plenty to eat soon."

When the trio finally walks off, I exhale as slowly and silently as possible. If it had come down to a confrontation, we might have been able to hold our own, but I'd rather not risk putting Yue in harm's way. Not now that she's so intensely vulnerable. What she needs is a place to lie comfortably, get a few hours of deep rest. If there are demons lingering around, it means the Maskmaker can't be too far ahead of us. We're catching up, and soon, we'll be able to sneak around and get ahead.

Everything's going according to plan.

What if it doesn't? asks a tiny voice in the back of my skull.

Doubt is nothing to despise. In fact, it's a huntsman's greatest tool. To always be on guard, to always be thinking of alternate plans—it's the thin line that differentiates between those who survive and those who end up buried.

But this time, there is no room for error. Not with the fate of the mortal realm, and perhaps even the Heavens above, hanging in the balance.

"See if you can pry those boards off the window," I tell Sooah and Wen. "We can't stay out in the open. They might double back."

We waste no time. Sooah and Wen rip the planks off, the rusty nails holding them in place offering up little resistance. Wen's the one who pokes his head in through the gap in the window to take a look at the interior.

"Is the coast clear?" I ask.

"Er . . . sort of," he replies, sounding heavily unsure. "Come see for yourself."

Cradling Yue in my arms, I step forward and peer inside the

stone house. It's plainly furnished, the tables and chairs crafted from light-grained wood. A thick layer of dust coats every available surface, an uninterrupted field of snow. For the most part, the house looks completely abandoned.

And then I notice the strange beings huddled together in the corner.

A family of souls appearing to watch us. Unlike the human souls we've encountered, these are nearly shapeless and lack any distinctive features. I can discern the outline of heads, and maybe arms, but they otherwise resemble shadows. I can tell that they've been here a long time given that they, too, are covered in dust.

I don't get the sense that they're hostile. Then again, I don't get the sense of much of anything from them. They're just . . . there. Defeated and fearful.

And then there's the Court of Fear, Kelai had said, *where most souls are haunted by their biggest regrets.*

"They won't harm us," I decide aloud, carefully transferring Yue to Sooah so that I can free up my arms to climb inside. Once my feet are planted, I take Yue back, holding on to her protectively.

As I suspected, the shades don't move toward us. If anything, they seem to press themselves up against the corner, cowering.

I take in our surroundings. This house can only boast a small gathering area and a single bedroom shunted off toward the back. Neither Sooah nor Wen argue when I take Yue directly there.

"Seal the way," I instruct them. "We won't be here long, but we best not risk any unwanted surprises."

Wen nods. "But what about these things?" he asks, gesturing to the shades. "They're unnerving."

"Keep an eye on them, but leave them be."

I nudge the thin wooden door to the bedroom open with my foot, relieved to see that there's a small bed to lay Yue on. There are no pillows or blankets in sight, but it's as good a place to rest as any. Given all we've been through, a safe place to sleep and four walls for privacy is, frankly, a luxury.

I sit on the edge of Yue's bed and watch her sleep, observing and then admiring the slow rise and fall of her chest as she breathes. I absentmindedly reach out to brush a few strands of hair from her face, noting the curl of her lashes and the gentle slope of her nose. The mask I painted for her is nothing short of a marvel, but that's not why I'm transfixed.

She once terrified me. And in some ways, she terrifies me still. But now it's not her teeth or her claws or her tongue lashings I fear, but that my heart is beginning to crave her warmth, the feel of her fingers pressed against mine, the fleeting glances she thinks I haven't noticed.

At the end of the day, I'm still a hunter. What will become of us when we finally leave this place?

If Yue returns to the mortal realm with us, there's no question that she'd have to return to the hunt. I'd be condemning innocent humans to her jaws.

She is at her most vulnerable now. To save those innocents, all I'd have to do is reach for one of my daggers and be through with it. But guilt won't let me do that, not after everything we've been through and everything she's done for us.

As I wrestle with my heart and my duty, a terrible pressure grows behind my eyes.

I don't know what to do. I don't deserve to sit by her side.

"Careful, Captain. You look like your head's about to burst."

I glance down at Yue and chuckle softly. Her eyes are open a crack. "What are you talking about?" I ask. "I always look like this."

She rolls onto her side to face me better, our hands barely a whisper apart. "You'll lose your hair if you don't manage your stress better," she murmurs. Yue lifts her little finger, and I reply by brushing the pad of my thumb along her fingertip.

"How long was I asleep?"

"We have time."

"That's not what I asked."

"I know, but I'm telling you that we have time."

She sighs. "Sonam, I'm—"

"How are you feeling?" I ask, unsure why my heart insists on pounding so loudly. A part of me is worried that Yue can hear it, her ears no doubt sharper than most.

She presses her lips into a thin line. "I'm cold."

I take her hand, carefully threading my fingers between hers. "Better?"

She shakes her head. "Still cold."

I pull my legs up onto the small bed and lie down next to her, holding her hand flat against my chest. There's still a whisper of space between us, yet that gap might as well be an endless void because I'm nowhere as close as I wish to be. "And now?" I ask, my throat uncharacteristically tight.

She slips her hand out from beneath mine and reaches up, using her fingers to trace over my chin. Her cheeks are flushed pink. "Much better," she murmurs. "Although . . . "

"Yes?"

Yue visibly swallows. Her stomach grumbles—and rather loudly at that—answering on her behalf. "I'm sorry," she says, shaking her head slightly. "Don't mind me."

"But I do," I say. "I mind you a great deal." I tilt my head to the side, exposing my neck to her. "If you're hungry—"

"Don't—"

"It's willingly given," I interject.

Her face turns bright-red, her brows pulling together into a frown. "You've gone mad. Do you know how easily I could kill you?"

"You won't." I peer deeply into her eyes, not searching so much as letting her in. "I trust you."

"A grave mistake."

"Yue," I say firmly but not unkindly.

Her gaze flits down to my pulse point, her breathing shallow and tight. "I don't want to hurt you," she confesses. Admittedly something I never thought I'd hear a demon say. "And it *will* hurt, Sonam. If you insist that I eat, you can give me your palm again."

"We both know that wasn't enough for you. You can have your fill this way."

"Has anyone ever told you that talking to you is like talking to a wall?"

"I could say the same to you."

"Are you always this stubborn?"

"A trait we share, it seems."

With a sigh, Yue rolls toward me, delicately pressing a hand against my far shoulder for stability. She leans in slowly. Unsure. The warmth of her breath tickles the thin skin of my neck, sending goosebumps trailing down my arms.

I never could have imagined myself in this position. To not only be this close to a demon, but to allow her to feed of my own accord. And yet, as Yue presses her lips to the crook of my neck, I don't panic. I don't even reach for one of my weapons in case she loses control.

Her teeth dig into my flesh, sending shards of glass shooting up my spine to barrage the inside of my skull. As a fox, she might have ripped the side of my throat away with her fangs, but this is little more than a puncture. The pain fades quickly into numbness. It's strange, in a way, knowing what I know. A demon's prey rarely lasts long, and yet I feel perfectly fine. Could it be that Yue's being gentle for my sake?

When she throws a leg over, straddling my hips, I know I've spoken too soon. She presses her full weight against me, pinning me on my back. Yue drinks greedily. Her teeth sink in deeper, her searing tongue swiping against my neck. Every gulp she takes comes with a pleasured, breathy moan. And although the sound ignites a firestorm within my veins, I dare not name the sensation.

Yue pulls away with a gasp, her mouth coming away crimson. She runs her tongue over her lips, careful to lick up every last drop. Her cheeks are flushed and her pupils blown wide. Yue looks every bit as wild as she is bewitching as she brings a hand up to apply steady pressure to staunch the bleeding, the pad of her thumb grazing along the line of my jaw.

Gods, she is a sight.

"Better?" I ask.

She nods. "Much."

I can't help but stare at her mouth. There's a strange heat growing in my core. It's terrible. And I crave it all the more.

"Will you tell me a tale?" she asks, her long lashes fluttering closed. Yue continues to lie atop me, resting her head against my chest.

"Which one?" I bring a hand up to find a lock of her hair, absentmindedly twisting it around my finger.

"Whatever comes to mind."

"A tragedy, then," I murmur, "of Houyi and Chang'e. Houyi shot down nine of the ten stars to keep the world from burning. He was awarded an elixir of immortality by the gods for his heroic deeds. Little did they know he didn't do it for anyone's sake other than his beloved. It was for this reason that fate decided to take a twisted turn, sending someone to steal what he loved most. Believing the elixir to be under threat, Chang'e drank every last drop rather than see it fall into the wrong hands. The magic within flew her away to the moon—and in that one moment, what Houyi loved most was stolen from him forever.

"He spent the rest of his life searching for a way to bring her back. He sought council with the land's wisest shamans and pleaded with the gods—but all to no avail. Houyi spent the rest of his years looking longingly up at the moon, setting out cakes and sweets Chang'e once enjoyed on Earth in offering. On the night he finally passed, it is said that the moon shone twice as bright and full so that he could look up one last time and know his moon goddess was watching over him."

"Yet another love story," she says, once I've concluded.

"As I said, every story is a love story."

Yue curls in a bit closer, the tips of our toes brushing up against one another. "I wonder what it's like," she whispers. "To be loved by someone so much that they'd be willing to kill the stars for you."

"Poets have tried putting it into words for centuries."

"But what about you? What does the great Captain Sonam think it means to be loved?"

I pause, turning her question over in my mind, though there is hardly a neat, simple explanation. "It's a great many things, I think. To be loved is to be seen. To be accepted. To be not only wanted but needed."

"Must be nice," she mumbles, her lips barely grazing my own as she speaks. It's not a kiss, not quite.

But I want it to be.

"What is this spell you have me under?" I whisper, more to myself than to her.

She laughs softly. "This is no spell."

"Yue, I . . . " I set my jaw, swallowing hard. The right words won't come to mind. As much as I want to lean forward and claim her lips for my own, I resist with just as much adamance.

Because there is only one truth: No matter how I yearn to know her touch, it doesn't change what we are. A demon and her hunter. What love could we ever hope to share?

Our hearts are made of different metals, hers forged from gold and mine from silver. We're destined to clash. Perhaps not now, when the light is dim and we're desperate for each other's warmth, but someday—and soon. We are reluctant allies here in Hell, but once we return to the surface, that is over.

We cannot change what we were born to be.

"I'm sorry. I—"

"It's fine," she says, pulling away.

The sudden distance between us leaves me empty. I expect to look up and see dejection. Rage. *Hurt*. Instead, I'm greeted with a resigned smile. And somehow, that's a million times worse, because it means she knows, just as I know, that we were never meant to be.

"We should get going," Yue whispers. She stands and leaves, stealing all the warmth of the room along with her.

39

Sonam

Hunting Log #399:
Almost there.

Are you hungry, Yue?

When Sooah says Yue's name, she uses the same sign as she does to indicate the moon as shorthand. She holds up a few scraps of jerked beef as we walk, but Yue shakes her head. Sooah takes Yue's hand and places the scraps in her palm anyway.

"Thank you," Yue says with a sigh. "Can you teach me how to sign that?"

The corners of Sooah's eyes crinkle as she smiles. She demonstrates, resting the open palm of her left hand over the closed fist of her right. Yue copies the motion.

"I guess ye really can teach an old dog new tricks," Wen says.

Yue laughs dryly. "Keep that up and I'll bite your nose off."

"Liar."

"You think I won't?"

Wen chuckles. "Deep down, I think you like me more than you care to admit."

Yue scrunches up her face as if smelling something repugnant. "Don't kid yourself. I barely tolerate your existence."

I'd take her at her word, Sooah says with a grin.

I'm the one to break up the conversation with a loud clearing of my throat. I come to an abrupt halt, looking around before glancing down at my palm. The welts have all but faded away, leaving a lone dot on the pad of my palm. We've followed the outer edge of the sixth Court of Hell, making sure not to venture too far in lest we somehow stumble our way into its trial.

"This is it," I inform the group.

"Are you sure?" Wen asks, an eyebrow arched skeptically.

I can't exactly blame him. I see no obvious entrance here. Just a high wall to our left, the rows of abandoned houses to our right, and nothing much in between. No gates, no doorways, no tunnels. Could this be another of the star goddess's tricks?

"Let me see."

It's Yue who speaks, her words soft as she takes a step toward me. She doesn't wait for permission. She takes my hand and inspects my skin with a furrow knitting her brow. My chest tightens. We haven't spoken a word to one another since we left the abandoned house. Where I might once have relished her silence, now it makes me anxious. By keeping her at arm's length, I've somehow bruised my own soul.

It's the only explanation for the way my heart twists when Yue refuses to meet my gaze; for the chill that slithers down my spine when she turns away without further acknowledgment. I was the one to put up the walls between us, but it is she who now reinforces them.

I tell myself it was the right decision. It had to be.

Yue sniffs the air, her eyes eventually settling on the jade tiles beneath our feet. She tilts her head to the side, contemplative, before tapping her foot. "There's a draft beneath us," she explains. "Does the Jade Palace in the mortal realm boast servant's corridors?"

Jun used to speak of the network of underground tunnels the servants used to get from one pavilion to the next like ghosts beneath the royal family's feet. How I wished to explore them, though Jun warned me that if I ventured down where I didn't belong, I'd get lost with no hope of return. It was a scary enough prospect that I soon abandoned the idea.

"They do," I reply.

We search the ground together, prodding tiles to see if any come loose. It takes us a few minutes, but we finally discover a cluster of four tiles that shift beneath our weight. Bending down, we lift one tile each, exposing a dark tunnel burrowed just beneath. The hole is exceedingly narrow, no wider than the length between my elbow and the tip of my middle finger. It's difficult to determine how far the tunnel goes or how steep the drop could be, but it's clear those aren't the most pressing issues.

There's no way I'm going to fit, Sooah laments. *None of us will. We'll suffocate down there.*

"What do you suggest, then? It's not like we have another choice."

We have the choice not to die beneath the Jade Palace, Sooah argues.

It's unlike them to bicker—perhaps Hell is changing us for the worse.

"Enough," I say tersely. "I have an idea."

I reach for my hunting log and rip out a few blank pages from the back. This will be an excellent test to see if the magic works on any type of canvas. I retrieve the Maskmaker's paintbrush and search my mind for sources of inspiration. Sooah's right. There's no way the four of us will fit through the tight servant's tunnels.

Four young children, on the other hand . . .

I can recall being around very few children in my life. My brothers were never around, several years older than me and therefore too busy with their studies to tolerate my existence. Even more so after I was sent away to live in one of my father's distant summer homes. Hidden away, along with my mother, as a disgrace. I was raised by a handful of maids and eunuchs, but there were precious few people my own age.

I recall one of the stable boys in training. I had wanted to be his friend, but he was always too anxious to play. I paint his face on the first piece of paper, scouring my memories to capture every little detail. When I'm done, I hand the freshly painted mask to Wen.

The next face I recall belonged to a servant girl. She was kind, if I remember correctly, though I rarely saw her. She was as quiet as a mouse and just as small—which I realize now will certainly work out in our favor. I paint the next mask, making sure to count out the three moles I remember so distinctly on the right side of her face before giving my newest creation to Sooah.

As for my own mask, what better choice of a visage than my own? I'm certainly familiar enough with it to paint a younger self-portrait.

Now, for the last and final.

I look up at Yue, disheartened to find her still staring off at nothing. She's a wilting flower, the slump of her shoulders and the droop of her head giving her whole body an unnatural lean to the side. I can't explain the terrible ache in my chest when I look at her.

I paint her mask with care, choosing the face of one of my earliest friends. A very distant cousin I haven't seen in many years. She was married off decades ago to a minor lord in the far north, but I still remember those precious summers spent under the care of the same history tutor. Cousin Xiao was always quite small for her age, a fact that will no doubt serve us well.

Approaching slowly, I clear my throat to catch Yue's attention.

"Will you wear this for me?" I ask. My words come out a near whisper, as if I'm afraid to disturb her mournful contemplation.

Yue sighs, nodding wearily. "Yes."

She removes her mask and allows me to trade it for another without protest. While I'm mindful of her true form, I'm by no means as afraid of it as I once was. I tie her other mask to my belt for safekeeping.

I don my mask and marvel at my own transformation. I've observed magic—rituals conducted by the palace shamans, my own demonic oath between me and Yue—but never before have I used it on myself. A warmth buzzes through my veins as the mask adheres to my face, sticking to my skin with a consistency close to honey.

The world around me grows larger, or perhaps it is I who shrinks. I peer down at my hands, watching with wide-eyed fascination as they transform into those of a boy barely out of adolescence. My clothes have changed, as well, lending themselves to my full disguise. I recognize the light blue robes I'm in—silks befitting a young prince. Gone are the hard edges of my thirty years. I bring a hand up to feel. My stubble-lined jaw is now smooth, my cheeks plump and round. I have even lost the aches and creaks of my joints, practically brimming with a youthful energy I thought long since tempered.

Sooah's and Wen's transformations are amazing, as well. A stranger might easily mistake us for a band of misfits. We'll be able to slip through the tunnels with ease. What truly spectacular magic.

I catch Yue staring at me. There's a slight furrow to her brow—or rather, my cousin's brow.

"Is something wrong?" I ask.

"That face you're wearing. It looks . . . familiar."

Behind us, Wen snorts. "Probably some poor kid you ate."

"I've never eaten a child," she answers curtly, as if the suggestion is an insult.

"It's my own," I tell her. "From when I was a boy."

Yue blinks, something flashing across her features. After a moment, she laughs. "Truly?"

"Yes."

She shakes her head with a gentle smile. "I'm glad you grew up to be such a good man."

I frown at her in confusion. What does she mean by that?

I'll go first, Sooah signs. *To make sure the path is clear.*

Wen follows shortly after. I watch my friends lower themselves into the hole, their shoulders scraping along the sides, before they disappear underground. I listen closely, sighing with relief when I hear both of them land.

"Are you alright?" I call down to them.

"We're fine! An awful drop, though, so be careful," Wen shouts back.

An odd sense of pride flows through me knowing the masks I've created work well. The thrill of creating any face I please rushes to my head.

I approach the edge of the hole and pause, turning to look at Yue. She hasn't moved an inch. I reach out to her reflexively. "Are you coming?"

Her lips part as if to respond, only to seal shut again. She eventually nods, though she walks past without taking my hand. Ignoring the sting at the back of my throat, I follow her down into the gloomy dark.

40

Yue

Hunting Log #400:
Curse my pride—I should have kissed her.

T***here's only enough space in*** the tunnel for us to follow one another in single file, crouched over slightly to avoid scraping our heads on the dirt ceiling above. Without our masks, we would never have fit. There is no light to work with, so we trudge forward in complete darkness, nothing but the walls at our sides to alert us of any turns.

Although I'm only barely able to sense his form in front of me, I'm aware of how frequently Sonam throws me a glance over his shoulder, as if worried I'll fall behind.

"Something's up ahead," Wen informs from the front of the line. His voice has become laughably squeaky with adolescence. "I think I see the light."

I bite my tongue. That's not as comforting to hear as he thinks.

The climb out is nowhere as steep as the sudden drop of the tunnel's entrance, so we're able to crawl out one by one with little difficulty. Sooah is the first to pull off her mask, panting as sweat drips down her face. Her large shoulders tremble as she stands to full height, no doubt elated to be free of the tunnels' tight quarters. Wen and Sonam take their masks off, too, looking relieved.

Before us lies a steep staircase leading up to the main pavilion of the monumental Jade Palace. I count at least ten flights, each separated by wide landings. At the very top sits a massive circular moon door. Three serpentine dragons are carved into the stone framework, the finer details of their eyes, claws, and teeth painted in gold. They glare down at us in judgment, as if daring us to complete our ascent.

At long last, we've reached the innermost circle of Hell, standing before the legendary gates to the mortal plane.

I take off my mask and toss it to Sonam, who easily catches it. I stretch out into my fox form, flexing my claws and uncurling my tails, grateful to no longer be cramped in the tunnels.

"I suppose farewells are in order," I say, attempting to keep my tone light. "Since I've had just about enough of you all."

Wen approaches me first. "You know," he mumbles, "I had you pegged all wrong. You're not so bad, Fox."

"I suppose you could be worse, too," I reply with a smile.

Sooah is the next to step toward me. *Thank you,* she signs before reaching up to scratch behind both my ears. She presses an affectionate kiss to the side of my muzzle. Sooah then brings three fingers up to her cheek, bending them like claws before rotating her wrist.

"What does that one mean?" I ask.

"She's calling you her big sister," Sonam translates.

Warmth blooms in my chest. Embarrassingly, my tails wag behind me, betraying my thoughts outright. I've never been anyone's big sister before, but if there's anyone for whom I'd be willing, it is Sooah.

They turn toward their captain expectantly. Sonam couldn't appear more uncomfortable even if he tried.

"I would like a moment alone with her," he says gruffly, his gaze cast to the ground.

Sooah and Wen shuffle off toward the staircase leading up to the gate, though they can't go very far. It's a good thing they weren't hired as spies, because they do not possess an ounce of subtlety. Sonam makes several false starts, clearly struggling to put his thoughts to words.

I offer him a reprieve. "You don't have to say anything—"

"I want to."

I shift uneasily. "Speak plainly, then." I know I won't want to hear his next words.

Sonam casts his gaze down, his dark eyes swimming in conflict. "Once we've warned the king and dealt with the Maskmaker . . . I want you to run. As far as the uncharted lands in the west, if you must."

I flinch. "You're sending me away?"

"You know this is the only way I can protect you," he says. "Once this fight is won and the king commands it . . . I will have no choice, should our paths cross again. I'm asking you—" Sonam takes a deep breath and lowers his voice to a whisper. "I am *pleading* with you: do not force my hand."

I should have expected as much. Sonam is too honorable, too stubborn—which also happen to be his best traits—for this to have gone any other way. It's even worse that his eyes speak an entirely different tale from his words.

It occurs to me then, how accustomed I've become to the harsh lines of his face. We've been in Hell for far too long, because I can no longer recall a time before Sonam marched so fiercely into my life. Where I resigned myself to my loneliness, I've grown spoiled through his companionship. Now he wants me to leave, and I cannot find enough anger to fault him, because there is no fault at all. He is right. Sonam is protecting me.

And breaking my heart all the same.

"Is that truly what you want?" I ask, so softly I barely hear myself. "To never see me again?"

There is much that can be learned in a man's silence. The next few moments are as suffocating as they are cold.

"Yue, I—"

A snarl interrupts him. Not my own, but from somewhere a distance behind us in the darkness. My ears twitch and my eyes go wide. I can smell them coming.

Demons. Too many to count.

They emerge from the shadows like ink drawn from wrung cloth, coming at us in one massive tidal wave.

"Up the stairs!" I scream at the humans, but they reach for their weapons instead.

We are easily overpowered. At close range, Wen's bow is rendered useless. It takes seven demons to pin Sooah down. I'm outnumbered and overwhelmed. With every head I bite off, it feels as though two more grow in the place of the fallen. My captain fights with every ounce of ferocity that I've come to expect from him, cutting his way through beast after beast in the hopes of coming to my aid.

"What are you doing?" I growl, my teeth no doubt coated in black. "Get out of here!"

Before he can respond, an imposing shadow looms over Sonam, bringing with it a terrible chill. The Maskmaker, pure fury in his eyes and a manic grin ripping at his lips. He wraps his hands around Sonam's throat and squeezes with a vengeance, his forward momentum sweeping the captain off his feet. I try to get to him, but the demons won't let up, practically climbing over one another at the chance to tear at my flesh.

"You have something of mine," the Maskmaker seethes. "First Yue steals my mask, then *you* steal my brush. You two really are of a kind."

"Get off of him!" I scream over the rush of blood past my ears. Sonam struggles furiously, throwing every strike and kick he can manage—to no avail.

"Did you think you were in the clear?" The Maskmaker laughs darkly. "I bet you thought you were clever, using those tunnels. Did you ever stop to wonder how I escaped Hell all those centuries ago? I dug those with my bare hands; dug until my fingernails peeled back and my skin was raw. But I did it. I escaped this wretched place. Escaped *Death*. If you thought you could give me the slip, you're an even bigger fool than I thought."

"Enough of your drivel," Sonam growls through gritted teeth.

The captain twists his body to the side, snatching up the dagger end of his rope dart to drive it into the Maskmaker's cheek. The star god flinches back, a massive hole opening in the side of his face as he does. Not a killing blow, but still just as satisfying to witness. Sonam wastes no time and stabs the Maskmaker again, blade sinking into his shoulder with a wet *thud*, red blooming from his fine clothes like a springtime azalea. The Maskmaker throws him off in a rage.

I snatch a demon up by the throat and shred it to pieces, throwing its limp body aside. "Sooah!" I shout. "Wen! Get him out of here!" They help him to his feet, but Sonam still has fight in him. I come up behind them before turning to face the onslaught. "I'll hold them off for as long as I can. Don't forget your promise to me, Wen."

Together, he and Sooah grab the captain by either arm and drag him toward the gate.

"Wait!" he shouts. "No, we can't—*Yue*!"

I look back at Sonam, desperately wishing I could hate him. It would be easier to part that way—if I hated him, I could accept that this is the last time I will ever see him.

"Go," I urge. "It's your only chance."

They drag him, kicking and screaming, out of Hell.

The blood oath we made now stands fulfilled.

41

Although the Maskmaker commanded her to, Yue did not eat the boy that day. Nor the day after, nor the next.

She was simply too fond of the child: The vibrant stories he would share. The assortment of hand-carved toys he would bring to show her. Yue had never met a human quite so energetic, so curious. Sonam was nothing like how the Maskmaker described humans to be, cruel and fearful and bloodthirsty. Creatures who lashed out at the faintest sign of a threat. If he was wrong about this, what else could he be wrong about?

On one fine morning, they spent the hours drawing together beneath the shade of a large ginkgo tree. Yue's hands were shaky, unused to holding things between her slender human fingers. These tools that humans used—paintbrushes—were very similar to the one the Maskmaker so often used.

"I'm going to send this one to my father," Sonam proclaimed, holding up his newest creation. A landscape painting, awash with a beautiful array of colors. Though she found the concept of art strange, Yue knew the boy had an undeniable talent.

"Do you not live with your father?" she asked.

The boy shook his head. "He lives far away from here in a palace made of jade."

She raised her brows. "What's a palace?"

Sonam laughed, bright and bubbly. "You're funny. A palace is a really big house. As big as a city, even!"

The fox's heart skipped a beat. A house as big as a city? She could hardly imagine it.

"I'm going to live with him one day," Sonam continued. "With my father and all my brothers."

"Why don't you live with them now?"

"I haven't proven myself yet."

Yue frowned deeply, terribly confused. Was this a common practice among humans? To shun their little ones until, by some arbitrary measure, they were deemed worthy enough to live with the pack?

"I'm sure that day will come," she said.

Sonam set his painting aside and smiled up at her. "I really hope—"

The fox smelled trouble well before she saw it. The Maskmaker. She spotted him across the clearing, hidden beneath the shadow of a drooping tree. Watching for her to complete her task.

But how could she go through with it? The boy was innocent. He had a long life ahead of him. It didn't seem right.

"Run on home," she told Sonam.

"But you said you'd play with me today."

"I'm sorry. I have something important to attend to, but I'll see you again."

"Do you promise?"

Her tongue felt heavy. She could not lie. But if she didn't know how things would unfold, could she truly be faulted when she nodded and said, "Yes. I promise."

Yue did not return to the Maskmaker until she was sure the boy was well out of sight. She approached with caution, wary of her master's brewing ire.

"You are so different from your sisters," he said, tone brimming with disappointment. "Give me your mask."

She did as she was told, removing the magic that concealed her true form so well. Her ears were pressed back, her tails tucked between her legs. It was the first time that Yue truly knew fear.

The Maskmaker pursed his lips and whistled sharply. Her elder sisters emerged from the shadows of the jungle, a terrible tension sizzling in the air.

"Why didn't you just eat him, Yue?" Qin asked her.

"You could have finished him in one bite," said Ahn.

"You'll starve to death if this keeps up," muttered Nuying.

"Leave her alone," snapped Lu, normally so softspoken. "I'm sure she had her reasons."

The Maskmaker shook his head. "That won't do," he argued. "Remember the oath we made. This *is what happens when you disobey me."*

With a snap of his fingers, fire erupted across Yue's face. It burned so hot that the flames appeared blue, singing through her fur and flesh even as she screeched in agony. She tried to put the fire out, jerking her head from side to side. She scraped at her face with her own claws, smashed her head into the dirt to stifle the fire. Yue could hear her sisters, all of them screaming, crying, pleading with the Maskmaker to stop.

After a minute, he snapped his fingers again, the fire threatening to eat its way through her bones snuffed out like a candle left out in a maelstrom. It was then that the family of foxes realized their mistake.

They hadn't struck a deal with a god, but the devil.

"Let that be a lesson," the Maskmaker said icily. "The rest of you, finish what your sister could not. Devour the whole village and leave no soul behind."

The foxes made no effort to move. How dare he order them around after harming their beloved little sister? They were a pack, a family; and threats against family, without question, were to be eliminated. The eight of them pounced with teeth bared and claws extended. The moment they dared touch their master—

They all turned to ash.

Yue could only watch as her sisters erupted into flames and just as quickly crumbled away, scattering upon the wind's breath. It took her a moment to comprehend what she'd just seen, to understand the finality of it. When they'd sworn their oaths, they had not exchanged their unwavering obedience for masks, as she first believed. Instead, it was a vow never to turn on their master. To attack him was to break their oaths—which, in the end, would destroy them.

The Maskmaker scoffed as he brushed ash off his clothes. "Now I must start all over again," he said with a heavy sigh. "No matter. This time, I know exactly where to begin."

Yue was frozen, drowning in grief, fear, and rage. Instinct told her to lash out, to take her own revenge, but if she so much as harmed a hair upon the Maskmaker's head, her demise would be just as swift as those of her sisters. So long as they both breathed, she was bound by the oath she made.

So she did the only thing she could think of.

Yue snatched up her mask and ran.

42

Sonam

Hunting Log #401:
It can't end like this.

Silver moonlight. A cool breeze. The soft orange glow of paper lanterns. All normally gentle, unassuming things I would have taken for granted, but after so much time spent in the expansive dark with nothing but the eerie green glow of Hell's Jade Palace, it's almost too much.

I'm on my hands and knees upon the polished tiles of the palace courtyard, sucking in long, deep breaths. Sooah and Wen are on either side of me, just as winded. We were running for our lives not a moment ago. I'm on edge, my mind still racing. I never thought peace and tranquility could be so unsettling.

"Sonam?" calls a gruff voice.

Shakily, I look up, confused to find my father looking down at me, a notch between his brows. He's still dressed in his flowing golden robes. My elder brothers are also here, staring at me with matching confusion. The palace shamans stand just to my right, bowls of ritualistic burnings still in hand from when we banished

Yue to Hell. It's as though we never left the mortal realm in the first place.

"How—how long were we gone?" I rasp. My throat is shredded. I've screamed myself raw.

It's the king who speaks. "But a blink of an eye. One moment you were falling, and the next, you reappeared here."

My heart rails against my rib cage. Overwhelmed. Disoriented. What were we running from, again? What urgent news sits so heavily on my tongue? My thoughts are scrambled, nearly impossible to decipher.

"Demons," I mutter. And then, in a breathless whisper, *"Yue."*

"What's he blathering about?" one of my brothers, Zhong, says, raising an eyebrow from above his large silk fan.

I struggle to my feet, desperate to have my father hear me. "You must prepare your soldiers. There's an army of demons coming from Hell. They'll eat everyone in their path if we don't stop them here and now."

"He's lost his mind," one of the palace advisors scoffs loudly.

"You dare make demands of His Majesty?" snaps Han, my second-eldest brother. With Jun gone, he's the one who now holds the title of Crown Prince, destined for the throne.

"Listen to me!" I hiss. "I was down there. I saw them with my very eyes. They're coming in the thousands. Sooah and Wen know it to be true!"

They both nod furiously, just as eager as I to get the message across.

What starts as unnerved chuckling in the courtyard erupts into incredulous laughter.

"He's gone completely mad!"

"Has Hell scrambled your brains, little brother?"

"An army of demons? Do you intend to return to the Jade Palace as court jester?"

"There isn't any time for this!" I shout. "Yue won't be able to hold them off for much longer."

"Yue?" my father says. "Who is this Yue you keep speaking of?"

I can't breathe. Every time I try to inhale, the air is so cold it slices its way through my lungs. "The nine-tailed fox," I wheeze. "She's the one who—"

Who sacrificed herself for us.

For me.

This is as cruel as it is unfair. They're not only laughing at my efforts, but Yue's, as well. If it weren't for her, we might never have made it out of Hell. They don't understand that she's the only one who's given humanity a fighting chance—a chance I won't allow them to squander.

"We need archers at every post," I say. "And we must evacuate the city. The demons will wear masks to appear human. If they manage to escape into the population, it will be impossible to tell friend from foe."

"Someone call the palace doctor," my brother Sìzi chides with a grating over-importance. "The *captain* needs his head checked."

My frustration gets the better of me. I charge at him, punching my brother with such force that I feel the pain lance through my knuckles and up my arm. It feels good to finally shut him up. If I can force him and all the rest into silence, perhaps then they will finally take heed.

But then guards surround us, dragging me off my sniveling brother. He spits out a few of his teeth, the gaping holes in his grimace bringing me only a sliver of satisfaction.

"Throw them in the dungeons," the king commands. "Their time in Hell has clearly driven them mad."

"You have to listen to me!" I scream at the top of my lungs. "They're coming! *They're coming!*"

If they expected this jailing to go smoothly, they should have done the smart thing and knocked me out beforehand.

It takes five of them to hold me down, face pressed against the damp floor of the palace dungeons, as one of them hastily pries my weapons off my person. They even take my hunting log and my paintbrush, removing any possibility of me having an object to beat them senseless with.

I get a good punch in at one point, and certainly a well-placed kick, but before I know it, the palace guards shove me into a cell made of thick iron bars and slam the door in my face. Sooah and Wen are similarly thrown into their own cells on the other side of the room.

There's a ringing in my ears. My muscles are so tight they threaten to snap. I pace around my cell, not that there's much room to begin with. I reach the back of it in little more than four steps.

"You know," Wen mumbles, "yelling our heads off about the demon army probably wasn't a good idea."

Sooah sighs heavily, as if to say, *Shut up.*

"They don't understand what we saw," I grumble. "What we know is coming."

Yue can't hold the Maskmaker and his army off forever—I try not to think about what will happen when they overtake her. If the king and the rest of the Jade Palace won't listen, then we'll have to do this on our own. But how?

If Yue were here, she would doubtlessly have chewed or slammed her way through the bars and barreled through the palace by now. But she isn't, and I can't rely on her strength to see us out of this. If only I were smaller, I could slip through the bars . . .

I notice our confiscated items piled high on a rickety wooden table to the right of my cell. It's well out of reach, but I have to try.

I lean against the bars and squeeze my arm through the narrow gap, desperately stretching my fingers in the hopes of grasping on to something. Anything. I can see the Maskmaker's paintbrush sitting near the edge of the table, but it sits at an angle, pinned down by the weight of our weapons and my hunting log. Sweat drips from my brow. Every muscle in my body strains, burning with the effort.

The tips of my fingers just barely graze the end of the brush's handle when the ground suddenly shakes. All around us, the walls and the ceiling of the palace prison tremble violently.

An earthquake?

No. The frantic, bloodcurdling screams that follow can only mean one thing: the Gates of Hell are open.

My stomach twists.

Yue.

But there's no time to mourn.

The tremors are so vicious that the table of supplies ends up tipping—in the wrong direction. I just manage to grab hold of the paintbrush, gripping its bamboo handle tight. I watch in dismay as my hunting log falls, open-faced, my life's work scattering across the floor. All the knowledge I've collected over the years, sentenced to lie in a crumpled, disheveled heap.

Above, the screams grow louder. The loud clang of the watchtower gongs ring loudly into the night.

Gritting my teeth, I snatch up the first piece of paper I can get my hands on and bring the tip of the brush down to paint. I don't need a reference. I can do this by memory alone. My work is messy and rushed, but this mask doesn't need to be perfect. I hurriedly smash the paper to my face and feel the magic rush over me like wildfire on drought-ridden land.

Wiry whiskers, tiny pink claws and feet, and ugly, matted black fur. A rat demon in all its horrendous glory. It feels strange, but not wrong, necessarily. Like putting on a borrowed cloak. A part of me is surprised. I thought the brush might not be able to recreate anything other than human faces, but now that I know what's possible, I realize the endless miracles of this tool. I jump through the gap between the cell bars with plenty of room to spare, ripping the mask off the moment I'm free.

"The keys?" I snap, picking up the paintbrush.

"I think the guards have them," Wen answers.

No time! Sooah signs.

She's right. I take a step back and kick, slamming the heel of my boot against the lock of Wen's cell. I strike with such force that it falls apart, bits and pieces of metal clattering to the floor. As Wen emerges from his cell, I do the same for Sooah, freeing them both.

"I have to find my family," Wen says.

I nod, already scooping up three fresh pieces of paper. I paint hastily, doing my best not to let my hands shake. "Find them. Evacuate any civilians you come across. Once they're out of harm's way, put these on and come find me."

They take their masks without question. We leave through the prison's main doors to find the halls empty. The guards have abandoned their posts. With one final nod to one another, they make for the city, while I race to find the Maskmaker with my weapon held tight in my hand.

Our chances of succeeding are slim, but we know what must be done.

43

Sonam

Chaos.

Demons drag themselves through the Gates of Hell. They come through all at once, the ground shaking beneath our feet so violently it knocks several soldiers off their feet. Our ranks are disorganized, fracturing. A dam about to easily be broken.

The demons look like spiders released from a gaping hole in their silken nest, crawling over one another, a tangle of arms and legs as their jittery bodies spill out into the courtyard. Swords and arrows and lances are all well and good, but not at the rate our enemies arrive. We're going to drown.

The masks they don may make them appear human, but there's no denying their monstrous hunger. Fallen soldiers are devoured without mercy. I cringe at the sound of crunching bones and blood-wet flesh.

"Fall back!" someone in the rear ranks screams.

"No!" I bellow. "Hold the line. We can't let them get into the city."

Even as I give my orders, I know they'll go ignored. I can read the fear in their faces. These men weren't trained as I was. They've never faced the horrors of the damned. One of them flees, then another. Before long, the demons push past, a rushing stream cutting through what should have been a wall.

The demons of Hell force their way through the courtyard gates. Screams rip into the air as they slaughter their way to freedom. We're outnumbered, and those still here with me won't be able to outlast the onslaught.

A feral demon disguised as a young woman throws herself at me, knocking me to the ground. She digs her nails into the flesh of my collarbone, licking her lips with delight.

"You look tasty," she says with a cackle. "What a waste of a handsome face."

I waste no time responding and slap a new mask onto my face. The moment I feel my transformation take hold—

I snap my jaws shut and devour, severing the top half of the demon's body with my jagged rows of teeth. The remainder of her corpse slumps to the side, black blood pooling beneath it. It's in this pool that I catch a glimpse of my reflection, my features highlighted by the silver light of the moon.

My bones continue to stretch and bend, but it's the furthest thing from painful. In fact, it's invigorating. I'm born again. I grow to double, triple, quadruple the size, casting almost half of the courtyard in my towering shadow. Six slanted eyes of white opal contrasting sharply with pupils of solid obsidian meet me in my reflection. My coat of fur is darker than the night sky. My claws are impressively sharp, each one curled like scythes. And behind me, nine sweeping, majestic tails that flow like war banners.

My sense of smell is heightened. My hearing is so sharp that I can hear the distant gongs signaling for the evacuation of the city. Most noticeable of all is my sight. I no longer have one pair of eyes, but three. I see the world in an array of colors I didn't even know existed.

This must be how Yue sees the world.

Saw the world.

For a moment, I almost hear her laugh, a distinctive cackle that was always high-pitched and dry, yet was so unabashedly joyful. I regret the way I treated her when she finally learned to trust me. I thought I was doing the right thing by keeping my distance. I mistakenly believed that we were too different, she and I. Now I know—all too late—that we weren't sword and shield, but the sharp edges of the same blade; stronger, fiercer, deadlier together than we were apart. Steel, after all, sharpens steel.

Now I will never hear her laugh again. I can never again earn one of her rare, genuine smiles. All the things I should have done and said weigh heavily on my heart.

When I see the Maskmaker rise up out of the Gates of Hell, I head straight for him. Demon, god, man, or monster—it matters not. I will hunt him to the ends of the earth for what he's done to me. To my people.

To Yue.

I race into battle, tearing my way through the endless onslaught. He sees me and laughs as he retreats, slipping through the turmoil with ease.

"Come back here, you coward!" I growl, slashing through every demon foolish enough to stand in my way.

The Maskmaker pays me no heed, heading toward the city center. I can't afford to lose sight of him.

Demons have forced their way past even the Jade Palace's tall walls, laying waste to everything they see. I've never seen such pandemonium. The streets are crowded with citizens trying to flee, some with their things hastily thrown into carts, most with nothing but the clothes on their backs. Distraught mothers call for their lost children. An elderly man trips over his own cane and is nearly trampled underfoot. Still-warm bodies litter the narrow roads, blood dripping into the watery canals of Longhao.

People scream when they see me. Most freeze, too terrified to move, while others run as fast as they can in the opposite direction—right into the jaws of a waiting demon.

Ten. Fifty. A hundred. No matter how many demons I tear apart with my teeth, with my claws, there's no end in sight. Even with my borrowed strength and size, I know I can't keep this up forever. Fatigue sets in. My muscles tire and my lungs burn. Though my heart isn't ready to surrender, my head knows this is a losing battle.

But if I don't keep fighting—if I don't give every last drop of my sweat and blood—then all is lost.

A terrible rumbling shakes the ground beneath me. For a moment, I fear what it could mean. Is it another wave of demons escaping from Hell? No, it sounds much closer than that. Like the stomping of large, hefty feet.

I see the threat all too late. A massive ox demon, his mask discarded. It seems he's given up on the pretense. With alarming speed, he charges at me, throwing his full weight into the tackle. I'm slammed into the building beside me, the walls crumbling with the force. The woman and little girl who were hiding inside let out a helpless cry. The mother has a kitchen knife in her trembling hand.

"S-stay back!" she stutters. "Please, don't hurt us!"

With a groan, I stand up on all fours, using my front paw to knock my mask askew slightly. The magic pulls away from where the paper has left my skin, exposing my true face. The woman stares at me, wide-eyed, when she realizes I'm not the threat she thought I was.

"It's okay," I wheeze. I think one of my ribs is cracked. "I'll draw it away. When it's safe to do so, take the little one and run. Stop for no one. Understand?"

She nods slightly, still in disbelief, but I don't have the time to explain further. I replace my mask and step out through the ruined wall of the house. The ox demon snorts, nostrils flaring. He's waiting for me.

"I could smell you a mile away, human," he says with a vicious smile. "You're fooling no one."

"Good thing that was never my intention."

"I'm going to eat you, and then the two lovely morsels I can smell behind you."

I bare my fangs. "I dare you to try."

He charges and swings at me with hefty fists, pounding at my skull like he expects it to shatter. The demon tears at my fur, yanking out tufts. When he grabs one of my tails, sending electricity crackling up my spine, I snap at him with my teeth, sinking my canines into the bitter flesh of his arm. We're equally matched, neither of us giving the other an inch. What in the nine suns am I supposed to do?

A thought occurs to me.

When the ox demon rears back to take another swing, I quickly tear off my fox mask. I shrink down to my normal height—well out of his reach. Unable to stop mid-strike, the boar demon loses his balance. He stumbles forward and falls flat on his face. Without hesitation, I reach for the Maskmaker's paintbrush and rush the boar, climbing over him like a hill. I knee him in the back of the neck, pinning him in place as I paint several quick strokes against the back of his bare head in lieu of a proper canvas.

The magic takes effect, the boar's massive form suddenly squeezing down into the body of a helpless little mouse. Before my opponent even has a chance to blink, I replace my fox mask, open my jaw wide, and snap him up in a single bite. He tastes particularly foul—like dirt and week-old milk—but the triumph that fills my chest is nothing short of exquisite.

A howl rips itself from my lungs—a fox's cry. Loud and sharp enough for all of Longhao to hear it. I want the Maskmaker to know. I'm still here, still alive—and he should be afraid.

Behind me, timid footsteps padding over rubble. The mother and daughter carefully emerge from their ruined home, giving me a wary nod before running off toward the outer walls of the city. With any luck, they'll be able to escape with their lives.

I sniff the air, trying to pick up the Maskmaker's scent, but something shatters my concentration.

A scream, much like the one I just unleashed. My hair stands on end, a shiver slithering through my veins. It wasn't an echo, of that much I'm sure. This call belongs to someone else. Another fox.

My heart stutters.

I know of only one other fox demon in existence, but . . . it can't be.

The howl comes again, and I know. I *know*. I can feel it in my blood and in my bones. As sure as the sun rises and the moon waxes and wanes. I turn in the direction of her voice and set off in a mad run to find her.

44

She traveled across the lands alone, searching for signs of the Maskmaker. She spent her mornings thinking of all the creative ways she might dispatch him and her evenings wondering whether or not to devour him fast or slow. But first, she needed to find a way to break her oath without suffering the consequences.

Many years passed, but not once did her burning hatred waver. If anything, it kept her warm. Yue was sure to find him. Until then, she'd continue her search.

She knew she had to be clever. Watching humans—studying them—was the wisest thing to do. The fox understood she couldn't risk being caught before she achieved her quest for revenge. She only ever took one meal at a time; she never went after children, nor the sick and elderly, for they only upset her belly. The best meals were the ones who wouldn't be missed. The ones whom even their fellow humans would be glad to see disappear.

One such meal was the madame at the local brothel. Yue had never met a crueler soul, save perhaps the Maskmaker himself. When one of the servant girls under the madame's care dared to speak out of turn, she had her tongue ripped out as punishment. Yue cared not for the way the madame laughed, or how she left the servant girl to bleed in the streets.

"This will teach you, Sooah," the madame huffed. "Never disrespect me again."

Yue returned later that evening, donning her beautiful mask as she passed in front of the madame herself.

"You there," the old woman crooned. "My, you're a beauty. I could use a girl like you. I bet all of Longhao will be begging at my doorstep to spend a night with you."

What a phenomenal example of how truly horrific humankind could be. Nevertheless, she had taken the bait.

"Let's take a walk," Yue said. "We can negotiate."

The madame's eyes twinkled, no doubt imagining the mountain of coins she'd earn with this new girl on her payroll. She didn't think twice as she followed Yue around the corner into a dark, winding alley.

There was no time to scream. Yue devoured the woman in two bites and carried on her way.

She wouldn't eat for another moon, but a pattern was beginning to emerge. Yue stalked the streets for her prey, listening carefully for signs of unrest. On one such occasion, she was attracted to the sound of a young woman crying by the canal. Beside her stood a rather unfortunate-looking man with a crooked nose and ears too large for his head.

"I don't want to marry that man, Wen," the woman sobbed. "I don't care how wealthy he is. My parents know he's an angry drunk, but they won't rescind the match."

"I'll help you run away," the man said. "Where is he now? I'm sure we still have time."

"At the teahouse. Drinking before the wedding tomorrow." The woman wailed into her hands. "I've been praying to the gods. I just want him gone."

Yue left without a sound, steering herself in the direction of the teahouse in question. She was no god, but in many ways, she was far more merciful.

45

Sonam

I *follow the sound of her* sorrowful song all the way across Longhao, bounding from rooftop to rooftop to avoid the roads full of fleeing civilians and ravenous monsters. It doesn't occur to me until I'm nearly halfway there that this could be a trick the Maskmaker is playing.

But I have to know. I *have* to.

I leap over a particularly wide canal, spotting a blur of white surrounded by a small group of demons. The sweep of the creature's nine long tails leaves me momentarily confounded, the violent swipe of her claws even more so. From her six obsidian eyes to the burns upon the right sight of her face . . . Her fur may be matted with black blood, whether her own or that of her enemies, but there isn't a doubt in my mind: it's her.

One of the demons, disguised as a hefty young man, lunges at Yue, releasing a sharp hiss. Before he has a chance to unhinge his jaw and sink his teeth into her, I pounce, crushing him beneath my front paws. I tear his throat out, throwing away his limp body without a second glance. Our remaining enemies are smart enough to flee. They might have been able to take on a lone fox, but two of us together?

Yue snarls at me, her hackles raised. She doesn't recognize me. That is, until she sniffs the air. "Sonam?" she rasps.

I approach, ripping off my mask to confirm her suspicions. Wrapping my arms around her neck, I hug her as tight as I dare in lightheaded elation. A soft laugh escapes me. "You're *alive*," I say breathlessly. "I was so sure you were . . . "

She drapes her chin over my shoulder, nuzzling her cheek against my own. "I'm here," she whispers, as if it's a secret meant only for us.

I take a step back, disturbed that my hands come away covered in black. Now that I'm close, I see the full extent of her injuries. She's covered not just in surface-level scratches, but deep, seeping wounds. It's a miracle that she's here, but even more so that she's standing. Yue is pushing herself well beyond her limit, battle-worn and well over the brink of collapse.

"We need to get you somewhere safe," I say hastily. "You can't fight in this state."

"I'm fine—"

"Don't be stubborn."

"You can't win this alone."

I set my jaw, fear piercing through my chest. "And I can't lose you," I say plainly. Honestly. Not only because we don't have time to waste, but because Yue deserves to know the truth. The words come rushing out. Everything I've wanted to say.

"I see you," I tell her desperately. "I accept you. I not only want, but I *need* you." I pull her closer, tighter. "You don't have to fight anymore, Yue. I have strength for the both of us. So please, just rest."

She breathes deeply, the warmth of her breath tickling my cheeks. I find myself leaning in, anxious to hear what she has to say now that I've laid my intentions bare.

"Are you sure it's wise?" she asks after a moment. "To choose someone like me."

"I have no doubts."

"It will be difficult," she insists.

"I've survived the trials of Hell. Loving you will be the easiest thing I ever do."

"You're not thinking, Sonam. What happens when the people learn the truth? That the Hunter of Jian holds a demon so close? Think of your reputation—"

"Screw my reputation."

"And what of your honor?"

"Back to Hell with it."

"And when I must eat?"

"For you, I will scour the lands for the cruelest souls and feed them to you on a platter. We'll rid the world of evil together." I stroke her old burns with the pad of my thumb. "I've already made up my mind. Whatever it takes, I will do it. For you."

Yue huffs a soft laugh, nuzzling my cheek with the tip of her nose. "You're right. I'm tired of fighting."

"So stay here and rest."

"But I won't leave you to win this battle alone."

"Yue, we just went over this—"

"I will provide support, but it's you who must kill the Maskmaker. I cannot raise a hand to him."

I frown. "Why not?"

"I swore a blood oath," she reveals. "Long ago. If I harm him—"

"You die," I conclude.

She nods. "I always thought revenge was something I needed to achieve alone. But I can't. I need your help."

It takes a brave soul to endure hardship alone and an even

braver one to reach out for a helping hand. I'm proud of her. "Then we'll do it together," I say resolutely. "Can you tell if he's near?"

Yue lifts her head and sniffs the air. "Yes. He isn't far."

I hurriedly replace my mask and shift into the mighty, majestic form of a nine-tailed fox. We look at each other. She is my reflection, my equal.

"How do we do this?" she asks.

"How does one do anything?" I say. "Afraid but willing."

46

Sonam

We chase the Maskmaker over the canals, around sharp corners, through narrow alleyways. The layout of Longhao is perhaps our only advantage. I know these streets. Every building and secret passage and dead end. Even though we no longer have to worry about the walls coming alive and turning us around, in many ways, this city is just as much a living, breathing thing.

Yue is hot on his trail, just within striking distance when the Maskmaker stumbles out into an open street. He turns toward us, eyes bloodshot and teeth bared.

"Imbeciles. You really think you can stop me? You're too late."

"Call off the attack," I growl.

"I have no control over them now, don't you see? They'll feast and feast until nothing—not even the Heavens—can stand in my way."

Yue snarls. "Then you'll be the ruler of nothing."

"I'll be the ruler of a world of my own making," the Maskmaker corrects. "Whatever I want shall finally be. These simple-minded fools are merely a tool. I've let them loose to blank the canvas."

Before either one of us can make a move, the Maskmaker holds up his hands. His palms burn red hot, the air around him sizzling. His whole body ignites into flames so intense he's nothing but a white blot upon my vision. I'd nearly forgotten that the Maskmaker, much like his siblings banished to Hell, was once a star god on high.

"You are nothing," he seethes. "I can't wait to watch you burn."

Flames erupt around us, catching everything they can in their wake. Smoke billows into the skies above, covering Longhao in an ominous black shroud. Fire consumes everything: the moon bridges, the drooping wisteria trees, the nearby buildings—people. If the demons don't destroy my home, this inferno certainly will.

Yue takes a step back, her ears pressed flat. My heart roars with fury. The Maskmaker knows how much she hates fire. But she stands firm nonetheless, growling with stunning ferociousness.

"I survived your first branding," she says. "I can survive another."

We leap together. We don't need to exchange words to know how badly we both want to tear this bastard limb from limb. Even with his almighty powers, the Maskmaker still runs—no doubt out of habit—and leads us farther into the hellscape. Little by little, inch by inch, the fires he's set turn the city into Hell itself.

We chase him through the streets, bounding down alleys and ripping around corners. Flames singe our fur and burn our eyes.

"A-Ba!" the voice of a child reaches my ears. I see a little boy, no older than four, pointing up at me with slack-jawed terror. "A-Ba, look!"

I come to a halt, claws digging into the roads. A man hurries out and pulls the boy into his arms and stares at Yue. I'd recognize that unruly hair and lean stature anywhere. It's Wen.

"We're going to lose him!" Yue shouts.

"Keep on him," I say. "I'll be right behind you."

She nods and dashes off, leaving the Maskmaker no time for reprieve. My heart worries for her, but I know she's capable.

"Where's the rest of your family?" I ask hastily, shoving my mask to the side. Wen breathes a sigh of relief when he recognizes me.

"Sooah saw them out to the jungle's edge. Lost my little one and stayed behind to find him."

"Get in the water," I command. "And tell anyone else you come across. It's too late to evacuate now. Climb into the canals, and the water will protect you until the worst is over."

"But what are you going to do?" Wen asks, already making his way to the edge of the canal wall. The water is deep and murky, but he knows how to swim.

"I have to help Yue," I say.

But the unspoken question lingers over our heads: *How?* To believe we can kill a god is both arrogant and foolish. And with enemies on all sides, how can we ever hope to gain the upper hand?

Behind us, a vicious growl. I turn just in time to see two demons disguised as humans, their hideous faces blistered and contorted by the very fire their master set alight. They must have brute-forced their way through the flames, driven only by their insatiable appetite. They dash toward us, eyeing the little boy in Wen's arms with keen interest, but I'll have none of it.

Drawing a dagger from my belt, I whip it toward them. It meets its mark, driving into the demon's chest directly in the heart. The second one doesn't so much as blink at the loss of his comrade. He comes for me, attacks me with his bare hands, but I rear back and land a flying kick. His neck cracks as his head twists nearly the whole way around before he slumps to the ground in a limp heap.

"When it's safe, get the boy out of here," I tell Wen. "Come back to help if you're able."

No sooner does Wen nod that I bring my own finished mask to my face and feel the transformation take hold. This—this is the only thing we have to turn the tide.

"Go help her," Wen says.

He doesn't have to tell me twice. Digging my claws into the ground for traction, I run off, leaving thoughts of the burning city behind me.

47

Sonam

They haven't gone far. Just a few city blocks and then around a sharp corner. She has him trapped in a dead end. With my newfound strength, I barrel toward Yue, swiping away errant demons with my razor-sharp claws.

The moment our eyes connect, I sense it.

A fiery determination. We're capable apart, but together we're unstoppable.

This ends once and for all.

The Maskmaker's lip curls into a sneer. I can't tell if his face is red and swollen with anger, or if his own fire is what's painting his skin such a vibrant crimson. "Having fun with what's mine, thief? I'm going to kill you both."

Yue's body is a coil, tightening like a spring about to burst forth. "No wonder the Heavens wouldn't take you," she says venomously. "No one could ever love such a wrathful god."

"That's rich, coming from you," the Maskmaker says darkly. "Don't tell me you actually care for these pitiful creatures."

"I respect them. Something you'll forever be incapable of."

The Maskmaker laughs maniacally. "They'll never let you forget what you truly are, you know. They'll turn on you the moment they have the chance."

I take a step forward. "I won't let that happen."

He scoffs indignantly. "Two fools. Fine. Come to me and die."

Yue charges first. I'm right behind her. We lunge at the Maskmaker just as he burns brighter and hotter, the flames consuming his body so scalding they appear blue. We come to a screeching halt. There's no way we can get close enough. Even if we do, he's ensured that we'll suffer for it. The Maskmaker isn't looking for a fair fight. Honor means nothing to him. The only way we're going to stand a chance is if we stoop to his level.

I take a deep breath and let out a howl so loud it seems to shake the city itself.

"What are you doing?" the Maskmaker snaps. "Crying for mercy already?"

I howl again, louder and higher, praying that they can hear me. When I hear a thunderous, mighty roar from up above, I know they've found us. Something swoops in from overhead, barely visible through the smoke. I spot a tail. A serpentine body. Blue scales as pure as mountain water.

A water dragon. Just like the one my favorite brother, Jun, saw all those years ago when he was only a boy. Just like the one I painted onto a mask for Sooah to wear.

She roars again, diving down beneath the surface of the canals, emerging with such speed and force that water trails behind her in a stream. It slides off her iridescent blue scales, arcing over the burning buildings with a whip of her long tail. She showers Longhao in a storm of her own making, quenching the city like a blacksmith's sword into ice cold water.

The Maskmaker, thoroughly drenched, can only manage the smallest of flames now. Steam rises off his body, droplets evaporating the moment they touch his skin.

"But how?" he asks, eyes narrowed.

"You lack imagination," I reply. "Leave it to a god to shape the world in their image. All these years, you only ever painted human faces. Never once did it occur to you that you could transform into anything your heart saw fit."

The Maskmaker clenches his fist. We've moved beyond words.

He deals the first blow, singing the fur on my arm with his iron-hot palms. Yue runs up behind him, sticking her tails out so that he accidentally trips. Not technically an attack—and therefore not a violation of her oath.

I bite his shoulder. The bitter taste of his blood coats my tongue. With a feral cry, the Maskmaker throws us off of him with immeasurable strength. He flings me into a nearby wall with such force that it crumbles, the structure weakened from fire and water damage.

The moment I'm back on my feet, I lunge for his throat. It won't be a clean kill, or an easy one, but that hardly matters. All my life, I thought I knew what it was to look into the eyes of a monster. But there is nothing more horrendous than a spited god. The world cannot exist in harmony while he remains. The Legendary Archer did not balk when he set out to kill the stars, and I will not dishonor his memory by giving up now.

While Yue and I do our best to slow him down, Sooah soars overhead, diving down with alarming speed to crush approaching demons from the palace with the weight of her body. She's as majestic as she is terrifying.

Our fight with the Maskmaker reaches a precipice. I can sense him tiring. He bats us away, throwing his fists and launching fire with fury, but his movements grow sluggish. He's out of breath. He may be a fallen star god, but Yue and I are both seasoned hunters. He can never hope to match our stamina.

I tear the first chunk off of him—more fingers from his other hand. Then patches of his face, his torso. All the while, Yue serves as a distraction, swooping in only to dash away, the swish of her tails leaving the Maskmaker disoriented. Before long, he looks like a decaying corpse.

"Enough!" he screams, snatching me by the throat. He violently tears off my mask and crushes my windpipe, lifting me off of the ground.

"Don't you dare touch him!" Yue shrieks. She runs, trying to remove me from his hold, but the Maskmaker drives his fist forward and sends her crashing into the building beside us. Its foundation can no longer support the weight of the roof, which comes crashing down over her head.

"Yue!" I try to call out, struggling against the Maskmaker's grip. I can't breathe. Black spots blot my vision. This can't be how I die.

The Maskmaker pulls me close and spits in my face. "I'm going to melt that blessing right off your bones."

"Do your worst," I rasp, spitting back. "You don't scare me."

"As you wish."

The hand he has wrapped around my throat bursts into flames. The fire climbs up the side of my face as though it has a mind of its own, searing into my flesh without remorse. I scream until my throat is bloody and raw. No matter how much I fight, I can't escape. He brands his hatred onto my skin, the pain so intense it knocks the air from my lungs and sends sharpened knives scraping across my nerves.

I should be dead. No mortal man could survive such a horrendous attack. And yet I remain to feel every torturous moment of it, the sickening smell of my own charred flesh filling my nose.

Something massive sweeps in from behind. I was too focused on staying conscious to realize the approach of the hulking creature.

With one giant hand made of bricks and wooden planks and terracotta tile, the beast knocks the Maskmaker to the side. I fall to the ground, finally free from his brutality, but I'm too weak to stand. I can only lie there, straining my neck to see what's going on.

It's Wen, masked as the Sleeping City itself. This mask was the most difficult to paint, but I'm glad to see the transformation suit him so well. He towers over all of us. Over Longhao, even. We stand eclipsed in his shadow as he drags himself forward, crushing demons too foolish or too slow to get out of the way.

Wen raises his monstrous fist of broken shanty huts and mangled roads and brings it down upon the Maskmaker with a mighty bellow. The star god narrowly escapes, fleeing for his life as he sends fire crawling up Wen's arm. Thankfully, he's drenched in the rain Sooah summoned. The flames don't catch as easily. We may stand a chance.

I try to lift my head, eager to return to the fight, but I can't feel anything on the right side of my body. My ears ring loudly. I can barely see out of my right eye. It's frankly a miracle I survived the Maskmaker's maiming at all.

The sound of shuffling rubble. Heavy panting. Claws clicking against broken cobblestone. Is that my name I hear? It isn't until I feel soft fur grazing my cheek and a wet nose near my ear that I am sure.

"Sonam," she croaks. "Sonam, look at me."

I do my best, but my eyes are swelling shut. I must look atrocious, judging by the horror in her six obsidian eyes.

"It's going to be okay," she says, though she can't suppress her whimper. "We're going to be okay."

I have just enough strength left to reach for something attached to my belt. A single needle—the very last one I have coated in Zhenniao poison. I held on to it all through Hell just in case, but now feels as good a time as any to use it. All it will take is a small pin prick, and the Maskmaker will fall. The problem is that I can't move anymore; my mind is too tired and my body too strained.

"Take . . . this," I murmur. "You have to do it. I can't—"

"You can," she insists. "I can't harm him, remember?" She gently grasps the front of my robes between her teeth and pulls me into an upright position. "I need you, Sonam. We can do this together."

With a groan, I stand, leaning heavily against her. I think of her pushing beyond her limits in the Court of Despair. She's right. I can still fight. We survived Hell together, which means we can survive this, too.

I climb onto Yue's back and hold on tight as she rushes in leaps and bounds. She jumps from one shaky rooftop to another, the rain and ash mixing to form a thick mud. Sooah, Wen, and the Maskmaker are near the docks at the furthest edge of the city. They're keeping him at bay, but who knows for how much longer?

The blue dragon dives toward him, jaws open wide to devour him whole, but the Maskmaker burns Sooah's mask off without hesitation. She transforms midair, plummeting into the frigid seawater. I breathe a sigh of relief when I see her breach the surface and start swimming toward the nearest moored boat. Wen keeps fighting, growling and snarling as he brings his arms down to swipe at the Maskmaker like a fly.

"He's distracted," I shout over the clamor. "We need to get up high!"

I'm not sure Yue hears me, but then she darts toward Wen. She runs with such speed that her claws barely have time to scrape the ground.

"Hang on!" she shouts at me as we climb up the Sleeping City's back.

She uses Wen as a ramp of sorts, putting us at a height advantage.

Using the hard ledges for purchase, she climbs her way up until we've reached the top of the Sleeping City's head. From this distance, the Maskmaker looks like nothing more than an ant. She jumps down without fear, much to my—and the Maskmaker's—stunned amazement.

This is my only shot.

Before he has a chance to react, I fling the needle from between my fingers—

And hit him in the throat with it.

Our landing is the furthest thing from graceful. Yue goes tumbling into the water. I land on the hard surface of the docks, rolling three or four times until my momentum finally comes to a stop. I can't feel my legs anymore. I wonder if I've broken my back.

I can barely see Wen taking off his mask, shrinking down to his lanky human size. I spot Sooah, too, hurrying over to rejoin the fight.

The Maskmaker lies on his back only a few arms away. Black Zhenniao poison crawls through his veins, a reaching spiderweb spreading out beneath the surface of his skin. He chokes on his swollen tongue, his bloodshot eyes bulging with terror. He sputters, grasping at his throat as it closes and the rest of his body seizes, twitching like a spider in its final moments. When he dies with his eyes open, it should feel like a triumph.

But my only thoughts belong to Yue.

Panic grips me as I look around for her. Where is she? Is she hurt?

"Yue," I croak. "Where—"

Something cold and wet brushes my arm. Fur, soaked in seawater. "I'm here," a voice whispers in my ear.

I give in to the weight of my eyelids and exhale heavily. If this is how I die, so be it—as long as my fox is safe.

For my beloved monster of monsters, I would kill the stars.

48

Sonam

She's making people nervous," comes a voice. "She won't let anyone go near him. Damn near bit the head off of one of the palace doctors when he came to change the captain's bandages."

"Yue ain't going to harm no one." This voice I recognize. Wen speaks with an edge in his tone. "Ain't that right, Fox?"

"He's never going to get better if those quacks continue to poke and prod at him," Yue hisses. "Leave him to sleep or I'll— What? I *am* behaving, Sooah."

"If it means no harm, why does it keep looking at me like that?"

"Ignore her," Wen says. "She has a staring problem."

I blink myself awake slowly, listening more to the rhythm of their conversation than to the meaning of their words. I feel . . . fine. Sore and stiff, but not in as much pain as I thought I would be. The right half of my vision is obstructed by several thick bandages, and I can feel a heavy layer wrapped around my chest. My mouth is terribly dry, and my head pounds with a fury, but I tell myself that these are good things.

Discomfort means I'm alive.

I'm not sure where I am, or even what day it is. The heavy

smell of smoke still lingers in the air, though it's not as noticeable as before. The low mumble of chatter fills my ears. It seems to be everywhere, distant conversations that I'm barely privy to. With a groan, I attempt to sit up.

Yue, Sooah, and Wen are at my side in an instant. Yue, I notice, has forgone the use of her mask. It hangs around her neck, tied loosely with bits of ribbon. I wonder whether it was Sooah or Wen who tied it on for her.

"I told you he'd pull through!" Wen exclaims.

I cough, looking up at them through my one unobstructed but bleary eye. "Don't tell me you were worried."

Sooah glances down abashedly, signing quickly. *Of course we were worried. You should have seen the state you were in.*

"How long was I asleep?"

"Nearly a week," Wen says. "They didn't think you'd wake at all."

I take in my surroundings slowly. We're inside one of the private rooms situated in the inner courts of the Jade Palace. It feels strange seeing daylight, as unnaturally orange and smoky as it may be, filtering in through the latticed windows. There's movement outside. Not just soldiers, but civilians, too.

"His Majesty opened the palace gates to the people for temporary shelter," Wen explains. "And the army's helping with rebuilding efforts."

"Does this mean the shamans were able to seal the gate?"

Yue nods. "It took them a few days, but they managed."

"That's a good thing, isn't it?"

A few hundred demons managed to escape, Sooah says. *Ran off into the surrounding jungles. Maybe even farther.*

I press my lips into a thin line. Not an ideal outcome, but I'm hardly in a state to go after them right now. Knowing what I know now about demons, I'm sure a great wave of them will be born of this tragedy. "And what of the Maskmaker?" I ask.

Yue shakes her head. "Dead. I dragged his body to the Gates of Hell and tossed him in before they sealed it closed."

I study her expression carefully, noting the sourness in her tone. I would have thought she'd be happy now that her tormentor is gone.

The doors to the room slide open. In steps a procession of handmaidens, a few advisors, and then the king himself. My father regards me with such a wide smile that the corners of his eyes crinkle. He's never looked at me with such pride before.

"I'm glad to see you're well, my son," he says before casting Yue a wary glance.

A eunuch steps forward. "Send that beast out. We won't have it near His Majesty—"

"She stays," I snap, forgoing the politeness normally reserved for my father's station.

"It's fine," Yue says with a huff. "I'll be outside."

She turns on her heels and shuffles out the door, her tails swishing in a wide arc so that she hits the eunuch in the face on the way out. He sputters but doesn't dare say a thing about it. I want to tell her to come back, that she out of everyone shouldn't have to put up with such disrespect. If only they knew what Yue had done for them, understood the part she played in saving our people, maybe then they'd treat her with the admiration she deserves.

"That demon can't stay," my father says gravely as he kneels by my bedside. "It's making the soldiers and courtesans nervous."

"*She* saved countless lives," I counter. "Hundreds more might have been spared if my warning had been taken seriously."

My father's face is impassable. He sits perfectly still, clearly contemplating what to say next. After a moment, he waves a dismissive hand to all still in the room. "Leave us. I would have a word with Prince Sonam in private."

Everyone bows, Sooah and Wen included. They leave in a hurry, vacating without so much as a peep. Once the door slides closed, my father arches a brow.

"That nine-tailed fox . . . " he says slowly. "You seem quite attached."

"I am," I say with unflinching pride.

Father's expression softens slightly. I'm not sure if it means I have his approval or sympathy—or perhaps even his pity. "You've grown into a fine man," he says. "Just and fair and good. I could use more of that in my court."

I furrow my brow. "You mean to have me stay here at the Jade Palace?"

The king nods. "You'd be a most welcome advisor. What say you? You could help me rebuild Longhao alongside your brothers."

The offer is tempting. It has been my dream ever since I was a child to rejoin my family here in the capital. I would no longer have to live life in the periphery of the king's attention, but front and center where I might flourish.

Then I think it over. Yes, it would be lovely to live in a palace where my meals are provided for me at all hours. To wear lavish clothes and jewelry and want for nothing.

But that isn't who I am. I have no interest in the internal politicking of the courts or the formality of palace life. Everything I truly want can't be found within these jade walls. What I want is out there—beneath the jungle canopy, the endless skies, and the soft grass beneath my feet.

"I must thank you for such a generous offer," I say slowly. "But I cannot accept it."

Father nods, as if expecting this answer. "Then I must ask you to continue your hard work, Hunter of Jian. Have you been informed of the demons who escaped?"

"I have. Rest assured, I'll deal with every last one."

"Every last one?" he asks, glancing out the latticed window toward a pair of pointed white ears poking out just above the windowsill. They twitch at his words. I wouldn't be surprised if Yue's been listening this entire time.

"Maybe not *every* last one," I say.

He places a hand on my shoulder and nods with approval. "Then I hereby task you with ridding our kingdom of its plight, though the Jade Palace will always welcome you, should you require rest."

I dip my head in lieu of a proper bow. "Thank you, Father."

The king stands and turns to leave, sliding the door open himself to step outside. He looks to his right at someone just out of view. "Take care of him," he says before walking away altogether.

Yue rounds the corner, padding across the wooden floor at a leisurely pace. There's a bounce in her step and a wag to her tails. She makes her way to my bedside and allows me to reach out, lifting her mask to place it gingerly upon her face. Once she's transformed, Yue takes a seat on the edge of my bed with a mischievous smile.

"How much of that did you hear?" I ask her.

"Only all of it," she replies coyly. "Personally, I think you're a fool to pass up an opportunity to live in the palace."

I laugh softly. "Between you and me, I've seen enough jade to last a lifetime."

"So, you're rather attached to me, hmm?" she says softly.

"Eavesdropping is rude, I'll have you know," I say, though my words lack any real heat.

Yue snorts. "To be fair, you were speaking very loudly."

"Was I? I can hardly hear myself beneath all these bandages." I reach up to touch the linen covering the right side of my face. It's terribly itchy. "We should call for a doctor to change them."

"Allow me," she says.

Yue moves with grace, unwrapping the bandages with an intense concentration. Little by little, the pressure eases. I can finally open both my eyes, and though there's a noticeable tenderness to my skin, there's no pain. The heavy smell of ointment and herbs hits my nose. The palace doctors must have tried their best to heal the burns, but to no avail. I don't have to look in a mirror to know the true extent of my injuries, but that doesn't stop my morbid curiosity.

"Is it terrible?" I ask her with a grimace.

She stares at me for much too long. I can't discern what she's thinking. After a while, she brings her fingers to the line of my jaw, making sure not to touch the burn itself. Yue doesn't seem alarmed or disgusted by what she sees. Instead, she slowly breaks into a smile.

"We match," she whispers.

Two simple words, and yet they mean more than the entire world. She sees what I am, just as I see her—despite our flaws, or perhaps even because of them. I comb my fingers through her hair and let her lean in close, kissing her as tenderly as I dare. It isn't long, however, before things give way to an uncontrollable heat.

She kisses like she fights. Fast. Aggressive. I can't say that I mind. I enjoy it, in fact, because it means I can be just as rough and greedy in return. My hand roams, coming to rest at the nape of her neck as she nips at my bottom lip. Too hard. I pull back with a hiss, the taste of iron coating my tongue.

"Sorry," Yue says quickly, her eyes wide in mortification. She shakes her head, begins to pull away. "I'm so sorry, I—"

"Do it again."

She stares at me, stunned. Her smile returns, delightfully mischievous, before she hooks her arm around my neck and pulls me back to her.

Logic might dictate that this is hardly the time nor place for such a passionate embrace, but I might argue that it is, in fact, perfect. I was foolish for not kissing her sooner.

An exaggerated groan disturbs the moment. Wen leans against the doorframe, arms crossed over his chest. He looks as though someone fed him some rotten fruit.

"If this is how you two are going to act around each other from now on, I'm going to have to start paying Sooah to knock me out," he says.

No need to pay me, Sooah says. *I'll do it for free.*

Yue laughs. "I'll help."

Wen rolls his eyes. "So, when are we heading out? We're getting reports of demon sightings as far as that new settlement in the North. Jiaoshan, I think it's called. A little village by some big old lake."

My eyes widen with surprise. It sounds like we have a great deal of ground to cover, and likely countless targets to track. I look at Yue and grin.

"Feel like joining me on a hunting campaign?"

"Do I get to eat what I kill?"

I nod. "Of course."

She grins, too, and I already know her answer. Just as the moon follows the sun, and the sun follows the moon—where she goes, I will most assuredly be.

Epilogue

Yue

Sonam and Yue's Hunting Log #1:
Why do we have to record everything?
So we have something to look upon and remember.
Seems foolish.
Indulge me, Fox.
Very well.

Through the narrow streets I stalk, drawn to the sounds of the water market. A year on, Longhao has nearly returned to its former splendor, not a hint of the Maskmaker or his demons to remind us of that fateful day.

Well, almost nearly.

Leaping from rooftop to rooftop, the tiles clacking beneath my sharpened claws, I observe the old man as he hobbles his way down the winding alley. His back is hunched, his weight supported by a sturdy bamboo cane.

A completely defenseless victim—the perfect lure.

The old man brings a hand up to stroke his bald head. "Oh, dear," he mutters, confused. "Did I take another wrong turn? I thought for sure the tea shop was this way."

I stifle a chuckle. What an adorable little snack.

As if on cue, a young man steps out from the shadows, seemingly appearing out of thin air. He isn't nearly as clever as he believes himself to be. I could smell him from a mile away. I don't act immediately, however, waiting for the right moment to strike.

"Are you lost, good sir? Maybe I can help you find your way."

The stranger has a charming, unassuming air to him. Full of youthful energy and a smile that can warm even the most frigid of hearts. I must confess, this is one of the Maskmaker's better works of art. The face the demon wears gives the impression of genuine friendliness, not a hint of underlying motive to be found. It's no wonder this one has claimed three lives this moon alone. Three lives we could have spared, yes, but from tonight, it will feast on no others.

"That's very kind of you, my boy," the old man says.

The demon approaches. Not so fast as to seem eager, not so slow as to give the old man a chance to slip away. "Worry not. These streets can be confusing, even for me. Where is it that you're hoping to—"

He comes within arm's reach, but before he has the chance to unhinge his jaw and take a bite out of the elderly man's neck, I pounce from the rooftop. I land with such force that I create my own wind current, the rush of air sending dust billowing up and outward.

With my claws extended, I swipe the demon's mask clean off his face, the magic washing away instantly to reveal the face of a toad. It's covered in a spattering of at least twenty bright-yellow eyes, hideous brown warts affixed to every inch of its thick skin. Toad demons are rare—and an incredible nuisance. No matter. This one is destined for death.

I eat, scarfing down my meal to leave no time to feel pain or sorrow. Even after all this time, I still see no need to toy with my food. Demon flesh is nowhere near as satisfying as a human's, but with Sonam's offering to feed once a moon, I'm not only able to subsist, but thrive on the abundance of qi he has to share.

As I lick my lips clean, the old man steps forward, reaching up to remove the mask he wears. Sonam ties it securely to his belt with a grin. "Another job well done."

"You make a very convincing senior citizen," I tell him once I've finished my meal in a mere three bites.

He folds his arms over his chest. "And you've been letting them get awfully close, Fox."

I sweep my tails from one side to the other. "Don't worry, Dinner. I was never going to let him hurt you."

Sonam reaches out and affectionately scratches below my chin. "Speaking of dinner, we should hurry. We don't want to be late."

I press my nose to his cheek. "Lead the way, then. I'm right behind you."

We walk through the narrow streets of the city together without our masks, making our way over moon bridges and down familiar passages. It's true that people stop and stare, but never out of fear. Not anymore. I am a familiar and welcome sight—one of the beloved heroes of Longhao—my captain always at my side. Our matching scars make us easily recognizable.

That, and the fact that I'm the only nine-tailed fox demon from here to the farthest corners of the land who protects mankind from the monsters who lurk in the shadows.

Sonam's posture changes ever so slightly when we're out and about. A little straighter, his chest puffed out with pride, a protective hand laid upon my side as if to remind me, *I'm here*.

I rarely hide my face anymore, though my mask still has its uses—like helping me fit through the small doorframe of Wen's family abode. Although there's plenty of space, I doubt they'd be pleased to find claw marks everywhere.

Sonam takes it upon himself to place my mask, adjusting it for me as one would a crown. There's warmth in his eyes as he brushes his fingers across my cheek, moving to tuck a few loose strands of hair behind my ears. He presses a tender kiss to my lips before we enter, and I make sure to relish the way he tastes.

Wen, his wife, Ling, their children, and Sooah all greet us with enthusiastic shouts the moment we step inside. An assortment of food sits out on the table—steamed vegetables, fried dumplings, noodle soups, and sweet buns all lovingly prepared by hand. It's not a banquet fit for a king—because in many ways, it's even better.

"Auntie Yue!" Cheng, Wen's eldest son, rushes up and wraps his arms around my waist in a tight hug. "What did you bring me?"

I scrunch up my nose. "Unhand me, imp. What makes you think I'd bring you anything?"

"Because it's my name day!" he says without missing a beat. "You *have* to bring me somethin'."

"It's a rule, is it?"

That's how humans celebrate their name days, yes, Sooah says with a wide smile.

"So I have to give you something—for free, I might add—just because your parents decided to f—"

Sonam clears his throat, interrupting. He reaches into one of the larger pouches attached to his belt and produces a small bag, something rattling inside. Handing it to the boy, he says, "This is from the both of us."

Cheng opens the bag and spills its contents onto the flat of his palm. A collection of small, colorful porcelain marbles. His face lights up. "Oh, wow!"

"What do you say, son?" Wen says firmly.

The boy hugs me again. "Thank you so much!"

How did the hunt go? Sooah asks. *We could have helped—*

"It was easily dispatched," Sonam informs her, "but we'll be sure to take you along on the next one. I've heard rumors of a large group to the west."

Wen's wife clicks her tongue. "No talk of hunting," she says, voice light and sweet. "Not with the children around."

Miyu, Wen's youngest, whines, "But I love hearing about their adventures." She's quite nasally, not unlike her father.

"Me, too!" Cheng boisterously adds as we all gather around the table, taking up our seats to begin the celebration. I take a seat beside Sonam, diligently placing bits of food into his bowl. I've grown quite fond of the ritual dinnertime brings, though managing chopsticks still proves a challenge.

"I want to hear about when all of you went to Hell," Cheng continues.

Their mother frowns deeply. "Don't say that word. It's terrible luck on a name day!"

"But it's our favorite!" he insists.

"Yeah!" Miyu says. "Won't you tell us the story again, Auntie Yue? *Please*?"

"Tell us about your sisters. And Uncle Sonam can tell us about Hell and the Great Fire!"

I groan. "Don't you ever tire of hearing it?"

Sonam leans over and kisses my cheek, whispering against my ear, "Humor them, my moonlight. We all know you tell the story best."

I sigh, but it's without any real irritation. I enjoy entertaining the little ones more than I'll ever admit aloud. That's why, even though it's the hundredth time I've told the tale, I glance to Wen and his wife for approval. When they both eventually nod, I clear my throat and begin.

"I like watching them. Humans. It's a cheeky little pastime of mine."

Acknowledgments

Thank you very much for joining Yue and Sonam on their hellish misadventure together. This next part is what I like to call my Oscar's acceptance speech. They're going to start playing the music soon, so let's get straight to it.

Firstly, thank you to my agent, Jim McCarthy. If it weren't for you, I'd still be toiling away as an anonymous ghostwriter. Thank you for giving me the chance to live my dream.

Thank you to my editor at Saga Press, Amara Hoshijo, for her guidance and support. There aren't enough words in the English dictionary to express how truly grateful I am. I would also like to extend my deepest appreciation for the team at Saga Press: Tim O'Connell, Joe Monti, Ritika Karnik, Jéla Lewter, Amanda Mulholland, Lauren Gomez, Olivia Perrault, Alexandre Su, Chloe Gray, Ella Laytham, and Mabel Marte Taveras.

A massive round of applause for the cover artist, Kuri Huang, who not only illustrated for *The Legend of the Nine-Tailed Fox* but for my firstborn, *The Last Dragon of the East*, as well! I am blown away by your talent and the beauty of your work every single time.

A million thank yous to my beta readers: Ashley, FER, Stephanie, Danielle, Jolie, and Minju. Thank you all for cheering so loudly that I never noticed those who weren't. You're all angels and I hope both sides of your pillow are cool for all eternity. Thank you to my street team, as well, for helping me spread the word about my book. I cannot stress enough that I simply could not have done it without you.

And last, but not least, thank you to my husband. You have the very unique experience of getting to see me at my highest highs and my lowest lows. Thank you for believing in me on the days when I couldn't do it for myself. Thank you for drowning out the chatter and helping me find my passion. You're right. I worked too hard for too long to give up. This is book #3 and I have no intention of slowing down.

And credit where credit is due: the translated quote from the *Shan Hai Jing (The Classic of Mountains and Seas)* is an excerpt from *A Chinese Bestiary: Strange Creatures from the Guideways Through Mountains and Seas* by Richard E. Strassberg (Berkeley: University of California Press, 2002).

See you in the next one!

About the Author

Photograph by Katrina Kwan

Katrina Kwan is the author of *The Last Dragon of the East* and *The Legend of the Nine-Tailed Fox*. After graduating from Acadia University in 2017 with a BA in political science with honors, Kwan spent the next six years honing her creative skills as a freelance ghostwriter. With several ghostwritten romance novels under her belt, she's ecstatic to finally be writing books under her own name.